DEEP INSIDE

A GOING DEEP FOOTBALL NOVEL, BOOK THREE

by

VIRNA DEPAUL

Deep Inside
Copyright © 2017 by Virna DePaul

This is a work of fiction. Names, characters, places, brands, media, and incidents are either the product of the author's imagination or are used fictitiously.

Editor: Lawrence Editing, www.lawrenceediting.com

DEEP INSIDE

Ruby O'Brien, NFL publicist extraordinaire, lives her life by three simple rules:

#1 - Never date a client
#2 - Never sleep with a client
#3 - Never fall in love with a client

The problem is, she never counted on Alec LeBrun

Alec, the cocky and talented tight end of the Savannah Bootleggers, repeatedly asks Ruby for a date, and no one's more shocked than Ruby when she finally says yes. Less than twenty four hours later, however, he's engaged to someone else. Lesson learned. Two months later, Alec's single again, acting like a publicity nightmare and requiring up-close supervision. Now Ruby has to help Alec fix his bad boy reputation, even as she protects her heart.

Alec watched Ruby from afar for months, long before circumstances got him engaged to his lying ex. Now he's free to pursue the only woman he's ever truly wanted. Ruby's smart, gorgeous, and super-professional, and he wants her with a hunger he's never experienced before. Too bad Ruby thinks he's still pining for another woman.

Now he has to prove her wrong. Jeopardizing their careers isn't part of the plan, but he also refuses to play by her rules—not when doing so means losing the woman he loves.

Can Alex convince Ruby that, sometimes, scoring in love means risking it all? And will Ruby accept that she's not second best, but the only woman Alec wants? For a lifetime.

1

Ruby O'Brien flashed her media badge at the stadium security booth before zipping into the Savannah Bootleggers' crowded parking lot. Pulling into her reserved spot, she turned off the ignition and rested her head against the steering wheel, listening to disgruntled Bootleggers fans returning to their cars after an unexpected defeat.

No wonder Alec was in a bad mood.

The mid-season loss, the recent breakup with his ex-fiancée, Colleen, the fact his own teammate had apparently been taunting him about both… It would put anyone in a bad mood, but unfortunately, right now, the reasons for Alec's bad mood didn't matter.

He had to straighten up.

Yes, he was obviously going through a lot, but he had choices. And choices, as a high-profile tight end in the world of professional football, meant everything.

Lately, his choices had changed him. The charming,

professionally-dedicated man she'd always known had deteriorated into a ghost of himself. For weeks now, Alec had wavered between his usual mischievous, easy-going self one minute and a short-tempered, troublemaking Hulk the next. The man was jeopardizing, not only his own image, but that of the entire Bootleggers franchise. Not to mention the reputation of her father's publicity firm, O'Brien PR. One more bad move on Alec's part, and the team's contract might not be renewed.

It couldn't happen. Not on her watch.

She had to get strict with him, and she had to start now.

As Ruby strode toward the Bootleggers' locker room, she focused on the job at hand. She tugged down the hem of her short skirt. She'd been in the middle of a date when her father had interrupted, a desperate phone call about Alec, urgently commanding her to "get that cranky-ass boy under control!" There'd been no time to change. So while she usually wore pressed, buttoned shirts and dark suits to work, right now, she was slaying a sexy black dress, strappy heels, and hair down in loose, fiery waves. Not how she'd choose to have a showdown with any client, least of all Alec, the man she'd crushed on for months.

She'd been drawn to him from the moment she'd first met him, but while he'd been friendly, flirty even, he'd never given her any indication that he was seriously attracted to her. Then, two months ago, after he'd broken up with his cheerleader girlfriend, Colleen, he'd asked her out, multiple times. And what had she done? She'd finally caved, despite the fact she *never* dated clients, because doing so violated her own rules, yes, but mostly it violated her father's business policies. In the end, it hadn't mattered. The date never happened. Instead, the next day, it'd been all over the news—Alec and Colleen were engaged and planning an early October wedding.

To say her heart shattered before it ever got out the gate was an understatement. *Water under the bridge,* Ruby thought. That weak Ruby was gone now, and she was the woman she'd always been. Professional Ruby. Ruthless Ruby. No-nonsense, Non-Heartbroken Ruby. *And here we go...*

Pushing those double doors open was the same every time: loud, bright, chaotic, and filled with the pungent smell of sweat and buckets of body spray. Ruby marched through the swarm of players, keeping her peripheral blinders on. *Do not look at the naked men. Do not, do not, do not...*

For a moment, a sudden silence overtook the locker room, followed by several low whistles. An elongated "damnnnn." Great. They were checking her out! She should've changed out of the dress. Oh, well, too late now. Her stride faltered, and a blush overcame her cheeks a split second before the catcalls ended.

"Hey, Red, 'bout time you got here." Martinez, the wide receiver from LSU who couldn't run a simple route to save his life, but could catch a ball with his pinky, shouted at her from his locker. "Ooo, LeBrun's in trouble now. Look how pissed she is. Ow!" he howled.

She breathed a sigh of relief that the men weren't going to razz her about her sexy dress. About Alec, yes, but that she could handle. Glancing in his direction but keeping her gaze aimed high, she waved at Martinez. "Be glad it's not you I'm after," Ruby said with a smirk.

Several of the boys chuckled. Notably, both quarterback Kyle Young and wide receiver Heath Dawson, Alec's best friends, were absent, as was Connors, the player Alec had fought with. Were they with him in the medic room? Ruby had already texted Richard James, Connors' publicist, and would be meeting with him after talking to Alec. As for Young and Dawson? They'd probably cleared out to meet their girlfriends. The men had recently found the loves of their lives and while they, unlike Alec, weren't letting their football careers suffer, they also made sure the women in their lives were given equal priority.

"We missed you at tonight's game, Red. We're used to you being in the stands but looks like you had bigger plans." That came from Plough, the left offensive end from Ohio State, who needed to get his hands up or he'd be knocked on his ass all season. "I think you're right, Martinez. She don't look too happy. Gorgeous but not happy."

"Hey, Red, how come you never come just to see us? Why it always gotta be LeBrun, LeBrun, LeBrun?" That was Hewitt, rookie quarterback the Bootleggers drafted first round from Stanford. Denser than a bag of bricks, but basically a nice guy who threw beautiful spirals to Alec every time.

"'Cause he's the only one who needs reprimanding, gentlemen." Her mind wandered, as she thought about all the ways she *wished* she could reprimand Alec for his misbehavior. In another world, another lifetime, where publicists and clients ravaged each other as post-game punishment.

None of that, Ruby. Keep it together. Alec just asked you out to fill in the space Colleen left behind when they broke up that first time at the end of the summer. As soon as he had the opportunity to get back together with her, he couldn't forget about Ruby fast enough. Hell, they'd never even discussed the fact he'd asked her out and she'd accepted—when she'd seen him again, she'd simply congratulated him on his engagement. And though he'd looked tense, like he wanted to say something more, in the end he'd simply said, "Thanks, Ruby," and walked away.

It hurt. Like a mothereffer. But Ruby was great at moving on, and so she did. Chin up and all that. She never should've agreed to a date in the first place.

Past the hoots and hollers, past the ass-staring—she knew they were doing it even with her eyes facing forward—past the not-so-clever quips, Ruby made her way to the medic room where she spied a man sitting on the exam table through the cheap, bent blinds. He faced away from her, as the team doctor dabbed a cotton swab to his cheek. She'd know that strong back anywhere—the twitching ripple of his muscles, the width of his shoulders, the expanse of his delts, the thickness of arms that would never, *ever*, wrap around her. There he was—Alec LeBrun in all his hot mess glory.

Time to put him in his place.

But then, Dr. Kelstrom—who everyone called Dr. K—turned away from Alec, revealing his exhausted figure slumped on the table. From the way he ran both hands over his face and shoulders, every line of his body defeated, she knew she couldn't be ruthless. *Crap, this guy needs compassion, not a tongue-lashing,* she thought.

When he turned his head slightly, she caught a glimpse of his profile and gasped. Not because Alec's left eye was swollen and bruised around the butterfly bandage covering what was surely a nasty gash. Not because his bottom lip—such a beautiful mouth—was split.

But because his whole being radiated pain.

And an answering pain began to squeeze her chest.

Despite the fact Alec was obviously mourning the loss of Colleen—it was a safe assumption given the timing of their breakup and Alec's recent behavior—Ruby wished she could console him. Not as his publicist, but as a woman. Just wrap her arms around him and tell him it'd be okay.

But she couldn't give into her stupid fantasies. She was here to protect Alec's career and nothing else. She could talk to him, figure out what was in his mind and heart, but only to do her job. After a deep, long breath, Ruby shoved the door open.

Alec straightened, shoulders stiff. "Is that her?" he

asked, peeking over his shoulder. His melodramatic tone clued Ruby in that, despite the hurt she'd witnessed on his face just seconds ago, he was going to play this off as cool.

Let the games begin...

Dr. K winked at Ruby then turned back to Alec. "It's her."

"Does she look mad?"

Ruby crossed her arms.

Dr. K glanced at Ruby, gauging her expression. "Oof. Very."

"Worse than when I got fined for celebratory salsa dancing with that Eagles' cheerleader in the end zone last week?"

Ruby rolled her eyes.

"Oh, yes. Much, much worse than that, Mr. LeBrun," Dr. K said with a severe tone.

The giant man with amazing dimples on the medical table shivered. "Worse than two weeks ago, when I took the Ferrari for a test drive a little too long the day before the big game?"

Ruby blew out an impatient breath. She'd almost forgotten that one. The man drove to Miami on a test drive. From Savannah. Georgia. To Miami!

Dr. K nodded. "Oh, yes. I would say five hundred percent worse than that." The doctor removed his gloves and tossed them in the garbage. He threw away the bandage wrapper, patted Alec on the shoulder, then gave Ruby his customary kiss on each cheek. "Give him hell," he whispered.

Ruby pursed her lips into a smile. "You know I always do, Dr. K. Connors?"

"Already been cleaned up and is meeting with his publicist as we speak."

"He look as bad as Alec here?"

Dr. K winced and shrugged, which meant Connors looked worst.

Great.

Dr. K slipped out of the examination room. As soon as they were alone, Ruby walked to Alec, heels clicking on the linoleum floor. She rounded the table, finally coming face-to-face with her battered target. She opened her mouth to speak but froze when Alec's eyes widened, raked over her, then widened again.

"Damn, woman. I know this means a lot to you, but you didn't have to dress up for me."

Her lips tightened. "I didn't dress up for *you*, Mr. LeBrun. I just came from…somewhere else." She avoided the truth, fearing it might prompt all sorts of intrusive questions, and frankly, her date was none of his concern.

"Was it a date?" He flashed that pretty smile, the one that rendered all the ladies useless. The one that had no effect on her tonight. Mostly. Partially. "Come on, you can tell me."

She ignored the question. "Would you mind telling *me* why you got into a bit of fisticuffs with Connors? You have a press conference in ten minutes, and you need to say *something*."

"You were on a date, weren't you?" His smile

dampened a bit. Was he mad about her being on a date? Because he had no right to be after he'd had the chance with her then blew it!

"If I answer your question, will you answer mine?"

His brown eyes disappeared into a narrow-eyed smile. "Always loved your deal-making ways, Red. Yes, I will."

"Fine. Yes, I was on a date. *Was* being the operative word. But now, I'm here. Dealing with a big baby who can't seem to stop getting in trouble."

"I don't know about baby," he said, jumping off the table, hovering near her at his full six-four height. "But you got the big part right." There was that smile again.

Ruby looked away, biting her bottom lip. She couldn't look straight at him, especially while he was half-naked, lower half wrapped in only a towel. She fished through her briefcase for a pad of paper and pencil, mostly to keep her eyes busy. "It's your turn, LeBrun. Spill. Why did you get into a fight? Can't make love to the woman you want so you've decided to make war—even with your own teammates now?"

He flashed her a dark look.

Ouch. That might've hit below the belt, but if he could give her a hard time about her date, then she could do the same about his breakup.

"Look, Red, I know things have been…weird. I know I've done a few wild things here and there. But I'm not sorry I hit Connors. Fucker deserved it."

"For what? What did he do?" Ruby asked.

"What did you eat at dinner? Was it lobster? Filet

mignon?"

"Why are you being difficult?"

"Why are you interrogating me?" Alec countered, leaning on the desk right across from her.

She felt uncomfortable with him so close, and moved away and into a chair, pretending like it'd been her plan all along. "Because it's my job to find out why you're having tantrums in public, Alec. Now answer my question," she demanded.

He ran his hands through his hair before they fell at his sides. "Look, I'm sorry."

"You don't seem sorry. You seem to want to make my job as difficult as possible. I know you're upset about...*things*...about Colleen. But this isn't the way to handle it."

At the mention of Colleen's name, Alec's expression immediately went blank. They stared at one another. And as the moments ticked by, she wondered if she'd suffered some kind of seizure and imagined the pure lust and near-uncontrollable desire that flashed in his eyes just then.

Was he mourning his broken engagement or not?

When it became apparent he wasn't going to say anything, Ruby took a breath and finally wheeled her chair closer to him. He smelled of fresh shower, soap, shampoo, and pure yumminess. *God help me.* "Alec, everyone has ups and downs, but broken heart aside, the public spectacles need to stop."

Alec's jaw clenched. "You don't know what you're talking about."

She cocked a brow. "I don't?"

"No. You think you do, but you know nothing."

"Well, talk to me then. So you didn't get into a fight because Connors was mouthing off about Colleen? Because that's the rumor that got back to me."

Alec closed his eyes in frustration. "Ruby…"

Her spine snapped straight, and she clapped her hands. "Okay, listen. The real reason doesn't matter. Despite whatever you're going through right now—and I'm sorry you're going through it, Alec, I really am—we need to focus on how to keep your career from imploding. That's priority numero uno. Got it?"

Alec stared at her, as if struggling not to say something, then he slowly transformed, as tension leaked from his body. The charming smile reappeared. That big, wide smile and those perfect white teeth. *Damn him. Damn him to heck.* He looked out from dark lashes, the ones he knew how to wield like a wizard's wand.

Resist, Ruby.

"Look, Red, I got into a little fight. That's all. Don't make it a bigger deal than what it is. Fans love that shit, too, you know."

"Maybe in the World Wrestling Federation, but not the NFL."

That shit-eating grin crossed his face again. He bit into it, then shook his head, repressing silent laughter. "Oh, man."

Her blood began to boil. "So, is that it? You think you can just solve everything with charm? Bring out the ol' smile, and everything is forgiven?"

Alec rubbed the back of his neck. "A little charm never hurt no one, ma'am."

Ruby frowned. "Don't ma'am me, LeBrun."

"Then don't LeBrun me." The chastising look he shot her may as well have been a hard slap to her ass. A rough clenching together of both her hands and a turning of her body to face a wall while he felt every contour of her body with those massive, athletic hands of his.

Ruby wiped a bead of sweat off her forehead.

She tore her gaze away from his and clicked her pen open. "Enough of this. We need to get you ready for the press. We need to find a way to spin why you were fighting with your own teammate."

"Do you want to get dinner afterward?"

Really? Asking her out while there was a crisis at hand? He had to be biding for attention. *Ignore him.* "Already ate." She brushed him off, determined to get through this process. "We know the fight with Connors is going to be the first thing they're going to ask you. There's no point in dancing around it, because that will just drag it out."

"Where'd you eat?"

"Bertoni's," she said quickly. "Okay, we can't go with the 'It won't happen again, it was just a one-time hot, stupid moment,' because this is the third moment in just as many weeks."

"With the breadsticks and the salad? Who'd you go with?"

Ruby tried to focus on her pen moving across the page, on the words that would appear, not only in print, but in audio clips across morning radio shows tomorrow. She resisted the temptation to meet his eyes. "My date. Can you please focus? Like, for two minutes, can you focus? Your public image is at stake here, Alec."

"Who was he?"

"Excuse me?"

"Who'd you go out with? I'm curious about the kind of man you'd date, considering how hard I had to work to get you to say yes to me."

She slapped down the pen and glared at him. "Ah, but the fact is I *did* say yes to you. You're the one who cancelled. Why was it again? Oh, yes, because you got *engaged* the very next day." *You dropped me like a hot potato for the bitchiest cheerleader of them all. Nice, Alec, nice.* "Can we drop the subject now?"

Damn it, she'd let him get to her. Her bitterness was showing, and now he could easily see how much it had pissed her off.

He stood and reached out to her. "Ruby—"

"No!" She backed up.

"I can explain."

The time for that was a long time ago, she almost said. "There's nothing to explain. It should've never happened. You're my client. I'm your publicist. One who's currently in danger of losing her job because my father doesn't think I can handle a hotshot like you."

"Is that what he said?" Something in Alec's face

seemed, for a second, to show remorse. Like, actual remorse for his chain of stupidities. "I'm so sorry. I've been fucking up, I know. But all this shit will get sorted out, I promise."

"It *has* to." She stared at him, letting that sink in. "Because if it doesn't, I'm out of a job, you could lose next year's contract, and my father's firm could lose theirs, too. This isn't a joke. It's time to cut the shit. Are we clear…Mr. LeBrun?"

If that didn't get through to him, nothing would.

"Yeah. We're clear." He folded his arms over his chest, boosting the thickness of his muscles, and holy hell, even his veins had veins on them.

"Good." She forced herself to look down at her notes, though everything on the paper was a blur. "So, about the press conference…you and Connor need to present a united front. Show remorse but shake hands and all that. It'll tell the reporters it was a minor scuffle. I just need to find Connors' publicist and confirm Connors will cooperate."

She made a big show about collecting her things, packing up, and pretending she didn't care he was staring at her with that inscrutable look on his face. But he was, and her chest fluttered with something she couldn't explain. Why—if ultimately, Ruby knew Alec was bad for her—did her body react so opposite from her brain?

Alec leaned into her. She smelled his goodness from a mile away. Her brain conjured up images of his arms around her, her hands running along that streamlined, gorgeous back, fingertips bouncing over those eighteen-pack abs. His scent made her head spin and thighs squeeze closer in aching need.

He picked up her hand, the one busy trying to zip up her case before the big bad wolf snatched her treats out of her basket. "Did you laugh a lot?"

She pulled her hand out of his. "What do you mean?"

"During your date. Did you laugh, smile, make him feel on top of the world, or did you put him through the ringer like you just put me?"

"I've had enough of this." Ruby stood, sending the chair spinning away behind her to clatter noisily against the wall.

"Because I kind of liked it, Ruby. I gotta admit. That was hot."

"You're impossible." She ripped her talking points from the notepad and shoved them against his chest. She didn't let herself feel his pec under her palm. Instead, she walked away. "Stick to the script. And please wear the suit I ordered you. The one that makes you look like a responsible man, not a child prone to playground fights."

At the look on his face, she almost felt bad for what she said. But then she remembered her date. Despite the fact she'd been bored out of her mind and half-glad her father had called her with an excuse to cut the date short, it was still Alec's fault she'd had to cancel personal time to deal with this. As such, *he* was the one who should be apologizing.

But those muscular thighs, defined abs, and wide

shoulders had no intention of apologizing. "Watch it, Red. I've had a hard day. Call me a child one more time…"

"And what?"

"And you don't want to find out," he replied. "I know you have to bust my balls a bit, because of what I did, but I'm warning you, you're pushing it with the whole mommy scolding thing. I told you I'll sort all this out. And a promise is a promise."

"Is that right?"

"Yes, that's right. I might seem like I don't care, but when I promise something, I stick to it." In his eyes, she saw he was dead serious. Still, she'd heard this one too many times.

Ruby scoffed. "That's what you said last time, Alec. You're all words and no action. See you out there." She turned at the door, happy about the way she'd handled the confrontation. Firm, not too weak, resolute. *Good job,* she congratulated herself.

But something she said must've set him off.

"Oh, Ruby…" he drawled, the warning in his voice crystal clear.

She slowed down to look back and check his face for clues.

"I'm *all* action, Ruby. Even after all this time together, I guess you don't have the faintest clue about who I am. We have to change that, don't we?" Then, he did the unthinkable. He dropped his towel, exposing the full Alec LeBrun, and headed straight for her.

Skin gleaming.

Muscles rippling.

Appendages saluting. And swelling.

And bouncing.

A child he wasn't. HOLY. HELL.

He paused, hands on his hips, willing her to look her fill, before he brushed past her and strolled out of the medic room.

Ruby swallowed the lump in her throat and tried to breathe. Just one breath would be good. Oxygen was her friend. But she couldn't speak, couldn't have the last word. Damn Alec. He knew the effect his stunt was having on her, too, because he turned around and caught her staring at his ass down the hallway.

His grin was no longer smartass as much as wolfish.

The game was now 6-0, and Alec LeBrun was in the lead.

2

Alec glanced at the suit hanging in his locker, still wrapped in plastic from the dry cleaners. The one Ruby said would make him look like a responsible man— the better to explain his irresponsible behavior when he'd knocked Connors on his ass after he'd taunted him about a woman. Not Colleen, mind you. Given his very public engagement to her and equally public split, he would've expected that one.

No, Connors had taunted him about *Ruby*.

"You played like shit today, LeBrun. What, were you thinking of finally fucking the team's publicist, now that Colleen's out of the picture? Can't blame you. She's hot as hell, and I bet she's feisty as fuck in bed, too. You know how redheads are."

That motherfucker.

Alec had been on edge the past month ever since Colleen had played him for a fool. In the end, it was good riddance to her, but it still burned that he'd lost his chance with Ruby because of Colleen, and Connors' asshole comments simply reminded him of that fact. Also, he *had* played like shit, so by the time Connors mouthed off like a stupid fuckboy in the locker room, Alec was ready for a fight. He'd swung with pure rage and every intention of breaking every bone in Connors' face. Connors blocked Alec, but Alec managed to get a fist into his nose anyway.

Blood flew. Bones cracked.

It had taken several of their teammates to pull them apart, as they glared and spat expletives, heaving chests and faces bleeding. Coach had nearly had a fucking stroke ripping into their asses after that, but Alec barely heard him. He was still too irritated about what Connors had said.

No one talked about Ruby that way. If one woman was off-limits and deserved respect in this crazy world of professional football, it was her. Connors, who'd obviously picked up on Alec's feelings for her, should have known that. But *how* had he figured it out?

Alec had only ever told his best friends on the team—and in life—Heath and Kyle, his feelings for Ruby, and they'd sworn never to say anything. They were also the only two people on earth, besides Colleen, who knew why Alec, less than twenty-four hours after he'd asked Ruby out, had proposed to Colleen in the first place: Colleen had told him she was pregnant.

As expected, Alec had reeled at the announcement. Not just because the prospect of unexpected fatherhood had terrified the shit out of him—what if he turned out to be as horrible a father as his own?—but mostly because he'd known instantly he had to do the right thing, which meant kissing any chance with Ruby goodbye and instead tying himself permanently to Colleen, a woman he'd slept with because she was gorgeous and good in bed, but had never developed deeper feelings for no matter how hard he'd tried to make things work between them. So he'd done what he'd thought was right. He'd proposed. He'd moved Colleen into his house and set a wedding date for the beginning of October, just two months later. But in the end, he hadn't been able to go through with it.

As much of a shock as an unwanted pregnancy had been, Alec had quickly fallen in love with his unborn child. And he'd come to understand that marrying Colleen out of obligation wouldn't create the kind of family he wanted his child to grow up with. So several weeks ago, just two weeks before the wedding, he'd told Colleen he couldn't marry her but was willing to remain an involved co-parent. She became incensed and admitted the truth— no baby. It'd all been a trap.

Alec had once again been floored—this time by how much he'd grieved the loss of a child who had never even existed. The loss of his chance to prove that he could indeed be a good father, unlike his own. His feelings had consumed him, making him drink more than he ever had, making him lose focus on everything else.

But it was time to pull his shit together. The drinking, the fighting—it had to stop. Not only for his career. But for Ruby's.

Ruby.

Clearly she was under the assumption—as everyone else was—that he'd loved Colleen and was devastated over their broken engagement, and that was why he'd been drinking and fighting so much lately. It was the natural assumption, of course. After all, he'd chosen not to tell-all to the public out of respect for Colleen. Yes, even after she'd shown her true colors, he still held integrity and divulged nothing to the press. But he'd shown a woman who'd lied to him more care than he'd shown Ruby, a woman who'd always earned his respect.

And, if he was honest to himself, a woman who'd always owned his heart.

With all the bullshit with Colleen, the last thing he'd been thinking about was dating again. Even Ruby. But that was before she'd walked in, looking gorgeous and getting in his face. It was as if she'd slapped him out of a trance he'd been in. For the first time in weeks, his vision had cleared and he was himself again. And he'd also been infused with purpose.

He'd come to want the baby he'd thought was his, but it was never meant to be.

That wasn't the case with Ruby.

He wanted her. And if the way she reacted to him— when he was wearing his towel and when he wasn't—was anything to go by, she still wanted him. He was going to make sure they both got what they wanted. That would mean sitting down with her and explaining what had happened with Colleen. It would also mean *showing* Ruby how he felt about her, which meant, as much as he hated it, taking things slow.

For starters, his breakup was still fresh, and people would talk about him. Also, his emotions were still raw from being played for an idiot. He needed to make sure the situation with Colleen was completely behind him before pursuing Ruby. Finally, he knew full well the reason he'd had to work so hard to get Ruby to say yes to his dinner invitation two month ago—her job, and her reluctance to cross professional boundaries.

Now, it would probably take a miracle to convince her to go out with him. He didn't want to fuck things up with her a second time. Women like Ruby rarely gave him another shot. Women like Ruby were too good for him. But it was time to move on now. Time to prove he had his and her best interests at heart, beginning tonight. All he could do was pray she'd give him a chance.

So Alec changed into the suit, appreciating the care Ruby had taken to pick out something that fit him perfectly, while at the same time replaying how fucking gorgeous she'd looked standing in front of him in that little black dress and heels, her hair long and wild cascading down her shoulders.

She was beautiful always, no matter what she wore, but given he'd only ever seen her in business clothes, it'd been a huge transformation.

It made him wonder how else she might transform. If they were in the bedroom, let's say. What would Ruby O'Brien be like between the sheets? Uptight? Innocent? Or full of piss and vinegar like she was every time he fucked up and she had to come looking for him? It was only about the thousandth time he'd wondered such things, and as always, he came to one conclusion. He'd bet his Super Bowl ring and every dime he had that a passionately aroused Ruby would be wild with desire, a freak in bed.

Maybe it was the way she always looked at him with those sexy, blue eyes, lips just barely parted in disbelief.

Or the way she'd stared at his naked body between the time he'd dropped his towel and the time he'd walked past her. She'd flushed, shocked eyes focused on his dick. Her breath had caught, and for a brief moment, he'd contemplated taking her square by the shoulders and fucking her right up against those lockers.

Maybe one day, dude. If you're lucky.

Looking sharp in his suit, Alec walked to the press room, where to his surprise, Connors awaited him alone. He had a butterfly bandage on his cheek, which covered what Alec knew was a nasty gash. He'd put it there. "Hey, man," Connors said.

"Hey." Alec kept a short distance from the shorter, bulkier player.

"You have a minute?"

"Not really." Outside the room, he could hear the reporters gathering for the press conference and wished he could just get this over with.

"Look, bro…normally, you're the ass, but tonight, I was out of line." Connors rubbed his chin and carefully touched his wound with his fingertips.

"Yep. You were."

"And my publicist just told me that if things get out about what I said to you, I might lose my endorsement to Hertz."

"Hertz?"

"Yeah. We can't all be Nike posterboys." Connors looked like he wanted to start another fight then remembered his career was on the line. "Anyway, I just wanted to say, why don't we get through this, salvage this situation, and be done with it?"

"Sounds good by me."

"You have my word I won't say anything about Ruby again."

Alec gave him a sharp look. "Don't even use her name around me, dude. Not even once. I'm warning you."

Connors lifted his hands in surrender. "Fine, fine. So you know, I only said those things because I was jealous as fuck. She's amazing and the way she looks at you... Well, good luck, bro. Truce?" He held his hand out to Alec.

Alec stared at it a minute, wanting to ask Connors how Ruby looked at him. God, he was pathetic. Instead, he nodded and tossed his hand into Connors'. "Sure, man. Truce. Let's go. I hear them coming." Sure enough, a moment later, the door opened and there stood a member of the press, letting them know they were ready.

Once the room had filled, Alec's gaze found Ruby, sitting in the back of the audience. He wasn't looking forward to standing in front of all those cameras, microphones, and reporters asking their questions, but one look at Ruby's face made things better. Despite the shit he'd pulled in the locker room, she smiled encouragingly at him.

Coach Reddick talked first. After he was done, he signaled for Alec to take the stage. Alec didn't bother to pull out the crumpled piece of notebook paper from his pocket, the one Ruby had shoved at him before he'd stormed out of the med room. He'd had enough experience talking to the press to know what to do. When it was time, he walked up to the podium in front of fifty reporters, photographers, and their camera flashes. He smiled and waved. And when the first reporter asked what had happened with Connors, Alec told them the truth.

"I hold myself personally responsible for the loss, fellas. I feel like I let my teammates down out there when all I ever want is to do the best I can for my teammates, for my fans, for the city of Savannah. Tensions and adrenaline were high, and it wasn't right, but Connors made a joke, and I didn't like it. We've already talked it through and put it behind us. We're good now, united in a common goal. We're going to demolish New Orleans on Sunday then go watch the new Marvel movie together. He's bringing the popcorn." Alec smiled, and flash bulbs went off.

Everyone in the room laughed.

Ruby smiled. Good. She was pleased. Alec couldn't believe how the sight of that smile affected him.

One reporter raised his hand. "Alec, what was Connors' joke about? Was it about Colleen? Are you still in touch with her, and is there any chance of a reconciliation?"

Alec had hoped that would be the end of their questions, but clearly the sharks hadn't had their fill of blood yet. At the question, Alec expected Ruby to shake her head, to frantically point at her notebook with her pen, reminding him to stick to the script. Instead, Ruby O'Brien, unattainable woman extraordinaire, watched him with wide eyes and bit her lip, a furrow between her brows. Anxiously awaiting his answer.

"No, Ben, there's absolutely no chance of a reconciliation. I wish Colleen well. Mutual breakup. But the end of any relationship is hard and I haven't been focused on what's important. That's about to change."

As he said it, everyone jotted down his words or recorded them with devices, all while he gazed across the room at Ruby. Sending an unspoken message. Guessing she probably wouldn't get it but trying anyway.

"What's important" was her. He was going to start focusing on her.

And if he had his wish, things between them were eventually going to change in a very big way

3

Ruby stood at the back of the press room, watching as Alec, Connors, and Coach Reddick talked near the podium. After Alec's articulate speech, Connors had taken the stage and basically backed up everything Alec had said. The reporters had all left, and although she should have already been headed home herself, she hung back, wanting to speak with Alec in private.

He'd handled himself well. She needed to tell him that after the hard time she'd given him. Tell him she believed in him and would do all she could to help him do what he promised—put the last month behind him and focus on what was important...his career.

That's what he meant, right?

Maybe it was wishful thinking, what with him staring straight at her during the entire press conference, but part of her wondered if he'd meant something else. If he'd meant that *she* was his new focus.

She had to admit, she was pretty darn pleased when

Alec had said there was no chance of him and Colleen reconciling. Considering everything that had happened between them and the fact Alec's statement hadn't addressed whether he still loved Colleen, Ruby's reaction to it only proved what an utter fool she continued to be for the man.

Finally, Coach and Connors left, waving at Ruby. She waved back and tried not to feel nervous about Alec walking straight toward her like a male model strutting down the catwalk, hands in his pockets. He stopped a few feet short of her but didn't say anything.

She cleared her throat. "You did great, Alec. You didn't stick to the script, but you did it your own way. I'm proud of you. Maybe now you can start over fresh." She hadn't meant that in a personal way—she'd meant it, as in his career—but now the subliminal message was out there.

Start over fresh, Alec. Start over with me.

"I meant what I said. I haven't been myself, but that's behind me now. I know it'll take work to repair the damage I've done to my reputation this past month—"

"That's what I'm here for." Their gazes locked. She had a hard time pulling away from those dark brown eyes and chiseled face. "I've already got some ideas. I just needed to know you were ready before I brought them up to you."

He smiled slightly. Not the shit-eating grin he usually wore but finally, a sincere one. "Well, I'm ready. And thank you for sticking by me. You're a great publicist, Ruby."

She mentally winced. Right. His publicist. *That's what I am to him. Remember that, Ruby! Ugh.* "Why don't I give you a call this week and we can schedule an appointment to talk about where to go from here? I—"

"Do you want to talk now?" He gestured to the door, as though they should get going. "I know you said you already ate, but I'm starving, and Giraldi's is just a couple of blocks away. Want to keep me company?"

"Alec…"

Would this be crossing the line? It wouldn't feel like it with any of her other clients, but she didn't have feelings for her other clients like she did for Alec.

"Strictly publicity strategy over dinner," Alec added, noticing her hesitation.

Ruby pondered the idea. It would be far safer if they scheduled an appointment and spoke in one of the meeting rooms in the next day or two. On the other hand, she was making this a big deal. The more she treated it like one, the more it would be. What happened to Focused Ruby? In-charge, Confident Ruby? "Sure." She smiled, plucking her bag from a chair in the back row. "Sounds great, Alec. Let's do this."

Twenty minutes later, they were sitting at a table, as Alec browsed a menu and Ruby pretended to check emails just so she wouldn't have to stare at Alec. He looked so incredibly handsome still in his suit, overdressed for this place, but then again, so was she.

It was almost like a redo of her date earlier with Greg, but instead of sitting across from a perfectly nice attorney who did nothing for her, she was sitting across from Alec.

Ugh, this is nothing like a date, Ruby! She nearly slapped herself back to center. This was business. Nothing but business.

Alec leaned over to look under the table. "You okay?"

"Yeah, why?"

"Your leg's shaking."

"Is it?" She laughed nervously. "Force of habit, I guess."

"So, you always shake your leg?" he chided her.

Or only when you're nervous? She could almost hear his thoughts. It was becoming more and more obvious that she was attracted to him and stupid to think she could make it through the entire meeting without giving herself away.

"Not always. Just when I'm thinking." *That's right, Ruby, you're a thinker. A smart, confident publicist, not at all a nervous woman on a date—business meeting!—with her crush.*

"It's good to think." He chuckled. "Good for the brain."

"Yes," she said. "You should do it more often."

"Oh!" Alec's eyebrows rose. He pointed at her with a smile. "Touché, Miss O'Brien. I will endeavor to think clearly and not fuck up your life from now on." He returned to studying the menu.

Ruby second-guessed everything about that exchange.

She loved that she'd regained the upper hand but hoped she hadn't come across as scolding him again when they had agreed to start over—start fresh.

"You sure you don't want anything?" Alec asked.

She shook her head. "Just a cup of coffee would be great. What are you going to have?"

"I'm thinking filet mignon, polenta, and a salad of some kind. What are your thoughts on arugula?"

She couldn't stop the laugh that burst out of her.

"What's so funny?"

"Endeavor. Arugula." She shrugged. "Who knew that Alec LeBrun had such an extensive vocabulary?"

He grinned. "Hey, I'm a man of many talents."

"That you are." Good God, she hadn't meant it that way, but there it was. It was the least she could do for taking two digs at him in the same minute.

He beamed, positively pleased with himself.

Was that sweat beading up on her forehead? She swiped at it, disguising it as fixing her hair. After he ordered, and the waiter brought her coffee, he leaned back and pinned her with his gaze.

"So, I get it. My behavior has been jeopardizing your job."

"Ah. I believe what I said was I was currently in danger of losing my job because my father doesn't think I can handle a hotshot like you."

"Evidenced by my bad behavior of late."

"Well, yes."

"Damn, sorry about the stunts. But they were great

stunts, weren't they? Especially the drive in the Ferrari."

"No, Alec, there was nothing funny about them."

"Not even a little?" He cocked his head.

Okay, she was starting to get it. Alec LeBrun liked to cover up pain. She totally understood how he would act up in the wake of his breakup—the joy ride, the fights, the excessive dancing in the end zone—but now that they were together, in private, he didn't need to call them "stunts" and pretend they were for show.

"Alec, I'm not the press. You don't have to slap on a charming smile and pretend it's all fun and games. You can tell me what's really going on. I can help you fix whatever is wrong. Fixing problems is my job."

He scowled, obviously bothered at the suggestion that he might be any kind of problem she had to fix. "Just life, Ruby. I'll get my shit together, don't worry. I always have."

And he had tonight. He'd pulled things together so well, it'd given her hope he might finally be on track. That was one thing she always liked about Alec, as evidenced by the suit, the apology, the action... It might take him a while, but eventually, he always owned up. The man knew when he was fucking up. He worked to fix it. If there was anything she hated, it was clients who never believed they were in the wrong.

"I believe you, Alec."

"Good." He gave her a soft smile, a moment of contemplation, then he folded his hands, ready to change the subject. "So, this thing about possibly losing your job, sounds like you have a complicated relationship with your dad."

She took a sip of coffee and shrugged. "My dad just wants me to do well. He's always been that way. Sometimes it seems like too much, but he's always believed in me. The last thing I want to do is disappoint him."

"You're not a disappointment to anyone, Ruby. You're the best. Everyone on the team says so. I'm sure your father knows that, too."

"Thanks, but I still have a job to do."

"And you'll do it. You already have. Eh?" He held his arms out, as if showing just how much she'd already reined Alec in. She'd dressed him up, cleaned him up. And damn, did he look hot as hell.

"Very nice, I have to admit," she replied.

"Thank you. But this is killing me." He loosened his tie, removed it, and unbuttoned the top button. Now, he looked more casual and relaxed but still super sexy. "There we go." He smiled at her. "Now, what do you want to talk about?"

She wanted to talk about a lot of things. But the only thing they could talk about was strategy. She folded her hands on the table. "Okay, so... I have some ideas to follow up on the positive turn you took at the press conference. Obviously, the past month has been an aberration, so we need to focus on what you've done so well in the past. Let's have you photographed attending a bunch of charity events, especially ones with kids but also—"

"Well, well. Look who we have here." A woman's voice interjected. High-pitched, Southern, and not at all welcome.

Immediately, Alec shot her an evil glance. Colleen stood a few feet away from their table, almost as if she was too afraid to come any closer. She wore jeans and a ruffled, yellow top, and a scowl. She was gorgeous. Tall and lithe, her skin a honey-brown, the epitome of an NFL cheerleader. Every inch of her, meticulously beautiful.

Ruby spotted two other women—her friends, Ruby thought—waiting for Colleen next to a column inside the restaurant. They must've just dined and were on their way out.

Alec's entire body became rigid. His face, which had been relaxed, amused, and dare she say...almost happy since the press conference...hardened. His jawline clenched.

Colleen's knuckles turned white because she was grasping her purse so tightly. Her gaze was on Alec as she shook her head. "I can't believe I've been calling you, and you haven't returned a single call. Yet you have time to be having dinner here with *her*."

As she spoke, pretty damn loudly, as a matter of fact, from the looks of restaurant patrons at nearby tables, it immediately became apparent that Colleen was intoxicated. *God, no, please.* This had the makings of disaster all over it. After the success Alec had had at the press conference, she prayed he and Colleen could act civilized while in public.

Maybe a friendly face would diffuse her? Ruby stood and held out her hand. "Hi, Colleen. I don't know if you remember me, but I'm Ruby O—"

"I know who you are, Ruby-O," Colleen hissed.

Okay, Ruby thought.

Alec stood and positioned himself between her and Colleen, facing his ex. His body language was clear—get the hell out and don't mess with my life. "What do you want, Colleen?"

"I want you to stop ignoring me."

"I'm not ignoring you. We're not together anymore, which is different. Now, please leave." Alec's voice was low and edgy.

"Alec...sugar." Her tone changed, as she approached him. Ruby got a sinking feeling in her stomach.

Note to self: *Never call Alec sugar.*

"I know you're upset, but we can work this out."

"No. We can't. And this is the wrong place to do this, Colleen."

"Alec, I was your *fiancée*. Doesn't that count for anything? Have you forgotten everything we had together?" Colleen pleaded.

"You *were* my fiancée until I found out you lied and betrayed me. Do you think I haven't forgotten that? What you did to me?" He looked like he wanted to shake her, his anger barely leashed. "Don't push me, Colleen. Just turn the fuck around...and go."

Ruby looked around, gave a gentle smile to the

onlookers, and wrung her hands. *Earth, swallow me now.* This was all she needed—another "stunt" to appear in the morning news. Luckily, there didn't seem to be any lingering reporters.

"I only did what I did because I love you and wanted you back!" Colleen tried to touch his face, but he jerked away. "It was bad of me, I know it. It wasn't the right thing to do, but if you'd just listen to me, I'm fixin' to—"

"You're fixin' to leave, Colleen. Right now with your friends. I'm not doing this again. I've moved on with my life."

"Moved on? Seriously? After only a month? And with this little slut?" She gave Ruby a pointed look. Colleen's scoff was the loudest thing in the room.

You could hear a pin drop, the silence was so deafening. Ruby wanted to stand up, yell, say something, but she couldn't. Her voice had been sucked from her soul. Slut? She gasped a breath, but Alec took over before she could say a word.

Alec blocked all of Colleen's nasty self from Ruby's view. "Enough. You just bought yourself trouble. First, you're going to apologize to Ruby. Then, if you want any chance of keeping the next victim you're currently seeing, you're going to leave right now, otherwise I will make what happened between us public."

Wait, what? What did he mean by next victim? What had Colleen done to piss Alec off so bad? And why all the hullaballoo if she was already dating someone new?

Alec's voice was harsher than Ruby had ever heard it.

She was glad that anger wasn't directed toward her. He practically vibrated with it. "Apologize," he prodded.

"I'm not apologizing for shit, and I'm not seeing Bryant anymore, sugar. I've already ended things with him. You're the one I belong with. I'm not giving up. I'm going to show you we belong together." With a final glare at Ruby, Colleen turned and left, her gait unsteady.

Ruby shielded her eyes from what would certainly be a train wreck any minute now.

"Do you think she'll be okay? She seemed pretty lit."

Alec shook his head. "Not my problem. Not anymore." Out front, they heard a commotion—the manager dealing with Colleen ranting and raving about Alec to her friends. Just on time, the waiter brought Alec his food, but he simply stared at it, his appetite seemingly completely gone.

"She lied and betrayed you?" Ruby asked, leaning in. Why didn't she know about this? And how come she wanted to know the details, not as his publicist, but because she cared? "Never mind. It's not my business."

"Actually, it is."

"What do you mean?"

Alec sighed and looked at her with his soulful eyes. She felt a flutter inside her chest. "I mean I'm into you, Ruby. I've *been* into you since the moment I first met you. My relationship with Colleen was already headed toward a close, but I made sure it happened sooner than later because I wanted to ask you out."

She stiffened. "You did ask me out. Then you got

engaged to her."

"Yes, but not because I wanted her more than I wanted you. I didn't want her at all, in fact."

"Alec..." Ruby shook her head. "You're not making any sense."

"I know. I'm going to explain. I wanted to wait to tell you, to prove to you that I was in a good place and had my shit together, but it doesn't look like that's the way to go. Because Colleen isn't going to give up, and before she messes things up for us even more than she has, I want to tell you the truth."

Messes things up for us? *What truth?* "I don't understand, Alec."

"I know you don't, but you're going to. It's just that— we were having such a good time. And I don't want Colleen to direct the show, if you get what I mean. I'll tell you on my terms, not hers. Can we just have tonight?"

Was this still a business meeting, or had Alec just turned it into a date? Because the truth was, Ruby would be perfectly okay with a date, except...she felt scared. Scared Alec would mess with her emotions again, claim to like her again, then run off when things got inconvenient again.

"For what, Alec? Just tell me your intentions, please, and make them clear, and be honest," Ruby said.

"Fair enough. I want this meal. I want to talk with you. I want to enjoy your company, if you'll let me. And then, I'll tell you everything. The reason I've been acting strange. I just need...your trust. Does that sound okay?"

Ruby stared at Alec, confused and her heart thumping, feeling as if something momentous was about to happen. She took a deep breath, then nodded. "Of course. You have my trust, Alec. But I have to say, this has been a crazy, wild-ass evening, and I'm going to need more than coffee."

Alec called the waiter over. "Hey, man, the lady and I will have a drink."

"Yes, sir. What would you like?"

Despite the weirdness of the night, Ruby was having fun with Alec. She bit her lip and shook her head. Somehow, he'd snuck his way into her life and claimed his date with her, after all. Not a bad way to end the night.

Or was it just beginning?

Before Alec could reply to the waiter, Ruby ordered for them. "Two shots of your best whisky," she said. "Actually, make them doubles."

4

Alec climbed out of the *Lyft* car and blinked up at the lights of the Bootleggers logo on the side of the stadium. Why were they here again? After his double whisky with Ruby, they'd talked, laughed, and had a great time, but when dinner was over, Ruby had bitten her lip in that sexy way she'd started to do since taking her first shot—since being confronted by Colleen—and said, "Want to get out of here?"

He'd hardened at her words. "Fuck yeah, Red." Though they weren't exactly drunk after their one and only double shot, they were pleasantly tipsy. Enough to take the edge off of running into Colleen. At one in the morning, the night was still young, and he'd go anywhere with Ruby.

He'd thought maybe she'd meant her place or somewhere sexier. He had no idea she'd choose the stadium on the *Lyft* app. Then again, they'd left their cars there.

"The game was over hours ago, guys." The driver poked his head out the window. "You sure this is where you want to go?"

"Yep. My car's still here," Ruby replied. "We walked to the restaurant. Have a good night."

"You, too." The man drove away, leaving them there alone in the cooling night.

At first, Alec expected Ruby to start walking to her car, but instead, she turned on her heels and headed toward the side of the stadium. "Where are we going?"

"You'll see." She smiled over her shoulder.

Amazing that they were together like this after she'd ripped him a new one earlier tonight. Even more amazing that she wasn't just okay with it—she'd instigated it.

"I love coming here after hours," she said. "But I can't walk with these damn shoes right now." She limped through the gravel and eventually gave up and took off her shoes, chucking them as far into the parking lot as she could.

He laughed out loud, the sound echoing through the lot. "Nice! Not a bad arm." Her shoes landed under the glow of a lamppost. Because he wanted to see her smile, he took off his own shoes and threw them into the parking lot as well. They landed a lot farther than Ruby's. "There. Now we're both barefoot."

She laughed then fished around in the jumbled contents of her purse for her badge. "I'm barefoot. You still have socks on."

"Fine." Alec took off his socks one at a time then

chucked those, too. He had no idea what the fuck they were doing, but it was fun. Besides, he'd rather be anywhere than back at the bar with Colleen stalking him. "So, you like coming here?"

"Yeah. Brings me back to when I was a kid, when I used to come with my dad after games. Roquefort was quarterback back then."

"One of my heroes." Alec smiled.

He remembered as a kid always watching Roquefort play on TV. Every time it seemed the game was over, he'd pull some stunt in the last seconds in overtime and tie the game or win it altogether. He remembered the way he couldn't breathe and his stomach would be in his throat and a single second would drag into minutes.

That pins-and-needles drama was how he felt when he saw Colleen tonight. When he'd looked over Ruby's shoulder and seen his ex standing there. What was she doing at Giraldi's anyway? She hated that place, preferring the high-end hotel bars in the trendy areas of Savannah instead. He knew well enough. Eighteen fucking dollars for rosé wine. Bullshit.

"Ruby? Would you ever pay eighteen dollars for rosé?"

"A bottle?"

"A glass."

"Bullshit."

Alec smiled to himself. Damn straight it was bullshit. *I adore this woman,* he thought. "Red?"

"Yeah."

"Should we have done drinks together?"

"It was just one drink, Alec."

"Yeah, one massive one." He chuckled. *Massive.* Like his cock watching Ruby walk ahead of him, her ass swaying gently from left to right. That girl possessed talents she didn't even know she had. Talents he wished she'd one day let him touch. And if it happened tonight, as much as he'd thought they should go slow, well, Colleen had changed all that. One thing was for sure, touching Ruby would certainly erase the Bootleggers' loss. Would erase the whole Colleen fiasco, too.

They turned down a hallway and unlocked a door with her badge. It was then he realized where she was taking him—the tunnel walk. It was the tunnel they ran through to get on and off the field. Normally, it echoed with the cheers of ten thousand fans cheering his name, but now it was silent. All he heard were his and Ruby's bare feet against the concrete.

They came out the other end.

Out on the field, it was dead silent. No blasting out behind his teammates. No shoulder pads and gleaming helmets. Only Ruby's dark silhouette outlined against the stadium flood lamps on the field. *Pure female,* he thought.

His eyes moved with the sway of her hips. As she reached up and tugged at her hair, he watched the knot she'd tied in the car fall, allowing those red waves to cascade over her shoulders. Damn. He stared in amazement at her delicate fingers loosely at her side. How would Ruby O'Brien use those fingers? Would she be gentle and inexperienced, or aggressive and fierce? Either way, his body shuddered with excitement.

Alec was used to his heart thudding in his chest as he made his way toward the field after coming out of this tunnel, but he was not used to it thrashing like it was about to leap out the way it was then. Ruby smiled at the edge of the turf, then stepped right onto the grass without hesitation. Like she played here every day. Like she'd been born on this field.

He followed her all the way to the fifty-yard line, toes enjoying the cool grass, as he slowed his pace to watch her find her preferred spot. Staring up at the stands that stretched high above, Ruby beamed at the lights that shone down on her, at the dome of night sky arching over them. Alec had been on this field a hundred times but would never look at it the same way ever again.

"I sneak in here sometimes when it's empty," she said. "I love it."

"Agreed." Alec joined her on the white painted hashtag marking the middle of the field. "But why do you do it?"

Ruby turned to him. Her lipstick—normally a glossy, vibrant red—had faded a bit. Alec liked it. It looked like he'd imagine it would if he'd been kissing her hour after hour, never getting enough of the taste of her. From the moment they were introduced, Alec knew he was going to have a hard time keeping business separate from pleasure. It'd been a year since they met.

"I don't know." Ruby smiled to herself. "There's just

something powerful about having this place all to yourself. You know what I mean?"

Definitely. So why had he never thought to come here after hours like she had? Funny that this woman, his publicist, loved the stadium more than he did. "If you were a guy, would you have played football?"

"Oh, yeah. Yeah." Ruby nodded. "I love everything about the game. As a kid, football, to me, meant having my dad all to myself on Sundays and Monday nights."

Alec could only watch her with a goofy smile.

Nothing sexier than a woman who loved his sport. He wanted to take her hand, wanted to kiss her here underneath the lights. That was one thing he'd never done—kiss a woman in his team's own stadium. Not even with Colleen. After the games, she'd take off as soon as she could.

Ruby looked at him with hesitation. Big blue eyes debating how much to share with him. How far she should open the door into the deepest parts of her heart. Gauging to see if he was worth it. He wanted to be worth her time. He knew he'd have to drastically change his ways, but he would do it if it meant having a chance with Ruby.

"It also centers me to be here," she added after some time. "In some ways, I feel like I'm always under attack. Do this, Ruby. Do that, Ruby. Better control that guy quick, or you're going to lose your job, Ruby."

It pained Alec to keep hearing he was almost the reason Ruby got in trouble with her father. But he also understood every word she said. He related to the voices, the yelling, the pulling and pushing in all directions except the one he wanted to follow. Coach wanted one thing from him. His agent wanted another. His fans wanted more, more, more. More catches. More yards. More fucking fantasy points. His friends wanted free stuff, season tickets, backstage passes, more and more free stuff.

Even Colleen still wanted him.

No fucking way.

It might've taken him a year, but he eventually realized what she was all about—his money, name, and status. She wanted him badly enough to lie. Because of her *bullshit*, he'd lost Ruby. Lost her before they even got the chance to get started.

"I know exactly what you mean, Red. We live similar lives. Just different sides of the same coin. Sorry for all the trouble I gave you. If you'll let me"—he moved in closer to her—"I'll more than make it up to you."

Ruby bit her lip, and Alec moved in a couple of steps closer, his hand reaching out to brush lightly against her forearm. She shivered under his touch. Maybe it was too soon, but it felt right. Here they were together sharing a moment. He'd do anything to taste those lips. Leaning his head down, he tipped the underside of his chin up toward her.

"The, um, the lights," she said, looking away shyly all of a sudden.

"What about them?"

"They're…they're pretty bright."

Alec dropped his hands and glanced up. He'd

forgotten where they were, standing in the middle of a wide-open football field under the glare of a thousand bulbs. "I guess they are." He chuckled, shaking his head.

Damn, that was close. So close that now his body needed her, wanted her so badly. What was it about Ruby O'Brien that drove him this crazy? He caught a glimpse of Ruby's eyes glancing up at him, as though gauging what he was thinking. His breath grew heavier, as he tried to force his heartbeat down.

"So...it's getting late," Ruby muttered. "Did you still want to talk about...you know?"

How fucking beautiful you are? Yeah, I do. And then I want to pull you into my arms, Ruby. Kiss you like you've never been kissed. Instead, all Alec could say was, "Yeah, sure. Let's talk business." He clasped his hands obediently, muttering in his mind.

This was Ruby. He wasn't going to be able to just say something suave to her then get her into bed. There was too much riding on this relationship. He'd have to play his cards right if he wanted this to ever happen.

"No, not business, Alec. Colleen. You were going to tell me what happened between you two, remember?"

"Oh, that." He felt like an idiot.

But Alec didn't start explaining about Colleen and how she'd fucked him over. Because in that next moment, there was a hum and then all the flood lamps extinguished as one. Once the flare of the bulbs died above him, Alec blinked in the new darkness. He could just barely see Ruby's shape still standing in front of him under the half cloud covered moon. He could hear her breathing, ragged and strained. Her chest heaved.

They stood there, blanketed by inky night. If she hadn't run screaming from him yet, he had no reason to believe she would. No, he wasn't imagining things. She wanted him—he could feel it. Even in the dark, he knew Ruby wanted him now.

Yes, finally.

Alec couldn't tell who crashed into who first, but they came together in a moment of pure release. Fuck it. All night, they'd been eyeing each other, flirting, and making their feelings clear. They'd talked about their current lives, about their work, and about their dreams. It had to come to this. They'd deal with the consequences, if any, later.

Right now, he just wanted to feel the warmth of Ruby's lips on his, feel her arms gripping his back, feel the swell of her ass, as he pulled her tighter toward him. Her gasp when she felt the push of his cock against her, proving how much he wanted her. The soft, loose strands of her hair caressing his hand as he touched her neck. Her tongue dragging against his bottom lip as he dug his thumbs across her hip bones.

God, he wanted her. So fucking badly.

Her moan drowned in the heat between them while his mind drowned in the intoxicating scent of her perfume that lingered just behind her ear. His hands felt every inch of her outer body, and hers explored his back and shoulders. When he panted, she pulled him closer, but there was no space left between them. That didn't stop Alec from trying to fuse as one with her there in the dark.

"Alec," Ruby gasped, as he nipped at her earlobe. "What are we doing?"

"Well, right now, I'm kissing the most amazing woman I've ever known."

"Alec, I'm serious."

"Red, I'm trying," he growled, as her fierce grip yanked at his hair. "But I can't stop. I just fucking want you so much. You don't understand how long I've wanted you. I've dreamed of it for so long."

"We had our shot. You threw it away."

"No. It just wasn't the right time." It may *still* not have been the right time, but he had to find out once and for all how she felt about him. So far, the feeling was pretty much mutual.

She kissed a line down the vein in his neck, kneaded his chest, and pushed up against him. Then, suddenly, she pulled away as if realizing this was all a mistake. They were a hot mess of heaving chests and lustful stares. Alec resisted the urge to draw her back to him, to his hungry mouth and growing erection. It took more strength than he'd ever expended in any weight room or on any field. His whole body was pulled taut like an arrow ready to be shot.

"Alec, if we do this, we'll have to deal with the consequences. This could be bad." Her breath shuddered.

"No. Nothing bad could come of us being together. Don't you want to just live in the moment, Ruby? Because you can. I won't let any harm come to you. Not because of me. I swear. Focus on now. Which is a pretty fucking sweet place to be, pressing my palm against your lower back." Alec's hand slid down her spine. "Right here."

Ruby looked up at him, and Alec thought he didn't see any of the apprehension, hesitation, doubt he saw in them earlier. He saw only openness and willingness and, above all else, desire.

"What else is happening now?" she asked in a whisper.

"Right now, I'm unzipping the back of your dress, Red." Alec's hands quivered as they slipped the garment from her shoulders. "It's a pretty sweet dress, but it's got to go."

"What now?" she asked, once the dress had slipped from her shoulders and opened up her entire, slender back.

"Now, I'm taking the whole thing off, so I can see your amazing body."

The black dress easily pooled at her still bare feet. Underneath, she wore a black lace bra and matching thong. Her body was tight, lean, with curves in all the right places. All he could do was suck in a breath at the sight of her, nearly bare for him.

Ruby's voice came from inside a dream. "And now?"

Alec made sure Ruby's eyes were on his, as he undid the button of his shirt and pants and let everything fall, one piece at a time, onto the turf below. "And now I'm getting rid of all this shit between us," he said, thinking how much these clothes were a metaphor for all the obstacles in their way.

As he worked to remove the last bits, she slid down her black panties, slowly exposing her silhouetted body, and plucked off her bra. The woman of his dreams stood naked before him. He shuddered and shook his head in disbelief.

"And now?"

His voice was husky. "And now I'm finally giving us what we both want."

Alec pulled Ruby to him and dragged her down on top of him on the turf. Ruby straddled his hips and grinded herself against his exposed erection. He moaned, as she moved again, his hands reaching for her breasts, cupping them each, playing with her hard nipples. She pulled his hands back and pinned them above his head.

So she was feisty after all. Just like he'd imagine she'd be. He could almost reach her tits with his mouth, the way she leaned over him, but they were just out of reach. His cock strained against her. He knew this would be fast and furious. If he ever wanted to take this more slowly, it'd have to be another night. Tonight, she was all about attack.

He could do attack. He loved attack. Especially when it came from her. The thought that this woman who worked so hard to keep appearances, who earlier he swore even hated her in that medic room wanted him made his head feel light.

"Here and now, I have to know. Are you sure you want to do this, Red?"

"Yeah."

"Why? Tell me why."

"Because I want you. I've wanted you a long time, Alec. I can't explain it."

"You don't have to," he said before kissing her hard on the lips.

She pulled away. "Condom?"

He couldn't believe what she was saying. Now that this moment had come, he wondered if it would end all too quickly. No point in worrying. He would enjoy every minute as though it were his last. "In my wallet. Can you reach my pants? Because I don't want to lose your beautiful breasts in my face."

She chuckled nervously. Good, at least she wasn't running far, far away from him. She reached a foot away for his pants, plucked his wallet from the pocket, took out a wrapped condom, and handed it to him. "Put it on."

Her demand sent a shiver down his spine. "Yes, ma'am. I mean—"

"Shut up, LeBrun." Her voice smiled in the dark, as she leaned back to give him space.

While he worked to roll the condom onto his leaking cock, he caught glimpses of her licking her fingers and rubbing her clit, as her back arched. For a moment, he worried he was going to explode before he even got inside her, but he knew he wouldn't. He would do this right. He would satisfy her, give her everything she wanted. Without question.

"Take what you want," Ruby said, still rubbing her clit in small circles just a hair's length over him.

Even in the near complete darkness, Alec could see the intensity in her gaze above him. The burning and pure desire. Taking her gorgeous hips, he guided her down onto him, but not before she wrapped her hand around him to test him out. "Let's go slow," he said, knowing his size could be a problem. "I'm on the big side."

"I already know what side you're on, Alec. I saw you tonight in full bloom," she said, meaning the moment he'd dropped his towel in front of her.

He smiled in amusement, as she dug her nails into his pecs—ah, she liked to scratch. He could get behind that—and barely gave her a moment to gasp before he raised her up and pulled her back down—hard.

She moaned, the sound of her cries carrying over the length of the field. He could already feel the muscles of her thighs squeezing around his hips. No, this wouldn't take long for him either. They'd both wanted this for a long time.

Ruby's head fell back, and the next time Alec drew her down, she thrust her hips forward, rocking back and forth on her clit. She moaned so deliciously, he recorded the sound in his mind to remember forevermore, in case this never happened again. He moaned at just the sound of her pleasure, the sight of her riding his throbbing dick, the whisper of night air through her fragrant, fallen hair.

"Tell me what you want," Alec managed to say through the intensity of heat pooling in his groin.

"I want your hands on my tits. Play with them, Alec. Please."

Please. No more demands. Now she was begging, which only fueled him further, set his desire for her even higher. God, he wished he could see her in the light. So many beautiful things he was missing, though he was grateful for the cover of darkness.

Alec cupped her breasts and ran his thumbs over her nipples, feeling the delicious hard flesh he longed to shove into his mouth. With nothing to taste, no skin to lick and essence to drink in, he panted, as he watched her. Without his hands on her hips, Ruby took over the rhythm. She lowered herself onto him until she was fully seated and then circled her hips.

Fucking hot.

She grinded against him in regular rhythms, as he watched her face in complete rapture. Loose strands of her hair had fallen across her cheeks, some stuck to the sheen of sweat across her forehead. Little gasps escaped from her quivering lips that she bit down to muffle a cry. When Alec pinched her nipples softly, she whimpered and grinded closer to her orgasm, so he did it again. Faster and faster, she picked up her pace, bouncing on top of him.

Ruby's thighs shook, as she rode him, her moans growing louder.

"That's it, Red. Give it to me."

"I'm close," she whispered, watching him carefully, looking for clues that might push her over the edge.

"Give me that beautiful, fucking orgasm, Red," he encouraged her. "Keep telling me what you want," he said, giving her nipples another pinch.

Ruby's hips rocked forward. "Make me come. Make me come, Alec."

Hearing his name used so huskily, so driven with desire, coming from the pouty mouth of one said Ruby O'Brien nearly made him spill inside of her. He needed no further instruction. He reached his hands around her ass and lifted her up to allow room for his hips to thrust up into her. Ruby's hands fell to his chest for support, as her hair haloed her face and as she squeezed her eyes shut. Her sweet pussy clenched around his cock in the most amazing of ways. Her mouth fell open, as she moaned loud and long. "That's it, Red. You did it. You came so good."

Almost crying, she collapsed on top of him. Her breaths in his ear as he carried her through her orgasm made Alec's movements uncoordinated. Ruby licked from his neck to behind his ear and whispered, "You come, too. I want you to."

"Don't have to tell me twice, love." Alec held tightly onto her ass, cried out her name, and came. Waves rippled up his balls and through his entire body, radiating into Ruby. He stayed inside of her as they lay together, chests heaving, bringing warmth to each other in the crisp and now cool early morning air.

Ruby shifted and raised her head enough to look down at him. "Touchdown?"

Alec groaned.

She laughed. "Too far?"

"Way too far." He grinned then slipped his hand behind her neck and pulled her down into a gentle kiss.

Ruby's lame joke wasn't the only thing that was way too far. *He* was way too far. The things he felt for her now, that he'd *always* felt, were coming to fruition. For so long, he hadn't allowed himself to feel any of it, believing his chances with Ruby to be over.

Now, life was giving him a second chance. It was happening. Here she was in his arms. For the moment, Ruby O'Brien was a reality. *Actually in his life.* All he had to do now was figure out how to keep her there.

5

Who let in the sun?

Had she fallen asleep with the windows open? Funny, it almost seemed like she was asleep outdoors. With a groan, Ruby shifted and felt socks on her feet. Socks? She never wore socks to bed. Something hard and plastic dug into her upper shoulders. Sometimes she fell asleep with a book or tablet on her chest if she stayed up late working, but that wasn't it exactly. She shifted and tried to snooze through it.

Birds chirped.

Birds?

You know, you could just open your eyes and end this blind investigation. With a groping hand, she felt around to pat down the covers, only there weren't any. Instead, she touched something that made her eyes fly wide-open—the fluffiness of cheerleader's pom-poms.

How much had she drunk last night?

OH. MY. GOD. That's right. She and Alec had gone

out to eat after the game, then they'd done a couple of shots after running into Colleen, then they'd returned to the stadium to get her car, only they didn't get her car. Somehow, despite her best efforts to keep things professional, they'd ended up having sex.

On the field!

Ruby looked around. They were outside in a courtyard that had access to the football field on one side and a door to the Bootleggers' locker room on the other. She was lying on a pile of clean clothes knocked over from a laundry cart next to her. And lo and behold, Alec LeBrun was lying next to her. He was still holding the pom-pom, currently covering his manhood. Well, not quite fully covering it, since he was so well-endowed in the length *and* girth department. Her eyes traced an equally impressive set of abs up to a wide chest and then up to a familiar face and an even more familiar grin.

"Like what you see?" He flexed his chest.

Ruby screeched then threw the pom-pom at him. A myriad of emotions flew in her face. Excitement over finally hooking up with Alec, disbelief because now they'd crossed the professional line, mortification because she was naked though wearing shoulder pads and football socks.

"Wow. I barely remember putting this on last night. I didn't think we drank that much." She sat and slipped out of the shoulder pads, reaching for her dress and using it to cover her upper body.

"Not that much, but we were tipsy. And delirious. *And*

exhausted from amazing sex."

"Wow." Ruby covered her blushed cheeks. She looked back over Alec, who was still staring at her, half like she was a piece of fine art in a Paris museum, and half like she was a frustratingly difficult math problem. "It's fine, Red. We had a great time. We really did."

"Please stop staring at me like that," she said shyly. It wasn't that she didn't like the attention. It was just that they shouldn't have done this—both the hooking up and the hooking up in the outdoors where anybody could've found them.

Alec looked at her with honest confusion. "Why? This is a dream come true for me right here."

"What do you mean a dream come true?" she scoffed.

"Look at you. Wouldn't you stare if you were me?" His eyes followed the lines of her exposed body. "I mean, Ruby *fucking* O'Brien is lying next to me right now naked, except for shoulder pads and knee-high socks. There's no way this is real life. It has to be a dream."

Ruby tried to stop the grin forming on her face. "Stop, Alec. You've had better, I'm sure." She reached for her purse and phone.

"What did you say?" He sat up and peered into her eyes. "You're kidding me, right?"

She began threading her arms through her dress. It was Monday morning and time to get home, shower, and get ready for work. She'd fucked up. She'd crossed the line and slept with Alec. Worst of all, it'd happened in a field, out in the open. "Stop. I'm not one of your cheerleader ex-girlfriends. What time is it, anyway?" She logged into her phone.

"Hey. Hey. Look at me. Remember yesterday when you told me to focus? Now, you focus." He covered her phone with his hand, then slowly began pulling away the dress, revealing her body. Hungry eyes roved over her. "You are gorgeous, Ruby. You're hardworking, passionate, and damn, girl...you're HOT." With one finger, he poked her and pretended to get burned.

A slow smile unfurled on her face.

"I'm serious. You, the way you climbed on top of me last night, touching yourself...oof."

Was this the acting Alec? The one who could get reporters to chuckle in the face of crisis? Or was he serious? Was he really that into her? Last night, he'd said he was. He'd said he'd always wanted to get with her, but then why run back into Colleen's arms? He'd yet to explain what happened.

"You know what I was afraid of?"

"What?"

"I was scared that when I woke up, you'd be gone."

She watched him.

Eyes were more than just windows to the soul—they were lie detectors, Ruby had always felt. And watching Alec's eyes as he said that, she knew he was telling the truth. His other hand covered her hip, as close as he could get to her skin without actually touching.

Ruby shivered. Just above her goose bumps, Alec slid his hand along her bare leg without actually touching her.

She followed his eyes, as they followed his hand like it was leading him to water after days upon days in the desert.

"Scared that this body…" His voice was just above a whisper, as his hand traced back up her leg, across her stomach, and toward her breast. "Would be missing from my life. Scared that these eyes…" His hand scooped the shape of her face without touching it. "Would go home, leaving me to deal with the fact I'd fucked up yet again."

"I wouldn't do that," she said. "I wouldn't just disappear and leave you alone."

"You wouldn't. But other women would. The ones you mentioned would."

She couldn't believe he was giving her goose bumps without even touching her. Ruby felt herself arch into the elusive touch of Alec's palm, but he pulled his hand back just enough to make himself still out of reach. Without the ghost of his touch, her nipples hardened and Alec's fingers flexed just millimeters from one's peak.

"I'm scared"—his gaze moved to hers as he held his hand perfectly still—"that if I try to touch these lips, I won't feel smooth delicious silk. They'll disappear before my eyes."

No, I'm still here, Ruby thought. Somehow, as crazy as this all was, she was still with him. That familiar heat was growing between her legs, slick and warm. And her heart began racing, as her nipples yearned for his touch, or tongue, or teeth grazing them. Hell, anything of Alec's, on her tits would feel nice.

But her mind wouldn't let her relax. It had just been a double shot of whisky, but things got crazy after that, and... "Alec," Ruby began, "we had sex on the field, right?"

"We had *great* sex on the field," Alec corrected, leading his hand down her thighs and smoothly into the cleft between them. Slowly, he began moving the pads of his fingers in slow, achingly slow, circles over her clit.

Ruby lost her train of thought and melted into the muscles of his chest. Such a wide, strong chest. She imagined waking up to it every morning. How awesome would that be? But no. She had to think this through.

"Do you realize how risky that was?" she asked.

"I do. But I thrive on risky, Red. You know that."

"Yes, but I don't." A terrible thought entered her mind just then. *What about when he starts acting up again, Ruby? You want to be with a man who only pulled himself together for one night, long enough to get with you? What if he goes back to the same shit as before?* "Alec." She pushed his hand away gently. "As much as this is one of my favorite places in the world and I don't want to ruin it, we need to talk."

Alec stared at her. "Ruin?"

She sighed. "Look, last night was amazing, but it was a mistake."

"Wasn't a mistake to me, Red."

"You're wrong. It's bad enough we overstepped boundaries last night when we decided to throw caution to the wind and have drinks together. Fine. So we did what we did. But now, let's think this through. Okay?"

Last night had been a fluke. Their desire had gotten away from them. Their bodies had taken over, all rationalization left in the dust. Fine. But now she—they—had a choice. They could go back to being professional, get back on track.

The man who could've been carved from marble, that was how hard he was, softened, muscles relaxing, as a sigh escaped his lips. "Okay. Let's talk."

Ruby curled up, using the dress as a blanket. "Look, last night was fun. It really was. And I'm sure right now could be really fun, too. But we can't do this again."

"Why not?"

Ruby didn't know why not. In her heart, she felt a sad pang that she couldn't give him a clear answer, but the truth was, she hadn't known Alec for long in this intimate respect to figure out why. There was definitely fear inside of her. But fear of what, exactly, she didn't know.

Instead, she went with the known variables. "Plenty of reasons, Alec. I mean, first of all, I'm your publicist. You're my client. We agreed just yesterday that we needed to get your career back on track. Mine needs to get back on track, so I can prove to my father that I'm capable. And I mean, holy shit, just a month ago, you were engaged, and—"

"I didn't love her."

Ruby scanned his eyes, his face, again. He was telling the truth. "You didn't love your girlfriend and fiancée?"

Alec sighed, lay back against a mound of clean

jerseys, and placed his hands behind his head. From this angle, his body was even more incredible.

Focus, Ruby. "How am I supposed to believe that? People don't just go around proposing to women they don't love, Alec."

"She was pregnant."

Oh.

It was a good thing Ruby was lying down, because that thought never crossed her mind. She couldn't say anything. All she could do was imagine Colleen with a tiny baby growing inside of her. A baby Alec had put there. She felt herself draw in.

Alec noticed her withdrawal and added, "Except she wasn't."

"What do you mean?" Ruby's eyebrows furrowed together.

He squeezed the sides of his head, and Ruby could clearly see his anguish. "I mean, it was a lie. She lied to me, Ruby. She did it to get me to marry her, so of course, when she told me she was pregnant, I did what good guys do—I proposed to her."

"Wow, Alec." That must've been when he cancelled the date on her. He must've just found out because soon after, they were engaged. Holy shit. Pieces began falling into place in her mind.

"Yeah." He nodded. "She even got one of those ultrasounds from the doctors. A fake one. I totally believed it, Ruby. I bought the whole damn lie."

"How did you feel at first?" Ruby asked. She wasn't

sure why, but it was important for her to know how he reacted to the news that he would be a father.

"At first, I wasn't ready for a kid. Hell, I don't know if I'll ever be. This career is hectic as hell. But I also knew there was no way I wasn't going to support her. One way or another, I would figure it out. I wasn't going to be like my dad." He scoffed.

Ruby had never heard Alec mention his father before, not to the press, not to his friends, not to her. She could only connect the dots and realize his father had never been there for him, so, at the very least, Alec wanted to be better than that. Five hundred points for him right there.

"So I did the right thing. Do you understand, Ruby? I did the right thing. I proposed to Colleen, news got out that we were engaged, I even started a savings, planned a nursery with her, and read a fucking parenting book. No, two fucking parenting books, and all for what? It was all a fucking lie." Anger oozed from his voice. He shook his head and crossed his arms over his chest. Ruby could see the strain of his muscles in his arms.

"How do you know it was a lie?"

He gave her a look like he wasn't stupid. "She told me."

"She told you?"

"Yes. The whole time we were planning a wedding, I kept thinking this isn't right. I don't love her. I never did. She was my girlfriend, and we made a high-profile couple, but I'd always known she wasn't my future. So two weeks before the wedding, I made a decision. I couldn't marry her. I would support her, be an involved father to the baby, but I couldn't take part in a marriage where there was no love." Alec looked at her then. Until now, he'd been speaking to the sky, as if a therapist sat there. "Do you blame me, Ruby?"

"Me?" What did she have to do with anything? That was his and his decision alone. "Whatever felt right to you, Alec."

"Well, that's what felt right to me. I'd never get it off my conscience if I'd gone through with it. So I told her one night. And she fucking blew up. Threw napkins in my face, a plate against the wall, and told me I was the biggest asshole she'd ever known. And oh, yeah...the baby was a lie. In fact, she was on her period right then."

Ruby shook her head. This was high drama that could've so easily hit the press, yet he'd managed to keep it down. Maybe Alec could act responsibly when he wanted to.

He continued the story. "At first, I thought she was making it up. She was lying about not being pregnant just to piss me off, but then I saw the texts."

"Texts?"

"To Margie, one of her friends who works at an OB-GYN. I looked through her phone later that night. She'd asked her to procure some fake ultrasounds for her, and that's when I knew it was true. The whole thing had been a fucking lie. We broke it off that night."

Everything fell into place—the fighting, the drinking, the crazy behavior that ensued...all of it.

"Alec, I didn't know."

"Nobody did, except for my buddies. I worked my ass off to make sure nobody found out, even though part of me wanted to expose her for being a liar and a fake so badly. But that's not me, Ruby. I treated her respectfully in the public eye, and I still do. And even when she comes around like she did last night, looking for trouble, I still treat her with respect."

Ruby couldn't believe it. All the while Alec's life was imploding, he was exploding. While he worked to keep his true feelings for Colleen under wraps, his anger toward her, he was acting out in other ways.

"To make it all worse," he said, taking her hand and kissing the top of it. "I wanted you the whole time."

This is where Ruby normally would've rolled her eyes at him. *Yeah, sure, but you were engaged.* It didn't make sense. But…now, things were clear to see.

"After the first breakup, I was happy to be free, happy to finally pursue the woman I was really interested in. That's when I asked you out. But Colleen couldn't handle the fact that we were done, so she made up the pregnancy, and when I saw the ultrasound, I believed it was over. You have no idea how sorry I am that I hurt you." He grazed her cheek with his fingertips.

Ruby looked up in an effort to keep her eyes from welling over.

She'd been through so much during that time, too. Here the man she'd been interested in had gone back to his girlfriend after claiming he liked her, and he'd come across as a player and a liar the whole time.

"Can you forgive me? Can we start over?" Alec's eyes were full of hope.

"I can forgive you. But there are other things in play. I'm your publicist. I have my career to think about. And guess what? I have yours to think about, too."

"We'll keep it under wraps," he said. "We'll make sure the media doesn't find out about it. That will protect your career and mine. But I'll do anything for this, Red." He turned her chin toward him with a gentle touch. "I'll do anything for *you*."

Looking into those earnest eyes that seemed wholly satisfied to see only her for the rest of their existence, Ruby wanted to believe him. She did. She truly did. She wanted to guide his hand back to the wetness between her legs and stare into those eyes as he undid her completely, right then and there. She wanted to walk into the press room, filled with people who knew nothing about their liaison, turn to Alec, and share a knowing wink about their steamy secret.

"Can we start over?"

A secret relationship. Ruby thought about it. In some ways, it could work, but that was the thing about secrets, though. Eventually, they came out. Usually in unpleasant ways.

"Alec, I'm sorry for what happened to you. I really am. You don't know how many times I wanted to console you while you were going through all this, and I'm so glad I know the truth now. But nothing more can happen between us." Hardest words she'd ever had to say. She wanted so much to fall into his arms and make her dreams happen. But Alec had already been through so much. She owed it to him—and yes, herself—to do what was right for both of them.

Alec stared at her, then sighed. He brought in his knees and covered himself with the pom-pom again, almost making her smile.

"Fine, I get it," he said. "I'll play by the rules. For now." He gave her a pointed look. "But we *will* revisit this. Fair?"

She wanted to agree, but at the same time, she knew what was best, and that meant accepting the hard truth. Before she could reply, however, they were interrupted by a door opening nearby. Muted voices flooded within the stadium walls, as Ruby scanned around for a place to hide. Shit, it must've been later than she thought. Were those players coming in for practice? But then, Alec would've known about it. How the hell was she supposed to escape this without anyone seeing her?

Panic filled her chest. Getting caught naked with a Bootleggers player? With Alec LeBrun, no less, who'd just gotten lots of negative press for other "stunts?" Who also just happened to be her client? Her father would disown her. She'd be blacklisted from every agency in America. There would be absolutely no coming back from this.

Alec saw the panic in her eyes and pressed a finger to his lips. "Don't worry. I'll handle this. Get dressed."

Someone walked through, opened the locker room door to the outside area they were in, kept talking, and propped the door open. Maybe it was the cleaning crew. Which meant they'd soon come looking for the laundry cart. Ruby quickly put on her clothes behind the cart.

"What are you going to do?" she whispered.

"Same thing I always do." He flashed his sexy smile. "Talk my way out of it. Just need one thing."

"What's that?"

"A kiss." Alec grinned and indicated the open door space through which Ruby could see the cleaning crew starting to work. There wasn't much time. "Come on, Red. They're coming!"

Ruby wasn't used to shenanigans. Ruby was straight as an arrow, but she had to admit there was something fun and spontaneous about this that made her feel adventurous. Dangerous, but adventurous.

"Fine, I'll still do it without the kiss," he said, grabbing the pom-poms, his pants, shirt, and jacket.

Ruby couldn't let the man who'd take the fall for her go without reward, so she sighed and leaned into him for a quick peck. But the second her lips touched his, Alec slipped his hand behind her neck and his tongue inside her mouth with such deliciousness, she thought her legs would give out. Wetness flooded her again, and she moaned against him.

Then, suddenly, he was gone, leaving a cold, empty space where His Royal Hotness had been a moment before, and her heart continued to pound. At the door to the locker room, Alec gave her that infuriating grin with those goddamn adorable dimples, then disappeared into the room.

The second he left, buck-ass-naked, she wanted him back. She wanted him back with a passion greater than she was willing to admit. Oh, yes, they would table this. They would revisit this decision in the future. Because there was no way she wouldn't. Nobody had ever made her feel so alive in all her life.

"Hey, so glad you guys finally got here," Alec spoke inside the locker room. "Got locked in last night. Those buddies are mine, such practical jokers. Do you have any idea how hard these benches are to sleep on?"

When someone from the cleaning crew apologized to him for getting locked in overnight, Ruby knew that was her cue. Straightening herself out, she slipped past the door and snuck into the exit hallway. She'd escaped one problem. But how many more had she created for herself?

6

Alec was beginning to feel like himself again.

For the past month, Ruby had stayed by his side, navigating him through one press event after another. Doing all she could to get his image back on track. Giving him the chance to make things right: with his career, with himself, and with her.

In return, he'd been playing by Ruby's rules, giving her space, not once mentioning what had happened between them that night at the Bootleggers' stadium. That didn't mean he couldn't remind her every chance he got with a quiet look, making it clear he intended to share moments like those again with her someday—when she was ready for that, of course. But for now, he was content to spend time with her, though granted it was almost always in the presence of her photographer, Mike, who acted like some 1950s chaperone hell-bent on keeping Alec out of Ruby's pants.

You can try, Mike, but you are so going to fail at that

particular endeavor.

At the thought, Alec told himself to cool his engines. Now was not the time.

"I'm open, Alec!"

"Right-O, Luke," Alec called to a happy eight-year-old. He was currently attending one his favorite charities in a local park for kids with cancer. Luke had just finished chemotherapy, and his bald head gleamed in the sunlight. From the moment Alec arrived, he'd instantly attached himself to his favorite football star.

Today's event had been on his schedule long before Ruby's quest to prove he was still a good guy began, and in truth, he'd been reluctant to have her photograph it.

"Not everything's about my image," Alec had told her. "I'm doing this because I want to, period. Find something else to photograph."

"I know you're not doing this for your image," she'd replied. "But the best publicity is about showcasing the best in you. Yes, sometimes it seems contrived, but that's the last thing this will be. You care for these kids. Let the world see that, Alec."

In the end, he found he had a hard time saying no to Ruby. He didn't know what that meant for their future together—he just knew there would be a future, whether she knew it yet or not. On that front, he was going to come out the winner.

For that to happen, he had to play the long game.

His gaze sought her out where she was sitting in the park bleachers, talking to some of the parents. Immediately, his mind went where it shouldn't given what he was doing—their night at the stadium when he'd kissed those luscious lips, touched her impressively athletic yet curvy body, heard the sounds of her climax resonating all throughout the empty stadium. Nobody had ever scored on that field the way Alec did that night.

But he couldn't dwell on it. He must stay focused. If he played his cards right, he might just hear that beautiful noise again one day, but for now, he had to prove his worth.

Alec tossed the football back and forth to Luke, enjoying himself immensely. Within minutes, a few other kids had joined them and they begged Alec to teach them how to tackle. The kids, due to their various states of health, couldn't engage in rough sports. But a little bit of roughhousing wouldn't be so bad, would it? After all, today, they just wanted to be kids.

He made a big deal of showing them what to do, cautioned them to go easy on him, then yelled, "Release the Kraken!"

Suddenly, Luke and an entire crowd of kids tackled him to the ground by surprise. He laughed, and the kids climbed over him like puppies. "Ruby! Help me!"

Ruby shook her head, then got down from the bleachers, heading his way. Though she was smiling slightly, she couldn't hide the worry on her face.

Oh, shit.

"Alec," she called, as she walked up to the scene. Along the bleachers, one or two parents might've had concerned looks on their faces, but most were into it, taking pics and having a fun time. "You know we talked about *not overdoing things*," she admonished.

For a second, Alec felt guilty, but that changed as soon as he saw how happy the kids looked. "Guys, let's all give Miss Ruby the sad look. Come on, you know the sad look." He pouted and gave Ruby puppy dog eyes. The kids—three boys, including Luke, and two girls between the ages of four and ten—all followed suit.

Ruby rolled her eyes, fist at her hip. "Alec…"

"All right, all right," Alec said, breaking through the kid pile, knocking them down one by one in fits of glee. "You heard the Big Bad Wolf. No tackling."

Ruby bristled at his comment.

"I know, I know," he said, standing and whispering in her ear. "I'm making you look like the bad guy. But you gotta admit it's fun for them. Fine, and me."

"Fun is one thing, but sometimes fun can do more damage than we think." At her contemplative tone, Alec stiffened, immediately getting what she was hinting at. He didn't like what it told him. That even as they'd been spending all this time together, a part of her was backing away from him.

"And sometimes," he said, "fun is what makes the difference between going through the motions and having an amazing time in life."

They stared at one another before she stepped back,

clapped once, and faced the kids. Then, in her most excited voice, yelled, "Let's all go find where they've put up the piñatas!"

Nobody moved. Alec suppressed a grin.

"I don't want the piñatas," one little girl said, clinging to Alec's leg. "I want to keep playing with Mr. Alec. Pleeeeeease?"

"Come on now, sweetie. It's time for the piñata, but maybe if you ask Mr. Alec nicely, he'll take you there. Won't you, Mr. Alec?"

"Of course I will," he said, then murmured to Ruby, "And afterward, we can talk more about the merits of fun time." He winked.

Ruby bit her inner cheek then pulled out her phone and looked at it like there was something important there.

Sure, Ruby. You can run, but you can't hide. He laughed inwardly.

Luke crossed his arms. "I don't want to play with the piñatas either."

"I don't blame you, buddy." Tearing his gaze from Ruby, Alec looked down at Luke and touched the young boy's shoulder. "Piñatas suck, but you want to know a secret?" At his ballsy proclamation that piñatas sucked, Ruby's head snapped up.

"What?" The boy looked skeptical.

"I was the reigning piñata champion in fifth grade. I could beat that fluffy papier mâché donkey till it bled candy. So you know what I think?"

"What?"

"I think you're scared."

"I'm not scared."

"Yeah, you are. You're scared you can't beat me—"

"I can beat you! Just watch me!" Luke ran after the rest of the kids, determined to prove to Alec that he could beat him at piñata-whipping.

"Go get it, kid! Proud of you!" Alec yelled after him then, hands on hips, he turned to Ruby. "So, about fun. I think you and I—"

Quickly, she said, "I didn't especially like that you undermined my authority with them, but I'll admit that was impressive. You're good with kids." For a moment, Ruby looked like she wanted to eat her words, like maybe mentioning kids or babies wasn't a good idea in front of Alec.

She was thinking of Colleen and what she'd done to him.

Damn his ex for interfering, even when she wasn't around.

Since she'd seen him and Ruby having dinner, Colleen had been blowing up his phone. At first, it'd been too easy to engage with her. For every little thing Colleen jabbed at him, he jabbed back. Until he realized that was what she wanted and stopped replying to her texts altogether. Just like little kids who behaved bad in order to get attention, Colleen was doing the same. She was having way too much fun accusing Alec of being the worst ex ever.

Yes, he'd dodged a bullet with that one.

Then there was Ruby, ultimately and genuinely caring about his career with no ulterior motive other than to be the best publicist she could be. But more than that, she cared about him as a person. As a man. Hell, she was afraid her even mentioning he was good with kids would hurt him.

He hesitated and dug deep, relieved to find the pain of Colleen's betrayal was only a dull throb now rather than a burning wound. Ruby had helped him get there.

"Nah. Kids are easy. They're basically small versions of football players: they love sports, food, and yelling."

She laughed. "I don't know if that describes all kids, but I appreciate you getting out there with them. Not a lot of players do. Being with the little ones makes some feel vulnerable."

"That's because kids tell it like it is. If they don't like you, if you come across as fake to them, they'll let you know."

"Most guys come to these events, take a few photos, and then hop back into their sports cars or go back to their villas in France."

"My villa is in Spain," Alec said, deadpan.

Ruby laughed, which made Alec smile. If he could make Ruby smile like that each and every day, he would've fulfilled his life's destiny. What was it about her that made him so intent in impressing her? "How about you go help the kids with the piñata? That'll make a great photo op." Ruby waved to their photographer, Mike. "Hey, Mike, time for some piñata smashing! Get a few of Alec laughing with the kids, and if they can all jump on top of him, that'd be even better."

Alec side-eyed Ruby. "We'll talk later, Red," he said meaningfully.

As he walked toward the pavilion where piñata-smashing was about to begin, he felt Ruby's gaze checking him out and his chest radiated pride. Despite the excellent job she was doing keeping things strictly professional between them, she was doing a terrible job acting like she didn't find him attractive. All day, she'd been checking him out. It was sexy to see her eyes wander all over his body.

"Want a Jolly Rancher?" Luke held out a wrapped green-colored candy.

Jolted out of his thoughts, Alec popped the candy into his mouth, making a face at the sour taste. The surrounding kids all laughed. He really did love their silliness. They sat in the grass, the kids munching on way too much candy and eyeing the piñata. Getting the hint, Alec stood and clapped his hands much like Ruby had done earlier.

"Let's do this." Alec reached for the baseball bat, showing the kids how to hit the damn piñata and how to stay far away so you didn't get hit by a wild swing. He handed the bat to Luke, who wound up like a major league pitcher and let the poor paper minion have it. Its body split on the side, but he had to hit it a few times to get it to crack open. "Not bad," he told Luke.

"See, I told you I could beat you."

The whole time, Mike took shots, and Alec had fun with it.After the kids ran off to find their parents, Mike followed, snapping photos here and there. Ruby emerged from a public bathroom and walked toward him. Alec definitely noticed the additional application of shiny lip gloss, which made her smile look like a million bucks.

Part of him wanted to take her behind a tree and take her hair down, find the sex goddess who'd shown up for a brief interlude the other night. Even as she looked now, with her hair in a tight bun and wearing a black suit with a gray silken blouse, she was hot as fuck.

"So?" he asked her. "What grade would you give me?"

"For what? Destroying the piñata?" Ruby tapped her bottom lip. "Probably a C. It took you a while to get the minion's head off."

"I was letting the kids do it, smartass."

She smiled. "Yeah, well, we'll take to Snapchat in the morning and see what people thought of your piñata skills."

He frowned at her not-so-subtle reminder that she was here as his publicist and nothing else. He'd been a good boy. It was time to show Ruby he could still be a little bad, and that she'd like it.

"Snapchat?" he said, even as they walked together. "What the hell is Snapchat again?"

Ruby may have sighed impatiently, but he still saw a tiny smile on her lips. "It's one of those things, on the Internet. You know, that thing people use all the time now?"

"Oh. I only just upgraded my rotary phone to a cordless one, so give me some time. I'm slow on the uptake. Just kidding. Jesus Christ, Ruby, I know what Snapchat is."

They laughed again, and Alec couldn't help but reflect on how right this felt. Making jokes, bantering, like they'd known each other for years. When had he felt this comfortable with another person? Probably never. He'd always been on his guard, wondering if someone had it out for him. Sadly, in his line of work, more often than not, women wanted something from him. Every woman he'd dated had wanted him for the fame or money that came along with dating him. Those women had wanted the man in him, too, but he knew, deep inside, they wouldn't have been as interested if he weren't a professional football player on one of the top teams in the country.

Ruby wanted something from him, too, but that was different. She was doing it for him, for both of them. Any other woman would've kept their relationship going, milking it for all it was worth, but not Ruby. She wanted to protect her own career and his. Protect her relationship with her father.

And, he suspected, most of all…protect her heart.

Somehow, as he and Ruby chatted, they ended up near a copse of trees that provided some amount of privacy from the event. Mike had disappeared—probably to get something to eat—and Alec realized Ruby hadn't noticed they were alone yet.

Then again, maybe she'd already noticed and had decided she didn't care. He felt like she was giving mixed messages, but maybe that was because he'd played things too well, and she didn't know where *he* stood. "You know, seeing you today, I couldn't help but wonder where that other Ruby had gone."

She swiveled toward him. "The other Ruby?"

"You know. The Ruby who demanded I touch her. The Ruby who grabbed my cock and made it fit, made it work, then worked *me*. The Ruby who screamed my name when I—"

She pressed a finger to his mouth. "Alec, there are kids here!"

"What? Red, they're all eating hotdogs like three hundred feet away. That's a football field, you know." He kissed her finger, dragged it across his bottom lip, but she pulled her hand away. "A football field is that place where people have sex. Usually with the woman on top. Her tits and gorgeous body on full display. God, I love football."

Ruby blushed fifteen shades of red.

"There, I wanted to see if I could still make you blush. And I can. Alec LeBrun takes the lead," he said, imitating an announcer's voice then faking a crowd cheering.

"You're the most arrogant, annoying man."

"And yet, you're still here. Isn't that amazing?" He flashed her his famous smile.

She opened her mouth, but then shut it with a snap. "I shouldn't be here," she muttered. "I should walk away and never look back. But I'm an idiot, apparently."

"You didn't answer my question."

"Which one?"

"I said, 'Isn't that amazing?'"

"That was rhetorical. It's not amazing. I have to be here. It's called my job."

"So you're saying if you weren't my publicist, you wouldn't spend time with me?" He cocked his head. Now, *that* was a valid question, and they wouldn't be going anywhere until she answered it.

"We have to get going."

"Not until you answer my question. If we didn't have this—this client-publicist thing going…would you go out with me? Remember I'm shy and delicate. Be gentle when you respond."

"Fuck no." She giggled.

Alec gasped. "Such language! Do it again. It's fucking hot. Come on. Say it."

"No way."

He couldn't stop himself from touching her silky soft cheek. In the afternoon light, he could see those microscopic tiny blond hairs illuminating in the sun. "Maybe I should get you to put your hair down again," he mused. "Is that the secret? When you have your hair up, you're a good girl, but when it's down, your bad side comes out?" He bit into his smile.

"Alec…"

"It is, isn't it? A-ha. I've unlocked Level 2."

"You haven't unlocked shit."

He reached to pull the pins from her hair, but she

playfully slapped his hand away. "Don't you touch the hair. Never, ever touch the hair, Alec. I'm warning you. Do you have any idea how annoying it is to redo it?"

"I won't touch your hair," he teased, "but only if you give me a kiss as payment."

"That's the second time you've asked for a kiss in exchange for doing me a favor."

"What can I say? I need your kisses, Ruby. They're like air. Or Wi-Fi."

"Yeah, but—"

"But what?"

"I don't want to feel like I owe you a kiss, Alec. If I ever kiss you again, it'll be because I want to." To his amazement and utter gratitude, she leaned closer...closer...they were inches away, and he leaned down to breathe in that sweet air right before a beautiful woman kisses you. Then, she ducked underneath his arm, laughing.

Before he could react, she'd scampered away like a mischievous little rabbit.

"You can run, but you can't hide, Red!" he called, but he was laughing, too.

She waved a hand over her shoulder, but she didn't turn back around. He sighed and, leaning against the tree behind him, he wondered what they would do next if he ever got her naked again. Whip her around against lockers and fuck her from behind? Throw her legs open and taste that sweetness in between? Watch those amazing lips of hers curl around his cock and suck it in deep?

Fuck.

Forcing himself to think of the least sexy things ever—cold showers, frogs, taxes—he finally got his unruly body under control so he could return to the job at hand—getting his life and career back under control, then focusing on winning Ruby's heart.

7

Ruby caught her breath after running from Alec. She had to admit—it felt great to forget about her worries for a minute and just play. So many responsibilities hung over her head that taking the time to laugh was a welcome break.

The park was alive with energy—people drinking punch and eating hamburgers, the smell of grass, smoked meat, and sunscreen filling the air. While Alec went back to the party pavilion, she sat on a bench watching two kids playing in the sandbox, not caring that they were sick. Seeing these determined kids in wheelchairs or on crutches reminded her that life was about making the most of your time. Part of her wanted to strip her career persona and just have fun.

I mean, look at them... Everywhere, kids played and families were having a good time. They kept her mood buoyant. Even Alec, now dancing the Electric Slide with a group of kids, made her smile. *He would make an amazing father*, she thought. She couldn't stop the image of him holding his own son or daughter in his arms, how he'd play and laugh and teach his child how to play football. For the thousandth time, she cursed Colleen for the trauma she'd caused him.

How could anyone lie about being pregnant? That was such a pure, joyous moment that so many people cherished and others prayed for, and here she was making a mockery out of it. He must've been so devastated when he discovered her lie. Seeing him now, one would never know what he'd gone through, which only made Ruby care about him even more.

But I can't let myself care that way. As a client, sure, but that's where it ends.

Yet it didn't stop her from wanting what she couldn't have. When he'd started talking about them together back there in the trees, her body had responded with a chemical pull. If they were in another world, one without client-publicist lines, she would've kissed him. She would've let the trees sway around them and taken in his scents, sights, and flavors. Alec wasn't just a handsome face and body on TV. Football players with good looks were a dime a dozen. No, what Alec possessed was definitely charm and charisma. She hated how well it worked.

Thinking about their near-kiss, her heart still pounded, and her body wished she'd lingered a little longer. The fact that Alec still wanted her and made it clear that one night would never be enough both empowered and aroused her. She definitely held the power in their relationship, if you could call it that, and the idea of that gave her goose bumps.

But their "relationship" was doomed from the start. She had to stop imagining herself in impossible scenarios with Alec. Sooner or later, Ruby was going to have to accept the truth—that she had to live without him.

Anxiety congealed in her gut where desire had been only moments earlier. *What am I doing?* She panicked. She looked out onto the charity event, unseeing, her thoughts whirling like a dervish. There was nothing funny or sweet or romantic about this. She shouldn't have slept with Alec. It'd been stupid and irresponsible. It'd been—

"Hey...Ruby!"

Turning, she saw a beautiful, curvy brunette with a young girl next to her. It was Camille Dawson, Heath's fiancée, and their daughter, Emma. "Camille, how are you?" Ruby and Camille had met when Camille had been hired to photograph a Bootleggers calendar a couple of months ago. In the time since, she'd been offered a permanent position as a photographer with the NFL, and most importantly, met and gotten engaged to wide receiver Heath Dawson in a whirlwind courtship. Last Ruby had heard, Camille was still negotiating the terms of her contract with the NFL; they wanted her, in spite of her engagement to a top NFL player, but she was taking her time putting the details in place.

"I'm great," Camille replied, her expression brimming with happiness. "Emma, you remember Ruby, right? We used to work together."

Emma was the spitting image of her mother, a spitfire who had her mom and Heath wrapped around her little finger. "Oh, yeah. I always want red hair every time I see you," Emma said.

"Funny, because I always want dark hair when I see you!" Ruby beamed. "But it's not all about hair. You have such an awesome, hardworking mom, too."

"Aww, that's sweet. Thanks." Camille bit back a smile. "Emma, how about you go get us something to eat over there? I think they have other things besides hot dogs."

"Okay!"

Emma ran off, and Camille looked on fondly. "She's going to be a handful when she's a teenager," she said with a sigh.

"Aren't they always? I know I was a real jerk when I was a teenager."

Camille laughed. "I find that hard to believe. You're the picture of professionalism and cool-headedness, Ruby."

Internally, Ruby winced. If only that were true. At the moment, she was also the picture of hypo criticism and indecision. "I don't know about that…"

"Seriously. Look at what a great job you've done turning Alec around. He was going through something hard, obviously, but you didn't give up on him. You're so loyal, as well as brilliant."

Ruby stared at Camille, wanting to tell her she was the furthest thing from brilliant. She had no one to talk to about her conflicted feelings over Alec. Building a demanding career over the last few years hadn't exactly given her enough time for friendships, and even if she did have friends she could trust, talking about her night with Alec LeBrun would still be considered the height of unprofessionalism.

Then again, if anyone would understand, it'd be Camille, who'd put her NFL job offer in jeopardy when she'd gotten involved with Heath. Plus, Heath was one of Alec's best friends. Still undecided on whether or not to tell her, Ruby turned to look at Alec, who'd joined another group of kids. No matter where she was, she was always drawn to him. No matter where he was, she found that charming laugh.

"Ah…" Camille tilted her head at Ruby. "I see now."

Ruby stilled. "See what?"

"Ruby, I've been there, done that. So, you and Alec, huh?"

It was as if someone had shot her with a bow and arrow. Stunned, then falling quickly to the ground. "Wait, what? Why would you say that?"

"Because I've been where you are. I may not know about lots of things, but one thing I do know about is falling for a guy I can't have. Or thought I couldn't have."

There was no escaping it. Camille knew. She may as well just admit it. "Fine," Ruby said with a heavy mind. She winced. "It was only once, I swear."

"I don't care if it was a hundred times, Ruby. Come on, tell me all about it. I'd have us go get drinks, but it'll have to be virgin cocktails for me."

They took a slow stroll around the park, as Ruby confided in Camille, telling her what had happened. If anyone would understand the situation, it was Camille, but she still felt strange bringing it all out into the open. As for the bits about Colleen, Ruby held back. That wasn't her secret to tell, but then again, Camille probably knew. Whatever Alec knew, his buddies would know, and their wives possibly as well.

"So yeah, whatever he went through, it changed him. He's determined now," Ruby explained. "Angry but also ready to overcome it. I guess I saw something in him that few people have never really seen."

"You don't have to tell me twice, girl. I get it."

"I know you do. And I appreciate that. I also slept with him, because for once in my life, I wanted to be spontaneous. This job of mine is super demanding. Sometimes I just need to let loose."

"Trust me, I hear you. No judgment here. What does Alec think of all this?"

Ruby sighed. "I told him we can't do it again, and he said he wants to 'revisit' the subject at a later time."

"He's not willing to give up easily."

"No," Ruby said. "So, now I don't know what to do. He's my client. I told my father I'd take on this project, that he could trust me, he didn't need to worry about me." She laughed bitterly. "And now, look at me."

Camille patted her hand. "You're still doing your job, Ruby. Alec's behaving like his old self. I mean, Heath had

been so worried, and I have to say, I'm glad he has you.
You're good for him, and, I think, he's good for you. I
mean, yeah, the client relationship thing is a little tricky,
but if there's something there? You'll figure it out. The
fact that you see Alec as more than a party boy with
money is huge. I don't think he's ever had a relationship
with a woman that was real."

Ruby wanted to argue that they didn't have anything
like a real relationship. One night of sex did not make
them real. But then, she thought about what Camille
said—how he'd never had a real woman, real relationship,
and that made her sad. At least she'd had Nick back in
college. Things may not have worked out between them,
but at least Ruby had known some form of love once
before.

"Thanks, Camille. It was awesome talking to you. I
knew you'd understand."

"Whatever you decide, I'll support you. You know
what's best for you, right?" Camille smiled then they went
on to talk about Kyle Young and his new girlfriend,
Arabella, a true-to-life princess. When Camille left,
however, Ruby couldn't stop wondering... Did she know
what was best for herself? At times she thought she did.
She thought she had her life all under control. But then
why, at times, did her feelings seem to spin out of control?

One night, she reminded herself, getting back on
track.

One night was all she and Alec were ever going to
have. People moved on from one-night stands all the time.

Some even went on to be best friends. She would do the same. Expecting anything more would be beyond foolish.

A few days later, Ruby was in her father's office giving him a report on her clients.

"Saw the photos from the charity event—great job, Ruby. You really nailed this one," Phil, Ruby's father, said with that pleased look that always made Ruby feel good inside. But part of her saddened. Would she ever stop wanting her father's validation?

Sitting on his comfy couch, going through her schedule on her iPad, Ruby kept her face down. She tried not to let her eyes sparkle anytime her father mentioned Alec, afraid that one wrong look, and her father would have her figured out. "Look at him, cavorting with the kids, back on track…fantastic."

"Yes. The response online has been very favorable," Ruby said with a nod. "There were naysayers, of course, but I think we're making good progress on shifting away from his previous issues."

Previous issues that no one knew about. It was infinitely harder to make the public empathize with her client when they weren't privy to the real information.

"Good. I know I was hard on you before, Ruby," her father said. "But I always knew you could handle him." Phil turned in his chair to face his computer once again. A good thing, too, because Ruby's cheeks flushed as she imagined herself "handling" Alec in just the right way.

"Thanks, Dad."

"Keep up the good work. And remember: there's a reason why these football players are so successful."

"Athletic prowess?"

"No, because they're charming and people are suckers. Don't be one of them, my girl." He winked at Ruby and went back to his work.

Ruby bit the inside of her cheek. She almost felt like she had a scarlet letter A tattooed to her forehead with a blinking sign that said, *I slept with Alec LeBrun. He charmed my pants off. Literally.*

If Phil ever found out she'd slept with him...

First, he'd kill her. Second, he'd fire her. And third, he'd be disappointed in her as a daughter, and nothing was worse than that in Ruby's eyes. Her whole life had been about winning Dad's approval, always proving herself to him. She'd never get to be partner at the firm either. O'Brien PR had strict rules when it came to client relationships, and anyone who crossed that line never got the chance to redeem themselves.

Ever.

As Phil's daughter, Ruby had even higher expectations to toe the line. One step out of bounds, and she'd bear the brunt of his disapproval. But no worries, because he'd never know. It was a one-time thing, and that's how it would stay. Now she just had to put an end to Alec's advances and tell him once and for all that it was over. And no better time to do that than at lunch.

Ruby drove to the Bootleggers' practice at the stadium. She was shown to a private room, while she waited for Alec to arrive. She might've been allowed to hang with him at charity events, but at practices, Coach was adamant about having only players on the field to keep them focused. As the players came in from practice and began dispersing all over the stadium to have their lunches, Ruby stood and welcomed Alec into the rec room.

"Hey, Alec."

"Red. Were you waiting long?" Alec entered the room, still toweling the sweat from his face. "I wasn't watching the time."

To her immense annoyance, she almost couldn't speak, as she stared at Alec. Today he wore a T-shirt that was practically clinging to his sweaty muscles, and his shorts left little to the imagination. Memories of their night together pummeled her brain. Trying to act like she wasn't ruffled, she started messing with the papers in front of her.

"No, I wasn't waiting long at all, actually." She kept her eyes down, as Alec took a seat in front of her. "Did you want to grab something to eat?"

"Nah, I'll eat in a bit. So tell me, how are the reviews, Red?"

"Good. Not perfect, but good. Your social media posts have been receiving positive comments and loads of shares, which is great. The more people see these photos, the better it is for us." She pushed her phone toward him after she'd pulled up a comment thread on a large celebrity blog site. "Read the next to last comment."

He did, his grin turning into a confused frown. "Alec LeBrun is such a fake," he read. "Do they think we'll forget that he assaulted multiple people? No way." He looked up. "I never assaulted anyone."

"Alec, punching your teammate is definitely assault."

"It's practically sibling rivalry," he countered, and Ruby sighed. "I understand, but it's indicative of what we're up against. We can't convince the entire world, but we can convince enough people that you're serious about this. A lot of people feel you're just washing away the dirt with a few good deeds. We need to up the ante."

"Which means?"

"We're going to have you do another interview, for one. And most definitely more photo ops, although I'm going to have you do some more low-key outings. Like grocery shopping in a quiet neighborhood. Something the average person would do."

He made a face. "That's it? I go to the grocery store and buy cereal and people will love me again?" Scoffing, he pushed her phone back to her. "I don't get this stuff sometimes."

"Me neither, but that's it. That's the gist of it. Considering where you were a few weeks ago, you've come a long way. I'd recommend continuing down this path. What we've been doing has been working so far, Alec."

And yet, he didn't look happy.

He leaned back in his chair contemplatively and blew out a breath. Ruby wondered where this Alec had come from. "What's wrong, Alec? Tell me."

"You know what's wrong."

"I don't, unless you tell me."

"You want me to tell you? Fine. Being with you these past few weeks, Ruby, has been the best time of my life. But it's also been the worst. I want you so much. Just being with you is damn terrific, but I'm selfish. I want more."

His eyes were killing her. So deep and soulful, so expressive and sincere. She'd been dealing with him so much lately, she knew when he was telling the truth, and Alec really did want more from Ruby.

"You know we can't do that."

He stared at her, looking like he wanted to argue, but then he nodded. "I'm accepting that. For now. But not before I get that kiss."

"What kiss?"

"The one you owe me from the park."

She opened her mouth, but quickly shut it. A flood of color reddened her cheeks, and she wished he didn't have the ability to fluster her so easily. She clucked her tongue. "You're like a kid with attention issues, you know that?"

"I thought we already established I'm nothing like a kid, Ruby." He stood and drew close to her. "Now, are you going to have mercy on me and grant me that one kiss?"

She wanted to say yes. He'd done so well these last few weeks, and she really wanted to reward him for his patience—oh, who was she kidding? She *wanted* him. He was so handsome and charming, and her attraction to him only increased with every moment she spent around him. Ruby shook her head. "You know I can't," she whispered, surprised to feel tears in her eyes. "This really is a case of 'it's not you, it's me.' Or it's the both of us. You get that, right?"

"No. I don't get it. Not at all."

"I think you don't want to get it. You're so focused on what you want that you're not seeing the big picture."

"Oh, trust me. I get the big picture, Ruby…"

Her phone rang in front of her. Dad was calling. She didn't want to answer it in the middle of a lunch meeting, so she declined the call.

"Isn't that a little harsh declining a call from your dad?"

"He knows what I'm doing. I'll call him back when we're done."

"Maybe it's important," Alec said.

He was right—maybe it was important. Especially when her father called back a second time instead of leaving a voicemail. "Give me a second." Ruby got up, walked to the corner of the room, and answered the phone. "Hey, Dad."

"Ruby, are you with LeBrun now?" His tone was fast and terse, and for a moment, she wondered if she'd been discovered and was about to get the tongue-lashing of the century.

"Yes. What's up?"

"Okay, tell him...that he got an offer from Sports Armour, the major clothing line. They have a big—I mean, BIG—sponsorship for him, Ruby. Huge!" She'd never heard her dad sound so excited. Her chest deflated with relief. "This is the biggest thing he's ever gotten offered, the biggest offer to ever come across our desk. They want him fully committed, excellent royalties and a huge advance. Tell him, and let me know what you both think. Well done, Ruby. Well done."

Phil hung up while Ruby stared at the corner of the room.

A big sponsorship was what they'd wanted.

But it also meant they'd have to move even farther apart. Under a sponsorship like Sports Armour, there was no room for error. They could never near-kiss under trees in the public again, couldn't date, and definitely never hook up again.

"Everything okay, Red?" Alec's deep voice from his seat only drove home how hard this would be.

"Yeah." She whirled around. "You got an offer. A big one."

"Who?" His eyes lit up like hope in the dark.

A slow smile spread across her lips. She loved that she would be the one to give him this fabulous news. It meant she could see him happy again, and she hated being the bearer of bad news, especially on a personal level. "Sports Armour."

Alec yelped, spun once, lifted, and hoisted her in the air, then caught her with a strong hold. All at once. Just like that. No big deal or anything. "Holy shit, Red! Are you kidding me?"

"Not kidding you." She laughed. Adrenaline shot through her body from having just been tossed around by a big, strong man. And not just any man. The one she so desperately wished she could allow into her life. "The deal is yours for the taking."

He shook his head like he couldn't believe it, then slipped his giant hands around her face. "Come here, you." The kiss was delicious and musky and scintillating and painful all at once. Painful because she wanted it to keep going. Her heart longed to accept his attention, go celebrate somewhere, make out all night, and maybe do a replay of their stadium tryst.

Suddenly, the door burst open, and Vince, one of the assistant coaches, stepped inside.

"Alec, you done yet—oh, hey, Ruby. Sorry, didn't know I was interrupting something." Just before he closed the door, he gave Ruby a lingering look that bordered on lascivious. Vince had always been a creep. "I'll leave you two lovebirds alone," he cooed before closing the door.

8

"No. No, no, no," Ruby whispered.

One glance at her, and Alec could tell she was about to lose her shit.

Her face was flushed, her eyes wide, her body frozen.

"Ruby, don't freak out," he said quickly.

The truth was, she had every reason to freak out. Not only was Vince a douchebag, but he was also the worst person who could've seen them in a lip-lock like that. The dude was a walking social media app, spreading news and lies and shit worse than any town crier. Worse than Nana, Alec's eighty-year-old grandmother.

"Don't freak out. Don't freak out? The question is, why aren't *you* freaking out? He just—we just—Oh God." Her eyes shot to the door Vincent had just shut then skipped to another door across the room that led to a maintenance hallway and then the parking lot. "I've gotta get out of here." Swiftly, she walked toward it, threw it open, then charged through it, Alec trailing close behind.

Before they hit the parking lot, Alec reached out and took her arm, stopping her. "Ruby, we need to talk about this."

She whirled around, causing Alec to drop his hand and step back. "What's there to talk about, Alec? He saw us kissing!"

He raked a hand through his hair. "I'm sorry, Red. I was excited because of the sponsorship news. Maybe Vince won't tell anyone."

"Vince will tell everyone!" Tears welled up in Ruby's eyes. Her mouth kept opening and closing, like she was trying to find the right words. She shook her head, pools of blue reflecting shame and fear. He hated knowing she found their being caught kissing as shameful.

He wanted so much to hold her, but when he moved toward her she took a step back. She blinked back her tears.

"Everything was going great. Your fans have been supporting you, you've been killing it on the field, my father's been proud of me for the work I'm doing, and then the sponsorship..." She shook her head. "My God, people will think I broke you and Colleen up. You'll lose the sponsorship before you even get it. And my father... Even if we explain the kiss was just a reaction to good news, that it meant nothing, I'm still screwed."

Alec scowled and crossed his arms over his chest. Damn it, he knew the kiss meant something to her. That *he* meant something to her. In fact, he'd begun to suspect that he meant so much to her, it scared her. That his proposing to Colleen had hurt her so much, it was the real reason she'd been holding off starting anything personal with him. Sure, the fact they worked together and she didn't want to disappoint her father was a convenient excuse, but she was probably far more terrified of what their kisses would lead to and how vulnerable it would leave her heart if she finally opened herself to him completely. He couldn't really blame her either. The idea of her having that much power over him wasn't the most settling feeling either. Even engaged to another woman, he'd thought of Ruby all the time, and that was before he'd even kissed her. Now? She was in his blood.

"I saw what those meaningless kisses led to, Ruby. I heard the way your heart beat and the way your hands trembled. You can't tell me it meant nothing."

She shook her head and threw her arms in the air. "I never said it meant nothing, Alec. But it's probably what we should tell people."

"I disagree. I think we should come clean about everything."

Her eyes widened. "Are you kidding? Your genius plan is to confess to everyone that we"—she lowered her voice only to hiss—"*fucked* on the football field because we were drunk off our asses? You're sure about this, Alec?"

Alec's jaw clenched. "First of all, we weren't drunk off our asses. We only had one double whisky each. And no, that's not what I think we should tell everyone. I think we should tell everyone we've been working together this past month, and as a result, we've developed feelings for one another."

"Why should anyone care about our feelings?" Ruby cried.

At least she didn't deny she *had* feelings for him. "People love a love story. Think about it. Me finding love again after a failed engagement? With the woman who's been by my side for the past few months, bringing me back to myself, seeing me at my best, being a positive influence. They'll root for us."

"That's a huge gamble."

He took her hands and placed them on either side of his face to feel her warmth. She didn't pull them away. "It's one I'm willing to take. It's also the smart move and you know it. Yes, we'll face criticism by some, and Colleen alone will lose her mind. But you know better than anyone that if we leave it in Vince's hands and rumors begin to swirl, it could be a thousand times worse. It's easier to do damage control than skirt around rumors. If we do it this way, our way, by being honest, then we can at least manage things. Play things the way *we* want to play them."

She stared at him for a second before closing her eyes and taking a solid breath. "You're starting to sound like me."

Alec smiled. "Right. Which means I'm making sense." He reached out and pushed reddish-orange strands behind her ears. "But I'll be honest here, Ruby, letting the world know we have real feelings for one another? It's not just about protecting our careers. I know you wanted to wait, but if this helps us start to explore what's between us sooner rather than later, I'm thrilled as hell about it."

She bit her lip, her expression still clouded with doubt.

"Tell me the truth, Ruby. If your job, my job, the public, Colleen, your father—if none of them mattered, if it was just you and me, and it was just a matter of what we wanted, what would you want to do?"

"If none of those things mattered, then yes. Of course I'd want to date you, Alec. I wouldn't care if the entire world knew it. But my father isn't going to be one of the people rooting for us. He's going to see that kiss as irresponsible behavior on my part. Even so, my job isn't the main thing at stake here. Don't you want to protect your image? Don't you want to protect your chances at winning this sponsorship? If people think you cheated on Colleen with me—"

He swiftly cupped her face, making her gasp. "Ruby, I want *you*. I let Colleen's lies mess things up for us before, but I'm not going to let Vincent, or your father, or this potential sponsorship with Sports Armour mess things up again. We're not fucking criminals, for God's sake. We didn't kill anyone. The worst we've done is get feelings for one another during a professional relationship. It's happened before and it will again. People will understand."

"Maybe at first. But what happens when things don't work out between us? A month from now—hell, tomorrow—you could be done with me. You could want someone else."

He cocked his head, wincing. "Is that what you think of me? That I'm that fickle?"

She closed her eyes. "Alec—"

"Ruby, I understand why the thing with Colleen makes you leery, but I told you the truth. It's you I wanted all along. I vote we take a chance. Take a chance on me. I won't disappoint you."

It was all he could do or say. All the cards laid out on the table. He'd made his feelings known. Now the ball was in her court.

She bit her lip. "I don't know, Alec. I just don't—"

Ruby's phone rang. She looked down at it and dread filled her face. "It's my father. Again. See? Look how quickly it's gotten to him."

"You can't know that."

"No. But I need to tell him what Vincent saw. I need to give him a heads-up."

Alec nodded. "Do it. But can I ask one thing? Can you put the call on speaker? Because I kissed you, and if you're going to have to face the consequences of that, I want to face them together."

The phone continued to ring.

Ruby stared at it, then at Alec, then at the phone again. Finally she bit her lip and took the call, hitting the speaker button.

"Hi, Dad."

"Hey, sweetheart. Do you have anything on LeBrun's

schedule for this Friday? I think it'd be a good idea to take him to that racing event that's in town. It won't take long and will work wonders in crossover sport publicity."

"I'll check in a minute," Ruby said. "But um... There's something I have to tell you, Dad." She turned to her side, as if to speak privately, but Alec was still privy to the conversation. "You might hear something today or tomorrow...something about me and Alec LeBrun kissing in the locker room. Don't freak out. There's an easy explanation."

Phil O'Brien was silent for so long, Alec winced. "What explanation, Ruby?" He finally said, his voice clipped.

"Well, see, the moment I told Alec about the sponsorship, he got so happy, he kissed me. Right at that moment, one of the assistant coaches came in. He might have...misunderstood."

Alec frowned even as Ruby glanced his way. Obviously it wasn't what he'd wanted her to say. He'd wanted her to trust him. Trust his idea. Take the chance on exploring what they could be to one another. But this was her father. Her career. She had a right to handle things as she saw fit.

Phil was once again silent for a few seconds, then he sighed. "All right, here's what we're going to do. Spin it that you're dating," Phil said. "We'll play the soul mates card. People will be all over it. The good girl who tamed the bad boy."

"What?" Ruby's eyes, which hadn't left Alec, boggled.

Alec raised his brows even as he suppressed a grin. Obviously, he and Phil O'Brien processed things in a similar fashion. The question was whether Ruby would go for it.

By the look on her face, her father hadn't sold her on the idea any more than Alec had. "Are you sure, Dad? It will be viewed as…unprofessional."

"It's fine, Ruby," her father said. "However, you will have to give up your position with the Bootleggers. Maybe take a leave of absence indefinitely from the first. You'll be let go from the firm immediately."

Phil's words immediately wiped the grin off Alec's face.

Ruby's shoulders slumped, but she nodded. "Okay. Who do I give my cases over to—"

"No." Alec swiped Ruby's phone from her. She tried to take it back, but there was no way he was going to let any harm come to Ruby. Even from her father. "That's not going to happen, Mr. O'Brien. Ruby stays. After all, it was her hard work that earned me a shot at the sponsorship. If she goes, I go."

"LeBrun, I believe this is between me and my daughter."

"That's where you're wrong, Phil. You're talking about disciplining her for something I did. I initiated the kiss, not Ruby. We don't have to say we're dating. Ruby thinks we should simply explain we were celebrating and went too far. That the kiss meant nothing. And I trust her, so if that's how she wants to play it, that's how I'll play it."

Alec felt Ruby place a hand on his arm. He looked down at her and sent her a silent message. He might have made the same suggestion as her father, but she was calling the shots here, no one else. And she certainly wasn't losing her job over any of this.

"No one's going to buy that and just let this lie," her father said. "Saying you're dating is the better strategy."

"Maybe. Like I said, that's up to Ruby. But no matter what she decides, she remains a Bootleggers publicist. She remains *my* publicist. If you fire her, I will fire you, and I'll take the Sports Armour deal to another firm. Is that clear?"

After a moment of silence on Phil's side of the call, he muttered, "Fine, Ruby stays on. But if you lose the sponsorship because of all this, there's going to be hell to pay." The line went dead.

Alec held out the phone to Ruby and braced himself for her anger. Sure enough, she snatched the phone from him and snapped, "Lord protect me from men who know best."

Alec winced. "Actually, I believe what I told your father was *you* know best. I was just making sure he knew I had your back while you decided what that was."

"Well, you shouldn't have told him that. I let you in on that phone call, Alec. I didn't give you permission to take my phone and hijack the conversation. That phone call was between me and my dad. My *boss*."

God, she looked so fucking beautiful when she was pissed off. Of course, he valued his life too much to tell her that, and anyway, the point she was making was completely valid. Even so, he'd do what he did all over again if he had to.

"Ruby, I'm sorry if that was pushy, but you weren't going to play hardball with your dad. I had no problem doing it. Your job is safe, no matter what. How we play things next is totally up to you. The question is are we playing it safe by brushing off that kiss, or are we going to start dating—out in the open, for real? And, Ruby, if you decide not to do the latter because you don't think it's the best move professionally, that's one thing. But if you decide not to do it because you're scared of what you feel for me, well...that's something else. All I can say is...don't. Don't be scared. Take a chance on me. You won't be disappointed."

She stared at him for so long, her gaze searching, yearning even, but she remained quiet. So quiet, he knew she remained unconvinced. She didn't want to take a chance on him. Not again. Not after he'd fucked things up, asked her out then proposed to Colleen, then been a complete asshat, jeopardizing his career and hers in the process. Fine.

He sighed. "Okay. We'll play it your way. I'll talk to Vince first and tell him the kiss meant nothing and we'll see what—umph."

All of a sudden, Ruby wrapped her arms around his neck and pulled his head down to kiss him. When she pulled back, she rested her forehead against his and said, "Let's do it. Let's date. Let's date the fuck out of each other and see where it goes."

Alec grinned and pulled her in for another kiss.

9

His kiss felt warm and toasty in the fall breeze, turning her weak legs and core into hot liquid magma. In the distance, a whistle blew out on the stadium field. Reluctantly, Alec pulled away and tipped her chin up to look at him. Ruby tried not to feel like another half of her had been ripped from her chest.

"Come over later? I'll make you dinner. We can talk about all this some more when we're not under so much pressure. But don't worry. It's all going to be fine, Red. Promise."

Ruby nodded. It was hard accepting that promise, because there were no guarantees. It was also hard hearing him say that maybe she was afraid of them two being together, but maybe she had been?

Maybe he was right, and she'd been using her career and her father's iron fist over her as an excuse not to get close to Alec, because even a reformed bad boy was still a bad boy. As Alec ran off in that perfect athletic gait of a seasoned football player, Ruby slipped into her car and let the captive air of her lungs escape.

"Holy shit," she spoke into the quietude of her car.

Excitement, worry, and pure lust all whirled together throughout her soul.

What was she getting into? Would he hurt her?

If she did this...if she agreed to date Alec...her world would change dramatically. Soon, she'd be in the public eye, not behind it. She'd appear in photos with Alec, accompany him to charity events, and people would come to know her as Alec LeBrun's girlfriend. They might even be known as "Al-Uby" or worse—"Ru-Bec."

Ruby cringed and started her car.

But would it last? She hated the possibility that she might just be Alec's rebound girl after Colleen. People might accuse her of having come between them. So many ulterior motives nagged at her, but her gut feeling told her Alec LeBrun was exactly who he appeared to be—a good guy who'd made a few wrong turns and was trying to find his way back to center.

Ruby just wanted to make sure that center was her.

There was no point in resisting him anymore. She'd always wanted him, and now that he wanted her, too, it all felt a bit overwhelming. It'd been one thing to fantasize that her handsome, charming client would one day look at her, but it was another knowing that he actually wanted to take it to the next level, wanted to please her, and not just sexually either. He seemed to genuinely care for her and loved the idea of the whole world knowing about it.

Now Ruby just had to chill out and enjoy it.

In the evening, she rang the gate to the swanky home in Thomas Square Streetcar. She brandished a bottle of wine, wore jeans and a flirty green top, nothing too sexy. Comfy, a little romantic, and *chill*, she thought.

I am chill. I am chillastic. I am the embodiment of chillitude.

By the time Alec answered the door thirty seconds later, however, she was a ball of nerves again. The door to the gorgeous mansion unlocked. A dangerously handsome man answered wearing jeans and a fitted T-shirt that highlighted his body. "There she is. My favorite redhead."

Alec.

There was that smile. It rendered Ruby boneless every time.

He looked even more amazing surrounded by the opulence of the home he'd earned with his own bare hands. A football had earned him all this. His hard work had earned it.

"Heyyy. If we're going to be dating," she said, stepping into the foyer with a grin, "I should probably be your favorite *person*, shouldn't I?" She laughed and handed him the bottle of wine, which he accepted before pulling her into a big hug.

"You're so right. Come here."

She melted against his chest. Damn, he smelled delicious, like rosemary and spice but also something unnamed. She knew she was in trouble. Good trouble. The kind of trouble that made you wish you'd be bad more often if the punishment looked anything like Alec LeBrun.

"Something smells yummy."

"Besides you?" He closed the door and led her inside. "Damn, girl. You're looking fine, finer than usual, that is. How do you keep getting more beautiful every time I see you?"

"Stop, crazy man." She blushed. Sure, he was flirting with her, and he could've just been saying pretty words, but she felt his words, too. She felt prettier every time she saw him, and maybe he was responsible for that. For pulling the natural magic out of her.

"You're right on time. The butternut squash is done roasting. I'll put the steaks on the grill now, unless you want to wait?"

He was saying something about food. She wasn't sure, because she couldn't focus. His house was incredible. She'd been to celebrity homes that were all gray or white, monochromatic, boring as hell, and devoid of feeling. But Alec's house was warm and inviting with wood floors, gorgeous modern paintings, and even a little kitty lurked in the shadows.

"We can eat now, if you want. I'm starving. Who's this?" She crouched to pet the all-gray feline with the green eyes sashaying up to her.

"That's Henna. She likes you. She never comes up to anyone."

"You're just saying that." Ruby scratched Henna between her ears.

"I'm dead serious. She's a feral cat I found in my yard

last year before the last hurricane that blew through here. I brought her inside to keep her safe. She's been with me ever since. She hates ninety-nine percent of the people she meets."

Ruby's heart warmed instantly, and the best part was, she felt it was true. She knew by the way he said it, not looking for attention or praise, just heading into the kitchen, that this little creature had been afforded a good life thanks to one said cocky football player. Briefly, she wondered if Henna ever liked Colleen, but as soon as the thought entered her mind, she pushed it away.

Colleen would not ruin another dinner of hers.

"Now, why didn't *that* story ever make it into the public?" she asked. "People would've loved that."

Alec shrugged. Ruby and Henna both followed him. "I don't know, but let's not share it. Henna's shy and wouldn't want the attention." He chuckled, then opened the oven and pulled out the roasted veggies.

"Fine, fine. That looks amazing," Ruby said. "I didn't know you could cook."

Alec flashed her a look. "There are lots of things you don't know about me, Miss O'Brien." The way he said it made her stomach crunch. Indeed. She was only getting to know this man, but so far, she wasn't sure what she'd been so afraid of. After heating a pan to cook the steaks and pouring Ruby and himself glasses of the cabernet she'd brought, he asked, "Do you have any pets?"

"Me?" She balked. "I wish." Henna jumped onto the counter and arched her back into Ruby's hand. Her bright eyes blinked happily. "My dad never let us have any. He always felt that pets would ruin the house."

"Wow. Was he strict when you were growing up? Your dad? Seems like it."

Ruby took a seat at the center island and watched Alec set the marinated steaks on the pan. "He could be, yes. I think he was harder on me than on my brothers, maybe because he figured it'd be harder for a girl."

"Well, it worked, didn't it? Because you're tough, you don't take shit from anyone, and you're the best in your field. In many ways, I admire the man. He raised you."

"I don't know if I'm the best, but I have a pretty good work ethic."

"A pretty good work ethic is a rare thing, Ruby."

She nodded. She didn't think it was, but then again, she didn't know where Alec was coming from. Maybe he was thinking about the women he'd known in his life. Maybe he was thinking about his mother. "What makes you say that?" She risked. He'd never talked much about his family and she'd always wanted to know.

Alec side-glanced her. "Let's just say one woman I know has worked her ass off all her life. You would like her."

"Your mom?" Ruby guessed.

"You got it."

"You don't talk much about her. I've been afraid to ask."

"She's private, and I strive to keep it that way. She's awesome. Raised me all without any help. She was, and still is, two parents rolled into one, since my dad abandoned her when I was a baby."

"Oh, God. I'm so sorry about that." A few pieces of Alec's puzzle locked into place. Hearing that he would be a father must've been scary for him. He must've wanted to right twenty-eight years of paternal wrong.

"Thanks. She taught me so much. About sports, about teamwork. She even taught me how to cook."

"Ah, so that's where it comes from?"

"I guess. Most of my friends were warming Hot Pockets after school, but my mom was showing me how to make pot roast, chicken parmigiana, homemade pizzas…" He poured some wine into the pan and scraped it down. "Reduction sauce, anyone?"

"Okay, now you're just showing off." She smiled, inhaling the delicious scents melding in the kitchen. "Seriously, I really can't wait for those steaks to be done." Her stomach was now growling, and she couldn't believe her luck. Gorgeous, athletic, and a talented cook. Even Henna meowed for a bite.

He smiled, leaned over the kitchen island, and petted Henna's head and back. Then, he kissed Ruby's forehead. "Almost done. I know hungry faces when I see them."

Oh, he had no idea. She was hungry in oh, so many ways. Driving here, she wasn't sure how far she wanted to take things tonight with Alec, but she did know she wanted to click with him first. Connect again like they had been doing the last several weeks. Whereas their first time had been impulsive, this time she wanted to go a little slower.

Find out more about him.

"So, how come you didn't become a cook?" she asked. "What made you go into football?"

"Because football was always my escape. Don't get me wrong, I love cooking, but as a kid, it was a chore, a survival thing. Football was the one thing that made me feel free, like I could act my age. When you're raised by a single mom, you have to grow up kind of fast."

Ruby nodded. She was lucky enough to have both parents and a normal childhood. They weren't rich by any means, but they had good times, good Christmas presents, and good vacations. She knew she was blessed.

"Your mom must be proud of you," Ruby said and meant it. If she had a son like Alec, she'd be incredibly proud of his accomplishments. She'd be worried as hell about his private life lately, but she'd still be proud. She didn't want to think too hard about Alec as a child, though, because that would make him more real in her eyes, and the realer he seemed, the more she'd want to help him, heal him and his heart. The more she'd want to become a part of his future memories.

I'm scared of falling too hard for him, she thought suddenly, sipping the wine mid-glass.

What was that smile on his face for? His eyes gleamed.

"What?" She smiled.

"Nothing. You just have this really content look on your face right now. I like it. You look relaxed."

"I am relaxed." And feeling even more relaxed by the

second after the wine.

She set about getting the salads ready, placed the roasted squash in a bowl on the table, and prepared the rest while Alec finished the steaks and plated them. *My own, personal chef,* she thought with a grin. It was so nice to talk, sit down with a fantastic meal—and it *so* was, the best she'd had in a long time—and just be with Alec. No worries, no talk about their kiss earlier or her father or any of the events that had transpired.

"To a new beginning," Alec said, raising his glass for toast. "We so needed this."

"We did." She clinked her glass against his. The wine was the perfect accompaniment to the even more amazing steak dinner. And the roasted butternut squash! Everything was superb.

"And I so need you, Ruby." He made sure to throw that one in there before digging into the meal. The idea wasn't lost on her. She knew his full intentions. It was she who had to decide how serious to get with Alec. Was she ready for him to go from crush to serious BAE?

Maybe it was the delicious meal, the sweet soundtrack playing from a speaker somewhere in the house, or the wine that shaved the edge off her nerves, but she settled in. Alec was funny and sweet and soon, she had no idea why she'd judged him so harshly. He was nothing like a child—something she'd accused him of several times— and now she felt bad about it. If anything, he hadn't had the chance to fully be a child. Instead, he'd been a boy caring for his mom, being a man way too soon.

"I'm sorry for giving you a hard time," she said after dinner when Alec pulled her to his back patio to look at the city lights as the sun went down.

"Me? For what?" He waited as she polished off her wine then took the glass from her hand and set it down on a patio table.

"For calling you a child a few weeks ago. I thought it'd be a good way to light a fire under your butt, but now I see how unfair that was. You've worked hard to get where you are, and that doesn't come by being immature. Forgive me?"

Alec looked at her a moment, scooped her off her feet, and placed her on a long chair where he curled himself around her. Here, under the stars, surrounded by the twinkling city lights of Savannah and the sound of crickets all around, she could easily fall asleep in his arms. Except the scent of his skin flooded her with warmth and sleep was the last thing on her mind.

His fingers caressed her hair, twisted it into a rope, and let it go again. "Listen, you were just doing your job. And a damn fine one, too. Don't apologize. I had to hear that shit."

"I can still be sorry." Ruby closed her eyes. It felt good to be so close to him. So safe, protected, and cared for. But his body also warmed her from the inside out.

"The only thing you should be sorry for is not wearing your hair in a bun today."

"What? Why?"

"Because I know your secret. I know when it's up,

you're in business mode, and when it's down like this..."
Burying his face in her hair, he inhaled her scent, as his
fingers traced a line down her jawline, tipping her chin up
to him. "You're more yourself. You're ready to have a
good time."

"Why should I be sorry about that?"

"Because I can't control myself when you're like this,
Ruby. You don't understand. I want you all the damn time.
So when you finally let me touch you..." With one arm
holding her around the shoulders, and the other slipping
around her waist, she felt captured and that was just fine
with her. "It makes me a little crazy."

"I can handle crazy right now." Crazy was her life at
the moment, and as the old saying went, *If you can't beat
them, join them.* She felt bold, brave. Maybe it was the
wine. Or maybe she was ready. "I can handle you, Alec."

It was as close to a declaration as she would ever get.
And to make it even clearer, she slipped her hand around
his neck and pulled him close. They met in a kiss that
lasted longer than she'd ever kissed anyone before. No
rush, no time limit, just the whole night ahead of them,
heat—fast and furious—spreading through her body like
wildfire.

His mouth and tongue explored hers, hungrily, blindly
seeking her main source, sliding over her neck and down
the curve of her breast. She arched into him, wishing she
could get closer. The buzz of the wine heightened the
sensations, and the stars seemed to shine just for them.
With every kiss, every undulation, she felt him pressing

closer, felt the size of him massive and impending. She felt drunk with lust and power over this highly wanted man, as he undressed her, removed her top, and slid his hand over her breasts.

He was hers, all hers.

"I want you to know," he said as he caught his breath. He looked up at her with that penetrating gaze. "That these are...without a doubt...the most luscious tits I've ever sucked on." He didn't wait for a response, only slid down the long chair and nestled by her side to suckle on one, taut nipple then another, squeezing and playing with each, giving them equal attention.

She reeled, gripping the chair, his hair. To say her panties flooded with her juices was an understatement. All he had to do was keep suckling her tits this way and touch her when the moment was right, and she'd go off like a bottle rocket. And from the way she fought for breath, chest heaving, pushing into his mouth, and fighting for more and more of him, he knew it, too.

His hand slid between her thighs, two fingers pressing against her core through the denim. "So fucking sweet, Ruby. You don't understand, you don't understand..." he kept saying, as if Ruby wouldn't know how much he'd been wanting her. Of course she knew. She'd been the same way, only more repressed about it.

As his mouth created a trail of fire down her body, past her navel to the edge of her jeans, she couldn't hold it in anymore. "I've thought about you every night for months now," she confessed. "Sometimes, I would touch myself thinking about it." It was a bold assertion, and she'd never talked to any guy that way before, but she felt the need to start out right, start sharing her deepest confessions right away, so they might have a true and honest start.

He needed that after what had happened with Colleen, and she needed it, too.

"Did you now?" He sat up, slid down her jeans so they were around her ass, then pulled them off completely. Seeing his big, manly fingers pull off her panties as well nearly pushed her over the edge. He was all man, all Alec, and she was completely bare beneath him. Bare and vulnerable. "Well, we're just going to have to do something about that, Red. Unless you want to go home and keep fantasizing."

"No. I want the real thing. I want you." Ruby braced for impact. She knew the moment Alec's fingers and tongue touched her, she'd be in trouble. The best kind of trouble there was. She sucked in a sharp breath and moaned softly. For Ruby, surrendering wasn't just hard—it was significant.

She trusted Alec. Now more than ever. She could do this.

She could do this every damn day.

He lowered himself so he was even with her aching pussy. God, she wanted him so badly. Risking a glance at him, knowing it would make her even wetter to see him between her legs, she opened her eyes to see the hazy, sexy gaze of a man who knew how to wield his power. His deep brown eyes devoured her, and slowly, his flat tongue pressed against her clit.

"Holy shit," she moaned, gripping his hair.

He began to lick. Slowly. Testing, gauging how soft or hard she wanted it, watching her reactions closely, sliding his fingers down her cleft and dipping it into her pussy. "You taste so good, Ruby."

She loved how he said her name. It sounded so lovely coming from his mouth. The mouth currently between her legs. So intimate. So happening at this moment. She tried not to focus on the obvious—it was Alec, Alec LeBrun, tight end of the Bootleggers—lapping up her folds. Her client, her crush, eating her pussy.

"I thought you might want dessert." She bit her smile. Yes, she was being cheeky now, and it felt nice for a change.

"You thought right, babe. My favorite, too."

She moaned in reply, as he softly flicked his tongue against her clit. Her fingers raked through his thick hair, pulling him closer, wanting to feel those shoulders, wishing she could rip his shirt off his back. Like he could hear her thoughts, he pulled it off in one swift movement without stopping his tongue for more than a second. Damn, he was good. His hand splayed across her belly, his thumb pulling up on her mound to give him better access, bury his face deep into her cunt.

Fiery breath against her skin sent prickles of heat up her legs, as he fingered her deeper, picking up rhythm as he went. She was close now. She'd been close to begin with. Without another thought, she ground her pussy against his face, holding his head in place, and giving him all of her. This was what he wanted—now he'd earned it.

"I'm going to come," she told him, feeling too damn good. She didn't care anymore about appearances, getting caught, getting found in the locker room, or anything. It was just her and Alec, Alec's tongue and fingers giving her what she wanted and didn't even know she needed.

"Give it to me," he mumbled against her skin, pulling that fire out from deep inside of her.

Yes.

It felt so…fucking…good.

The patio, the lights of the city, the stars, the cool air, the wine, and Alec's whole aura combined to create one vibrant painting to rival Starry Night. It swirled and swirled all around her, as she came, one wave after another, onto his tongue and his face. So intimate, so crazy, so right. Yes, it felt right to be with this man. She didn't care about anything else at that moment, because they were all that existed. This blinding, peaking moment.

Seeing his expression when she finally opened her eyes and felt him resting against her inner thigh, she knew she could do anything and Alec LeBrun would adore her. Where had this attention come from? What had she done to deserve it? She didn't know. All she knew was that he was at her mercy, and there was nothing sexier.

Once she came down from her high, she blinked up at the stars.

"Hi," he said after a minute, sliding up to kiss her deeply. From the passion in his kiss and the hardness in his jeans, she knew he wanted to go on.

"Hi," she said.

"Look at me."

She looked at him. But it wasn't easy. Just a few weeks ago, he'd been a fantasy to her, and now here he was. Here they were. And it was real. He was a real man with real feelings, sometimes with conflicting ideas, and that scared her half to death. But it was what it was—sensual, beautiful, and frightening as hell.

"What are you thinking?" he asked.

The million-dollar question. Ruby didn't know how to answer. All she knew was that Alec made her want to take risks. He brought out the spontaneous in her, brought out the real and maybe even slightly reckless Ruby, the Ruby she'd never given herself the chance to know. "That I want to go on. I want this to continue," she said.

"What we're doing now, or…"

"Everything, Alec." She breathed. "I want full in."

"Full in. I like that." He smiled.

And in that smile, she found a deeply devoted man. A rascal, too—one who knew he'd won for the moment. One who'd do anything to please her but now wanted his own pleasure in return. He brought out a sense of freedom in her, too. Yes, freedom. To be herself, finally, once and for all. "And right now, I want you to fuck me," she said, ready—so ready—for round two.

His hands dug into her thighs, reached underneath her ass, and squeezed. "Go big or go home. Right, Ruby?"

"Yes, sir," she felt compelled to say.

"Sir. I like that, too. Turn around for me, babe. And hold on to that chair."

10

Even though he was in a moment, as Ruby turned around in all her naked glory, Alec couldn't help but stop, his mind spinning a web of improbabilities. Here she was—the woman he'd pined over for so long, finally giving into him. Not just emotionally but physically, and in the most submissive sense ever. Tight ass up, arms folded over the backrest of the chair, as enticing as a woman could possibly get.

The elusive Ruby O'Brien, the one who told him this couldn't happen, because of their professional relationship, was poised and ready for his cock.

Was there anything more beautiful?

Had it been any other woman with her ass in the air, Alec would've grinned at this moment—*yeah, finally got what I want.* He'd admit it, other women were merely conquests. But with Ruby, he almost felt the need to bow down before her, literally kiss her ass. And so he did.

"This…" he said, placing his hands on either side of

her butt and lowering to kiss one cheek, then the other, "is something I've dreamed about for so long."

"You've dreamed of my ass?" She laughed.

"I've dreamed of you, giving yourself to me." He smoothed out her ass, feeling the roundness and perfect velvety softness of her skin. Had he been eighteen, he would've plunged into her already with no patience whatsoever, but he had to stop and admire the view, the pure vulnerability of the moment.

All in, she'd said. She'd get her wish.

"I trust you," Ruby said, glancing over her shoulder. He understood what she meant. She was talking about not using a condom. "You would tell me if you shouldn't, right?"

"God damn right," he said. "I'd never lead you astray." And he wouldn't. But he also wasn't sure he was ready to be a father. Not because he didn't love kids—he adored them—but because he wanted to do this right. He wanted to date Ruby first, then who knew? Marry her one day, then start a family. With Ruby, he wanted everything to be perfect. Because she was perfect in his eyes. "And you?"

"I'm on the pill. Just do it already, Alec."

"Do what, Ruby?" he teased. He knew she could hear it in his voice.

"Fuck me."

"I'm sorry, I didn't hear what you said. Can you repeat that?" Alec held his throbbing cock in one hand, pushing the head against her opening in big circles, teasing her entire cunt, feeling her twitch just beyond his reach.

She sighed slightly. "I said fuck me. Please."

Now she was talking. There was that word again, ambrosia spilling from Ruby's usually prim and proper mouth. "Oh, is it this you want?" He pushed in just a bit, hearing her moan with delight, then pushed in slowly some more. "Or this? Or maybe the whole thing..." He entered her all the way, a sword sheathing down to the hilt.

"Yessss..."

Good, she loved it. Her long, undulating moan made him so happy and fucking hot for her, he pulled out and this time, rammed her once. She cried out, fingers curling around the back of the chair, her back arching, wanting more. "You like it when I fuck you, Ruby?"

"Yes."

"Yes, what? Tell me..."

"Yes, I love it."

"Yes, you love it, what? What did you call me a minute ago?" he teased, holding his cock steady until she gave him what he wanted.

"Yes, sir."

Bam—another thrust, ramming his balls against her pussy. She cried out. Did it matter they were outside and neighbors might possibly hear her from several yards away? He didn't care. Part of him relished the thought. *Look at me, world, I finally got the woman I wanted.*

The woman I needed.

"Good girl," he said. Yes, they were playing minor roles of submissive and dominant, but Ruby seemed to love it. It was no surprise. After working in a powerful, controlling career all day long, it was no wonder she relinquished so easily. Her hips felt good under his hands, her body like it was made for him. For a better traction, he placed a foot on the chair and fucked her even harder.

And she'd started touching herself, too, which meant she might come again if he kept it up. "I know how badly you've wanted my cock, Ruby, so here it is again." He slammed against her again, pulling out and thrusting into her with purpose, each push sending a message. *You're mine. All mine.*

She rubbed herself with renewed enthusiasm, pushing against his every jolt forward, even reaching back to hold on to his legs and drive him in harder. She wanted him, every inch of him. She wanted to feel his cock hit her deep inside, and the demand sent a tightness coiling up his body and into his balls. They fucked hard and long, working up their heat until they couldn't take it anymore. Though he wanted so badly to let go, he wouldn't until she'd come.

He needed to hear that sweet moan again.

Finally, Ruby shifted to the right, draping her head over the edge of the seat, so she could lie flat on her stomach, squeezing her thighs together, as her fingers worked at her clit. He shifted accordingly, driving his cock into her pussy so tightly, it almost felt like he was fucking her in her ass from this angle, and the thought nearly pushed him over the edge.

But then, Ruby cried out. And stiffened. And when he heard that beautiful sound and felt her muscles squeeze all around him, he knew it was time to let go. His climax came from the underbelly of his long, aching need, from a place of which he'd been dreaming for months now—since Ruby had come into his life. From the moment he met her and wanted to possess her. They held their breaths suspended in unison. He bent low so he could hear the cries escaping her mouth, hold her hair and neck in place.

"Are you still all in, babe?" he asked. If she didn't want any part of this—because this was only the beginning of what she could expect if they were to be together—she should speak now or forever hold her peace.

"Yes," she breathed low and long. Music to his ears.

"Then I'll make it worth your while. More than worth your while." When she was ready, he helped her flip over, curled up beside her, and covered her with his body, keeping her warm from the cooling night. Part of him wanted to finish by saying he loved her, but he knew she wouldn't be ready to hear that.

In fact, he wasn't sure he was ready for it either, considering all that had happened between him and Colleen. Trust would always be an issue with women, as much as he felt that Ruby would never keep secrets from him. Still, he held back. *When the time is right,* he thought.

He turned her cheek and kissed her gently. He could've kissed her all night.

But between the big, healthy meal and the massive outdoor sex, they fell asleep instantly, and by the time they woke up in the morning, covered in a blanket Alec assumed Ruby had gotten in the middle of the night, news had hit.

The Internet—the world—knew they were dating.

Alec ignored his calls for most of the day. Knowing that Ruby was already a bit freaked out about their relationship going "official," even though her father believed it was all an act, he was hell-bent on making her feel comfortable. He didn't want her to regret her decision for one second.

They went out for lunch in the middle of town, and though he wished the two of them could continue talking like they had last night when he'd cooked for her, this time, it was evident that people were watching. And listening. When he'd reach for her hand or smile because he couldn't help himself—he was with the most gorgeous woman working in the NFL—he could feel the restaurant patrons taking secret photos with their phone cameras.

"It's fine. Don't let it get to you," he mouthed to Ruby across the table.

She'd pinned her ginger hair up into a bun, fussed with the scarf he'd loaned her because it had been chilly when they'd left—"It's my mom's," he'd quickly told her when she'd glared at him—and shook her head nervously.

"I don't know how you can be so calm about all this. I'm so nervous right now, Alec. What if Sports Armour revokes their offer?" She bounced in her seat.

With his leg, he steadied hers under the table. "They won't."

"How do you know?"

"Because I'm not fucking up, Ruby. Going out with you is so opposite of fucking up, it's not even funny. They're going to see what a good influence you are on me."

"Is that why you wanted to go out with me? For your image?" Even though she was smiling through her smirk, a little joke, he knew she was probably worried about this in the back of her mind.

He sipped from his glass, avoiding eye contact with a couple who walked past their table and perused them to make sure they were Alec LeBrun and his publicist who were reportedly dating, as of this morning. Once they were gone, he said, "Nah, I wanted to go out with you for your tits. Your tits are, without a doubt, the best part about you."

He waited for the evil glare and got a kick under the table instead. Right into his knee.

"Ow!" He rubbed his knee and bit his smile.

"You better watch out, LeBrun," she chastised, laughing. "I'm still your publicist and I will still knock you on your ass. Hear me?"

Alec nodded in surrender. "I hear you, loud and clear, Sergeant O'Brien. Holy shit. I love that you get my humor, Red. You know I'm pleased as punch that we're dating, because I damn well don't deserve you."

Her eyes softened as she gazed at him. "Is that what you think?"

"It's the truth."

"That's not true, Alec. I'm no better than you are.

We're equals."

He wasn't going to argue with her. Not on their first "official" date in public. But it most definitely was true. Ruby O'Brien was entirely out of his league, a fine woman who would be better off going out with a tax attorney, a banker, not a misbehaved, miscreant football player like him. That she had great tits was only the cherry on top of a highly unlikely hot fudge sundae. Two cherries, actually.

After their meal, Alec escorted Ruby out of the restaurant, his arm around her shoulders. He knew that some reporters waited for them outside and wanted to give them something to talk about. "You ready for this?" he mumbled into Ruby's ear.

"Not really," she replied nervously.

"Great. Here we go." They pushed out the doors into the gorgeous October day.

"Mr. LeBrun!"

"Mr. LeBrun!"

"Alec!"

At first, he thought it'd been a small crowd, but then he spotted a bigger swarm of paparazzi coming toward them with cameras flashing, mics extended in front of them, and video rolling. He sensed Ruby tense by his side. He quickly checked around him to see if there was any way to get away, but his car was too far. "Let's do this," he told Ruby, throwing on the smile he'd used a thousand times before, waving friendly-like as they reached him.

"Fellas." He used that charming southern drawl he'd almost forgotten wasn't his natural speaking voice.

"Lovely afternoon, huh? See that touchdown last Sunday? Pretty damn amazing, I know. Hey, who's got me on their fantasy team?" He knew they didn't give a rat's ass about his touchdown or fantasy football this time around, but he tried to distract them from making Ruby uncomfortable anyway.

"Mr. LeBrun, can you tell us how long you and Ms. O'Brien have been dating?" one of the paparazzi asked and another shouted, "Is it serious?"

So much for the distraction technique, Alec thought, his mind racing. It was hard to think with so many people crowded around, mostly people who didn't care about his feelings, who only wanted to make a profit off of his life's dramas.

Ruby took a step back, as the reporters fought for front line action, snapping their cameras and asking questions.

"Is she the reason for the recent good boy act, LeBrun?" They turned their attentions to Ruby.

"Yeah, have you been cleaning up for her?" someone else asked.

Alec glanced back at Ruby, who had moved behind him, somewhat shading her face. He reached back and gave her his best, reassuring smile before pulling her forward into the limelight. "Quiet down, gentlemen, if you want me to answer any of your questions." Once the crowd had quieted, he continued. "Like any relationship at its inception, it's full of possibilities. Miss O'Brien has worked as my publicist for a year now. We've always been friends."

"Are you sure it's only been friends?" some asshole asked, suggesting he'd been involved with her even during Colleen.

Alec did not give him the benefit of an answer.

"As you all know," he continued, unruffled, "she's had to work a little harder than usual to help me redeem myself after some bad behavior. And, during that time, feelings developed. It's complicated, what with her being my publicist and all, but if you think about it, it's perfect. I need someone working with me who understands me, who has my back, and there's no one I trust more than Ruby. So we're going to see how this plays out. From my standpoint, I only expect great things."

Everyone started shouting at once as casual observers started to fill the sidewalk all around them. Alec pulled Ruby closer to him. "One at a time," he shouted.

"What about Colleen?"

"I wish Colleen the absolute best, but there is nothing more between us."

"Why Ruby, Alec? Why not any other woman?"

Alec looked down at the woman by his side. His prize. "Ruby is an amazing woman who's always had my respect. No other woman can come close to holding a candle to her."

Ruby smiled. For a moment, it looked to him like she was trying to figure out whether he was saying this for the sake of the reporters or whether he truly believed it in his heart. She seemed to be searching for the answer and he hoped she could see it in his face despite the swarm of sharks all around them.

He hoped she could see the answer clear as day and would soon come to believe him. Ruby O'Brien made him not need to pretend anymore.

11

That had been, hands down, the scariest thing Ruby had ever been through.

Sure, Alec might be used to reporters and cameras, and Ruby was too—behind them—but she was rarely in front of them and being asked questions, too. She was glad not one reporter had thrust a microphone in her face, or she wouldn't have known what to say. Alec had done all the talking. And the things he'd said had sounded lovely.

But how many of them had he meant?

She had to admit it was difficult knowing where the honest Alec ended and where the limelight Alec began, but the more time she spent with him, the easier it was to define. When he was being honest, he wasn't smiling. That charming smile everyone had come to know and love, the one that plastered the front of sports magazines and graced commercial screens was Working Alec. The subtle, humble smile when he looked at her in front of reporters and declared that she was an amazing woman...that was

Real Alec.

"Your destination is ten minutes away," Siri informed Alec, as he drove away from the restaurant.

Ruby held on to the door handle, as he weaved through the streets.

"I know. Ten minutes till I get to kiss my favorite woman again." Alec smiled. "Hey, Siri. Text Ruby that she looks gorgeous today. I'm scared to tell her in person."

"Okay. I'll text Ruby that she looks gorgeous today, Alec."

A moment later, Ruby received a text from Alec LeBrun: *That she looks gorgeous today. I'm scared to tell her in person.* Ruby laughed and replied: *Thanks, dork.*

Yes, he was dead serious about her.

She almost felt bad for the question she'd asked him during lunch—was that why you wanted to date me? She wished she could kick herself now. In the car, heading back to his place, so she could get her car and finally go home, she turned to Alec. "I'm sorry about what I said during lunch."

"Which part? When you ordered the lobster cakes? Nothing to be ashamed of, Ruby. Really." He laughed to himself, looking straight ahead at the road.

"You know what I mean. When I said I suggested that repairing your reputation was the reason you were going out with me. I'm sorry I said that. Forgive me if I'm feeling a little unsure. I just…sometimes I can't believe it."

It was true. Today, at lunch, she'd wanted to pinch

herself. Especially standing in front of cameras and reporters. The whole time, she kept thinking, *Is this really happening? Am I really officially dating Alec LeBrun, tight end of the Savannah Bootleggers?*

True, she'd wanted to date a football player her whole life, but she also knew those had been her teen fantasies. Once she graduated from college, Ruby knew the possibility of dating one of her future clients would be close to nil. Still, memories from last night barreled her brain—the way he'd licked her to climax, the way he'd commanded her to turn around, the way it had affected her...

In real life, Ruby had always been in charge. But last night, there'd been something about Alec telling her to hold on to the chair, demanding that she call him sir, and hearing him talk dirty that totally drove her over the edge. She wasn't used to it.

But she wanted it again. And again.

"You? I'm the one who can't believe you said yes, Ruby. Even now, I look over at you and think, holy shit, this fine woman likes me. I mean, you do like me, right?" He shot her a few faux worried glances.

Ruby laughed. "Most of the time, yes."

"Oh! Fair enough, fair enough. I'll work on that." He chuckled, taking turns in his Porsche 911 like they were on rails.

"Stay in right lane," Siri said.

Yeah, Ruby, stay in the right lane. Make sure this is what you want. Don't take a wrong turn anywhere. With a sigh, Ruby leaned back and tried to relax. They'd had a whirlwind of the last twenty-four hours. Apparently, it'd taken Alec telling the whole world how he felt for her to truly understand he wasn't acting—he wanted her. Now she just had to get used to the idea—and the reporters.

"Was it okay? Everything I told the press?" he asked.

"Yes, though a few of them still seem to think I broke you and Colleen up. I was afraid of that."

"Listen, there's nothing we can do about that. People will believe what they want to believe, and those guys are just trying to stir up the pot, give people something to talk about."

"Because they get paid that way," Ruby added.

"Exactly. See? You understand this even better than I do. So listen, Red, let's not worry about it. In the next few days, we should be hearing from Sports Armour, shouldn't we?"

"You have a meeting with them in one week." She'd forgotten to tell him. Early this morning, as she'd gone to fetch a blanket for their outdoor chaise-bed, she'd checked her emails and seen the one from the SA rep.

"Seven days? All right…" He stretched his neck, and Ruby thought she detected a little nervousness on his behalf.

"It should be nothing. Probably they've heard about us and wanted to make sure you were still a good candidate for their ad campaign, which is squeaky-clean, sporty but also academic. They want a good guy for the face of their products."

"I'm a good guy," Alec asserted.

There was never any question, Ruby thought. Well, maybe a little. But now that she was getting to know Alec more than ever, she hated that she'd ever doubted him. "In oh, so many ways," she replied, giving him a sexy look.

Alec's eyebrows rose, as he pushed the car into fifth gear and reached for her hand.

"Your destination," Siri interjected, "is only three minutes away."

"One minute now," Alec said and punched the gas pedal.

Once they got back to his place, the plan had been for Ruby to go home, get some work done, then call him later on after practice was over. But the plan was derailed the moment they'd walked through the door to Alec's mansion and he'd pulled Ruby into his arms, giving her the deepest kiss of the day, luring her farther into the house.

What is he doing to me? Why don't I have any power to stop him? It scared her, the magnitude and speed with which she was falling for Alec.

He pulled her in, all the way to his bed. She never even had the chance to see all the amazing artwork and framed photos on the way to his room, but then again, there would be time to see them, because she hoped this would last a while. This "thing" between them. She had no idea what her future with Alec would be like, but for now, she was enjoying being with him. Being his official girlfriend, loving his attention.

For once, she felt relaxed, excited about the possibilities.

At one point, he pulled away and looked deep into her eyes. "You know, all that stuff about dating I told the reporters?"

"Yes?" For a second, Ruby thought he would say it was all fake, all bullshit. What would she do if he did?

But instead, he added, "We're not just dating, Ruby. Dating is for babies. Red, you are my *woman*. Every time I see you, I know it. I feel it. I've wanted you for so long, you're meant to be mine."

He kissed her hard then, imposing the gravity of his words, and it sent her body reeling, her core flooding with heat. Where this reaction was coming from, she didn't know. Words like those from anyone else in her past would've sent her into fits of laughter. But with Alec, they were real, said with meaning, and she believed it.

She believed she was Alec's woman.

He had chosen her, and there was no denying it at this point.

His kisses were long and controlled, and though she felt his body hardening the moment they landed on the bed, she loved the fact he restrained himself, didn't dive right in like they'd been doing, but instead took his time slowly. This time, he wanted to explore her, taste her, get to know the woman he'd told the world he adored and respected. And she didn't mind lying underneath him, looking up into his eyes, feeling every contour of his body, his weight pinning her down in the most delicious way.

He stroked her skin, sending goose bumps erupting all up her arms. "You don't know the power you have over me, Ruby." The admission seemed to come from some deep, dark place, and she knew she felt the same.

"I think I do. I know I do. You have the same power over me." As she kissed him, she ran her hands down his chest until she pulled up his shirt and touched his bare skin. So good, so hard against her fingers, like he'd been chiseled from stone.

Things quickly heated until Ruby's body felt like it was actually on fire. She could barely catch her breath—from Alec kissing her, to his hands cupping her breasts, to his hardness insistently pressing against her warm center. He stripped her of her cute top, the one she'd changed into on their way to the restaurant when she'd asked him to stop at her townhouse a moment. She returned the favor, wanting to see his naked chest.

She traced the lines of his pectorals. His skin was smooth with only a little chest hair, and she leaned forward to press a kiss over his heart. There, she felt his heartbeat pounding and knew none of this was an act. Alec really did think the world of her, a thought she had to force herself to get used to from now on.

As Ruby found his waistband and began to unbutton his jeans, he pulled away long enough to drop his pants, pick her up by her ass, legs wrapped around his body, and pushed her against the wall in his room.

He nipped at her neck. "Now, where were we?"

"I think I was doing this..." She reached underneath to palm his cock, stroke it with an upward motion, feeling herself fully supported by Alec's arms. His cock felt simultaneously hard as iron but soft as silk, and shivers traveled throughout her body at his touch. When she rubbed her thumb over the head of his shaft, he cursed underneath his breath.

"I'm not going to last if you keep that up," he warned her.

"Maybe I don't want you to last."

"Oh, you definitely want me to last, Red." He turned the tables on her and dropped her to her feet to undo her jeans, dipping his hand underneath her panties. "Damn, baby, you already this wet for me?"

"I can't help it. You always know what to say."

"Not just words, love. But I think we should get you even wetter."

She moaned, as he parted her folds with a gentle touch then slicked through her wetness, laving her with her own juices. She felt like she was going to burst out of her skin, especially when he began to circle her clit. Over and over again, but never touching it directly, he played with her pussy, as she dug her nails into his shoulders and undulated in time with his strokes. Her orgasm built, a wave that only grew higher and higher.

"Come on my hand, baby," he said in her ear. "I want to feel you soak my fingers."

She couldn't say no to that. She hit her peak, shrieking, and Alec covered her mouth with a fierce kiss as she climaxed. Just like he'd ordered her to. She barely registered when he set her feet on the ground to get a better hold of her, lifted her again, then wrapped her legs once again around his hips. His cock bobbed between them, and he rubbed his length through her still throbbing folds.

"I need you, Alec," she panted. "Please, I need you."

"I got you." He took ahold of his length and pressed it against her slick entrance. Slowly pushing inside her, they both groaned as he filled her. Ruby felt completely stuffed, down to her toes and fingers, so good and so full, she couldn't stop imagining him as some forest beast taking her completely, making her his.

Once he was inside her to the hilt, he didn't move. They both savored the feeling of being joined together again. Why had she been fighting herself for so long? This was pure bliss, this becoming one with Alec. She gasped, squirming, but he held her so tightly she couldn't get him to move.

"Alec," she begged. "Please."

He pressed his forehead against hers. Then he pulled out before thrusting back inside her. Waves of pure bliss rushed throughout her body, and she couldn't stop herself from making desperate, animal-like noises as he took her with relentless strokes. She grabbed his head and brought him down for a kiss as he pounded inside of her. Their tongues played, and she bit and nipped his lip, sucking on his tongue. It was alarmingly messy, but that was what Ruby liked about it—the raw fucking.

She didn't care that her back rubbed against the rough wall, or that the sound of their lovemaking could be heard by any of the lawn people outside trimming his hedges. At this point, she didn't care if Coach or Vincent or Heath or anyone on the team heard them. She didn't care if Siri was listening in either. She only felt completely satisfied that she was back in Alec's arms and nowhere else.

"Fuck, baby," he muttered, and his cock twitched inside of her, as he gritted his teeth and began to come.

She held him close, loving the way he surrendered himself to her embrace. This strong, vibrant, cocky man became putty in her hands when they were together. Her heart soared at that thought—*just like I'm his?*

He's mine.

He dropped to his knees, laying her on the floor, which made her gasp. Then she inhaled a sharp breath when he placed her foot on his shoulder, dropped to his elbows, and parted her folds, kissing her with hot, wet licks that sent her flying. He was relentless, flicking her clit with the tip of his tongue, pushing one finger and another inside her clenching sheath. The sound of her wetness only increased his fervor, and the sounds of his lips sucking and laving her only made her climb toward a second orgasm that much quicker. When it hit, it was almost painful in its intensity. She bit her lip to keep from screaming out loud, but her body shook so hard that Alec held her firmly in his arms.

Ruby wrapped herself around him, her mind soaring and body totally sated. When she finally came down from her high and Alec held her breasts close to his cheek, she let herself doze, feeling safe and cared for. There was nothing else. Only his body as he entered her. Only his cock as he plunged deep inside of her. Only his grunting and his animalistic possession of her, as he spilled his seed deep into her with a passion so complete, she nearly felt she was dreaming.

He claimed her.

And she let him. Because he'd won her, fair and square.

Ruby didn't give herself to random men easily. She didn't give her body or heart to anyone for that matter. But Alec had sworn to protect her. Sworn to adore her and treat her the way she should be treated, and for that, she would follow him to the ends of the earth.

12

That evening, on his way to practice, Alec sat in the Bootleggers' parking lot and stared straight ahead. There were still twenty minutes before practice and he hadn't talked to anyone since the news hit this morning. He knew exactly how most people would react. Heath and Kyle would be supportive about his dating Ruby, Coach would tell him to be careful, and Colleen...

Well, Colleen had been texting him all day at various intervals, though he'd done an excellent job of ignoring her. Aside from seeing her name pop up on his notifications, he hadn't delved into her texts to read any.

Quickly, he glanced at her last text, not wanting to give her any more energy than was necessary. She had texted: *Hope you're happy.*

Actually, yes, he wanted to tell her. More than he'd ever been, and things had only gotten started. But so far, he'd gotten Ruby to go out with him, had gotten her into his bed, and both had been part of his dreams. He could only imagine the amazing things to come.

But more important than Colleen was his mother. How could it be that twelve hours had passed since the first website SportsBlog.com had reported about him and Ruby, it'd been shared a thousand times all over Instagram and Twitter, yet Mom hadn't found out yet?

If he waited any longer, she'd give him an earful.

In the solace of his car, he called his mom and waited. She answered almost immediately. "I was wondering when you'd call me. I'm the last to find everything out, as usual."

Damn, she'd already heard. Alec winced. "Sorry, it's been a hectic day."

"Too hectic to call your mom up and tell her you've been dating someone new, I guess." She sighed. The sounds of pots and pans being shifted around the kitchen sink echoed in the background. No matter how many housekeepers he hired for his mother, the woman insisted on handwashing every night after dinner.

"Mom, why don't you let Celia do the dishes? I got her so you wouldn't have to do any manual labor."

"What's wrong with manual labor, Alec? I'm not allergic to it. And I've told you a thousand times, it gives me something to do. Besides, I let Celia go home early and you're avoiding my question."

"Actually, you never asked a question." He chuckled under his breath. It was his job as her son to give her the hardest time possible, always. "But I did call you before you called me. Don't I get any points for that?"

Mom's voice softened. "Well, when you put it that way." That was the beauty of his relationship with his mom. She would get her beef out right up front then give up the ghost. She could never be mad at him for too long. "So, tell me what's up, Alec. And please don't say it's a publicity stunt, because that would break my heart."

"What do you mean?"

"I mean, I hope to God you're really dating that girl, not just pretending to date her to improve your popularity ratings, or my hopes and dreams would be crushed."

Alec's jaw nearly dropped. Since when had his mother held an opinion on the matter of Ruby O'Brien? "Wait, you *want* me to date Ruby?"

"Alec, I've never met her, but from everything I hear, she's exactly the woman you need. Hardworking, no-nonsense...a girl to keep you in line."

"I-I couldn't be any more shocked right now," Alec scoffed, rubbing his chin. "How do you know anything about her if you've never met her? I think, in the last twelve months, I've maybe mentioned her to you like...three times? And all three have been about how she's given me hell when I haven't behaved."

"Exactly. That was my first clue. Also, several of your teammates' moms are fond of Ruby. One mentioned she thought Ruby would be perfect for you. I have to use the pieces I'm given, Alec."

And this was why he could never pull any wool over his mother's eyes. "Mom, why don't you have your own private investigation company again? With the way you pry information out of other people… Good God, woman. You and Nana both."

"Good thing I do, or I'd never know what's going on with you. About football and other things, sure, but not about your love life."

It was true. As much as Alec adored his mother and called her on a weekly basis, he never told her about his romantic involvements. She'd been through enough for one lifetime with Alec's biological father leaving when he was a baby, all the way through his college years, when she struggled financially, sometimes working three jobs just to support him. It just seemed, to him, that his mother wouldn't want to hear about his personal train wrecks.

Besides, there was never anyone to tell her about. He had never even mentioned Colleen, until he had to, when she told him about the "baby." And that had made Alec realize he couldn't marry Colleen. He'd never even invited her to come meet his mother.

"Because there's never been a love life *to* talk about."

"Hmm."

The sound of water running then his mother sighing seeped into the line. He could tell she was finishing up in the kitchen to get comfortable in her chair where she usually watched a previously recorded Hallmark movie, never on the Sunday when it aired, because Sundays were reserved for watching him on TV.

"So, Ruby O'Brien, huh? Irish, I take it?"

"Irish descent, most likely," he replied, realizing he'd never asked Ruby. Suddenly, he wanted to find out everything there was to know about her. "With gorgeous red hair and blue eyes."

"Of course."

"What do you mean, of course? I've never gone out with a redhead before."

"Yes, you have."

"When?"

"In pre-K. Sonia Jones had red hair."

"Mom, Sonia Jones was four years old."

"She had red hair, Alec. And she was the first girl I could tell you really, really loved, even at that tender age. You would come home and talk nonstop about her, then one day, I found my roses cut right out of the vase. The same ones you had given me for Mother's Day. But come Monday morning, they became Sonia's roses."

Alec threw his head back and laughed. "I did not."

"Yes, you did." He heard the smile in his mother's voice. "And the teacher called me after school to tell me it was sweet what you did, but you really shouldn't bring anyone roses unless you had enough for all the girls to share."

"Are you serious?" Alec laughed. "That's so wrong."

"And that's how I knew I had to watch out for redheads. Or girls who loved football, either one. That day, I cried like a baby."

"Why?"

"Because I knew one day, it'd be for real. Maybe not Sonia, but some day, someone else would steal your heart, and I wasn't ready for that."

"No one will ever take your place in my heart, Mom," Alec replied.

"I know that, Alec. And when the right woman comes along, I won't mind sharing your heart with her one bit."

Why hadn't he ever made that connection with Sonia Jones before? He'd completely forgotten about her being redhead and how much he followed her around the playground, so much that poor Sonia had told her parents, and the next day, Mrs. Brenfeld moved his desk to the other side of the room.

"So, you haven't been by in over a month," Mom said, taking him further along on this guilt trip. "I have some things I need your help with, unless you're too busy for your dear old mom?"

"No, ma'am. Never too busy. I'll come by this Saturday. What do you need from me?" Alec heard the first whistle blow and knew he had to get going soon or practice would start without him.

"The porch screen is torn in one corner," she said, "and the dishwasher keeps getting stuck on the same setting. A bunch of things. I have a whole honey-do list for you."

"I'll be happy to take care of those, Mom. Listen, I gotta go. Just wanted to be the first to tell you about Ruby, but I guess I failed you. At least I was the first to tell you that it's real. Not a publicity stunt. Does that get me anything?"

"A knuckle sandwich." She laughed. "I know, honey. I'm just giving you a hard time. She's the one, by the way."

"What?" he asked, shocked that she would make such a proclamation without even knowing her. "The one?"

"Yes. The one, the love of your life…"

"How do you know that?"

"Because," she said with all-knowing motherness. "You gave Sonia my roses, and now you gave this Ruby my scarf."

"Your scarf?" He had to think for a minute. Oh, right. The scarf from this morning. The reporters had already posted the pics from this afternoon. "Damn."

"Damn is right." She laughed. "And, Alec?"

"Yes, ma'am?"

"Bring Ruby on Saturday. I want to meet her."

13

Ruby stared at her laptop screen, trying to focus on work, but her mind raced with a million different thoughts. The biggest one burning her brain: if it wasn't love, then what was it?

It was difficult for Ruby to consider that maybe she was falling hard for Alec LeBrun, but what else could it be? She thought about him nonstop. He made her feel so loved, he cared about her, even bragged about being with her, treated her so nicely, and he was amazing in bed. And *out* of bed, too. The back patio, the wall in his room... Check, check, check, check!

But for how long?

What if he was being a total sweetheart *now*, only because he was going through a good period? Because she'd agreed to date him? What guarantee was there that he wouldn't resort to childish antics again when things didn't go his way? There was no way she could date the old Alec, the Alec who just made headlines a couple of months ago. And *not* for good reasons. How could she be sure he'd always be the man she needed him to be?

There were no guarantees.

It was still early, she reminded herself. Romantic feelings were one thing—true love was something else entirely. Even though she'd only had one real boyfriend in her life, she knew enough not to trust those initial honeymoon feelings. Though several friends had called her during the day to find out the juicy bits about dating Alec LeBrun, she couldn't honestly tell any of them what she was feeling in her heart.

One phrase kept repeating itself: *Yep, it's true! Let's see where this goes.*

Yes, it was too early to tell if she loved him. She was going to have to test him out and see. Give herself time to grow into loving him. Find out what he was really made of. That's what any sensible woman would do, and Ruby was a sensible, practical woman. No need to jump to conclusions and claim love just yet.

That was her plan, and she would stick to it, she told herself.

Shaking the thoughts from her mind, she went back to putting together a PR plan for another client. She kept reading the same sentence over and over again, because all she could think of was Alec's laugh, Alec's smile, Alec's face between her legs, his eyes whenever he looked up at her, his tongue lapping her up and taking her to that point of no return.

"Fuck, Ruby," she chastised herself. "Concentrate."

As if she needed further distraction, her phone rang. Annoyingly reaching for it, she stared at the screen. Her father. "Ugh, don't feel like dealing with this right now," she mumbled, but she had to. He was also her boss. "Hey, Dad. Kind of in the middle of something."

"How's my sweetheart doing?"

"Your sweetheart is working her ass off."

"Yes, she is. Saw the pieces on you and LeBrun this morning. I gotta tell you, pure genius, Ruby. How you guys walked out of that restaurant looking like you'd been dating for months is beyond me. Maybe you should've gone into acting?" He was in a rare jovial mood, which she knew had to do with the Sports Armour offer.

"Ha, yeah. Totally."

"You heard from Sports Armour about the news?"

"No, I haven't, but our meeting is in a few days, and the rep just emailed me the paperwork, so I'm assuming it's all still a go. I'll let you know how it goes down then, okay?"

"Yep. Let me know. Oh, and, Ruby?"

"Yes, Dad?"

"I appreciate you going through all this just for the firm."

"What do you mean?" *The firm?*

"The whole Alec LeBrun thing. I know you would never be caught dead dating a guy like that, and he doesn't deserve you. But you're doing it for me, and I appreciate that."

Ruby nearly choked on her coffee.

Was that what her father thought? What would he think if she confessed she actually *did* have feelings for Alec? That she was purposely dating him? That she could conceivably see herself in a long relationship with him? That she had possibly *begun* a love relationship with him and hadn't told him yet? Maybe she underestimated her father, but she felt for certain he'd be disappointed in her.

He said it himself—*he doesn't deserve you.*

Well, now she knew what her father truly felt, and that only made things more complicated. She wasn't sure if Alec deserved her quite yet—it was too early to tell, but she knew she loved being around him. He made her smile and feel like her true self. He took her out of her head and made her have fun. He made her take down her hair!

There was enough going on in her mind without her father's opinions adding to the mix, so she cut the conversation short. "Sure, Dad. We all benefit from this, don't we? I'll talk to you later."

Hanging up, she leaned back in her chair and blew out a long breath. Man, this was getting crazier by the day. *Take it one day at a time,* she told herself. That was all she could do. A moment later, her phone rang again, and she answered brusquely. "Ruby speaking."

"Hey, Red."

"Alec!" She caught the excitement in her own voice, felt it change tones from annoyed publicist to grinny, goofy girl in love. She toned it down before his ego got any bigger. "How are things on your end? Your tight end. Ha—get it?"

"You made a funny, Red. That's so cute."

"Shut up. Tell me what's up."

"My mom. She wants to meet you when I drive up to see her this Saturday. Want to come with me?"

"Saturday, as in three days from now? But we're getting ready for the Sports Armour meeting."

"That's not till Monday. Come on, Red. A drive to Charleston, just you and me in the car. I'll even steal a Ferrari for the joyride. It'll be fun."

Though she knew he was joking, she couldn't help but imagine themselves riding along the highway, stuck in a car for hours, talking about life and maybe getting a little sexy along the way. The idea of a trip appealed to her, but to meet his mom? Already? "Alec, are you sure it's a good idea? What if your mom doesn't approve of me?"

"What if my mom totally loves you like she already does?"

What was he talking about? He sounded like a kid who'd gotten his Christmas presents a little early this year.

"Trust me on this, Red. She already knows about you, and she's thrilled. I'll pick you up early around eight. Sound good?"

Words tried to come out of her mouth, but suddenly, her stomach ached. Everything was changing so fast, Ruby wasn't used to it. Things rarely changed in her world, and when they did, they took a long time. But all of that changed when she said yes to Alec that fateful day.

And nothing had been the same since.

"Super cute." Ruby smiled.

When Alec's car pulled up to the charming but modest two-story home in Charleston, South Carolina, Ruby couldn't help but wonder why Alec hadn't bought his mother a bigger house. Most of her famous clients did once they had big money. It wasn't like Alec couldn't afford it. Then again, maybe his mother hadn't wanted a new house. From everything he'd told her about his mother, Carolyn, on the drive up, she wouldn't be surprised if Mrs. LeBrun had refused any kind of charity from her famous son altogether.

Butterflies fluttered in her stomach, as they got out of the car, pulled out their bags, and walked up to the front door. "Ma!" Alec knocked three times. "That's how she knows it's me," he whispered to Ruby.

"Ah. Not because of the crazy man screaming at the front door?" Ruby winked, and Alec bumped his side against her. They'd been having fun the whole trip from Savannah, and Ruby gathered it was because he was helping her feel at ease, knowing she'd be nervous about meeting his mother.

A small woman with short, neatly coifed hair opened the door. "There he is! My boy!"

Alec dwarfed his mother with an enormous hug, even lifted her off the ground while she shrieked, then set her back down again.

"And you must be Miss O'Brien."

"Oh, call me Ruby, Mrs. LeBrun. Please."

"Then you must call me Carolyn." The woman spoke in a Southern accent thick as Georgia molasses. "Come in, come in, before the bugs eat you alive. The mosquitoes have been slow to leave this year."

Ruby couldn't help but smile at the woman's Southern hospitality. "Thank you. You have a lovely home." She really did. Inside was immaculate with humble, beautiful furniture and framed photos of Alec when he was little.

He saw her noticing the photos and blocked them with his wide shoulders, eyeing her. "Do not look at the kid pictures."

Ruby laughed and whispered, as Carolyn led them through the living room. "I'll look at them when you're not looking."

Carolyn spoke over her shoulder. "I've lived here since Alec came up to my knee. A long time ago, as you can imagine. Did you want me to make you sandwiches?"

"Oh, no, Mama. We already ate on the way up," Alec said, and Ruby noticed he had a different way of talking to his mother than he did with...pretty much anyone else. Not only was he respectful, but it seemed to Ruby he turned into a shy ten-year-old around his mother.

"That's a shame," Carolyn said, entering the kitchen. "Then, you'll have some sweet tea I brewed especially for y'all?"

Ruby wasn't a huge fan of sweet tea, but if Alec's mama made it, then she would try some. "Oh, yes. That sounds nice. Thank you."

Carolyn showed them to the kitchen table where they

sat by a window. A small but colorful garden was just outside that made Ruby smile.

"So, my son tells me you're working to get him back in line?" she asked, pouring the tea into three glasses. "Has he behaved himself so far?"

Ruby almost laughed at the sight of Alec's wide eyeballs upon hearing his mother's comment. "Oh, yeah. He's been great," she replied, her voice almost a wheeze. "One of my best clients."

Obviously, his mom knew he was more to her than that, but it wasn't like she could say he was the best lover she'd ever had. Alec's eyes gleamed as he looked at her from across the room. "Ruby's been working hard, Mama. I made a real mess of things, you know."

"I do know, just like when you were a little boy. Always getting into people's gardens and stealing flowers to bring home." She smiled at the memory. "Did he tell you about Sonia?"

"Mama, not now," Alec warned.

"Who's Sonia? Should I be worried?" Ruby smiled and exchanged winks with Carolyn. She loved this woman already and immediately felt at ease.

"Oh, honey, why not? It's the sweetest story," his mother said. After passing out the sweet teas, Carolyn sat at the table and lifted the lid on a lovely small lemon cake. Presumably homemade as well. "Fine, I'll tell her some other time. Then again, Alec always brought me a bouquet, so I couldn't get too mad at him."

Alec rolled his eyes as they exchanged memories.

Ruby listened intently as the conversation continued. It was obvious that Carolyn and Alec were devoted to each other, and Ruby couldn't help but envy him. She loved her father, of course, and he loved her, but Carolyn supported her son through thick and thin. Whereas Dad was critical unless she did things his way.

"So, Ruby…Alec tells me you're absolutely perfect in every way."

"Mama!" Alec LeBrun, tight end of the Savannah Bootleggers, actually blushed.

"What? For goodness' sake, Alec, that's exactly what you said to me the other day," Carolyn said, shaking her head and turning to Ruby, as if only Ruby and Ruby's opinions would be heard from now on. "Does he take care of you? Because if he doesn't take care of you, I will see to it that he's cut off from the homemade goodies I send him."

"No! Not the homemade goodies. Come on, Ma!" Alec pretended to be woefully offended and winked at Ruby. "Anything but the homemade goodies ban."

Ruby laughed softly to herself, hand over mouth, and turned to Carolyn. "He's great. He treats me really well. So far."

Alec shook his head then laid it on the table over his folded arms. "I knew this wasn't a good idea to bring you here."

Ruby laughed so hard with Carolyn that she had to admit, she was having a great time. This could work to her advantage. There was nothing to make a man straighten out better than his mama. "Hey, you wanted me to come. Now, here I am." Ruby reached out and tousled Alec's hair, which made Carolyn blink lovingly behind her knowing smile.

They talked all afternoon, and Ruby had never felt so comfortable with any boyfriend's mother before. She could see this woman as her best friend, especially when they both ganged up on Alec, making him shake his head or leave the room in mock protest.

After dinner, cleanup, and some time by a small fireplace, Carolyn turned to Alec. "You're not playing tomorrow, are you?"

"No, it's a bye-week. So I'm yours, whatever you need me for."

"Great. Well, I'll see you in the morning then. You two can have the guest room upstairs."

From Alec's shocked look, Ruby gathered that was a big deal to be allowed to sleep together in the same house. "Don't you want me sleeping on the couch downstairs, Mama?"

"Oh, heavens, no. Ruby can't exactly keep an eye on you if you're not with her, can you, Ruby?" Carolyn paused at the stairs, pushing her reading glasses down to see Ruby's face.

"No, ma'am. Whatever you deem right, Carolyn."

"Sleep together." His mother waved the issue away with her hand. "We're liberated women, aren't we, Ruby?"

Ruby nearly coughed up a lung. "Yes, ma'am. Have a good night."

Once she was gone, Alec and Ruby looked at each other, both relieved to let their guards down.

"Whoa, that was stressful," Alec exclaimed then led Ruby outside to give her a tour of the neighborhood. Although the house was small, it had been well-maintained, and Carolyn's garden in the backyard was more beautiful than through the window. Ruby admired the roses situated behind the house, and she bent to smell a large red one.

"Your mom seems like an amazing lady," Ruby said as they strolled the street. Fireflies were beginning to emerge from the grasses, blinking lazily as the sun went down.

"She is. You remind me of her in a way. Hardworking, respectable." Alec put his hands in his pockets as they walked, as Ruby wondered. Did she want to be known only as hardworking and respectable? She'd seen the kind of women Alec used to date in the past, and they'd been sexy, hot women. She wanted to be sexy and hot for Alec, too. "I didn't know how hard she worked when I was a kid," Alec continued, this time taking Ruby's hand. "I mean, I knew she worked a lot, but I didn't know she did it all so I could play football."

"Wow, that's really admirable."

"Thanks. Yeah, she worked herself to the bone for me because she always believed in me." He shook his head. "I owe her everything."

"I'm surprised you didn't buy her a big, flashy house, knowing you."

He laughed. "Hey, what do you mean, knowing me? I'm not too flashy. And I tried. But she said she was going to die in this house that she worked so hard to buy, and I didn't have the heart to press the issue. I did buy her a brand-new car, though."

"And she never has to work another day in her life again," Ruby added.

"That's true. I don't ever want to see her struggle again. Worked my ass off to make sure I changed that." They fell into silence as they meandered. Ruby took in the neighborhood, enjoying seeing people rocking chairs on their porches or taking evening strolls. It was a serene neighborhood in Charleston, and she could understand why Carolyn hadn't wanted to leave it.

"You know why I really wanted to play football?" Alec said with a sad smile.

"Cheerleaders?"

"Not even close." Alec's whole demeanor changed. Serious, unloading truth. "When I was a kid, I hoped to get into the NFL so when I got on TV, my dad would see me and regret that he'd walked away in the first place."

Ruby stopped mid-stride and touched Alec's cheek. Her heart ached for him. "That's so sad, Alec. I'm sorry to hear that." It was such a touching story, one that would have benefited him to use for PR purposes. Not Alec, though. He wanted to keep his personal life, especially his mother, out of the public eye, and she respected him all the more for it.

She'd worked with a lot of famous people, most of

whom wouldn't think twice about using their families for a great story to enhance their personal image. Yet as she walked alongside Alec, and they began to return to Carolyn's house, she couldn't help but admire his integrity. He would protect his mother to his last breath, leaving her out of the picture, the media, everything, and even though he could easily persuade her to do an interview that would easily gain him sympathy, he refused even to consider it. He'd rather have a tarnished image—and career—than potentially damage his relationship with the person he probably loved most in this world.

Her heart twisted at that thought. What would it be like to be loved by a man like that? A man who would do anything to protect her? It was a dangerous thought, one she wanted to push far away. After all, she'd decided to just have fun for now, not think about things too seriously with Alec. But it hung about her throughout the rest of the evening as she did some work on her laptop, as Alec puttered around the house, helping to fix his mother's porch screen, tighten a faucet, and other things she needed help with. This man was a do-er. He hadn't just landed a position on an NFL team. He'd earned it through hard work and dedication, and she respected him all the more for it.

At one moment, watching him fix a molding that had popped out of place, seeing his muscles ripple and his beads of sweat from his exertion, she knew this was the kind of man she wanted. A man who loved his mother would love her the same way. No, she wasn't just open to dating Alec LeBrun—she was falling in love with him.

Hard.

Despite her plan to wait for further information.

For a moment, she couldn't breathe. It was like all of the oxygen had been sucked from the room. The truth hit her hard, and when it did, she couldn't focus on her work anymore. She had to take this man—this beautiful, sweet man—upstairs right now, right this second, and make love to him.

14

He wasn't sure what made Ruby walk over to him, pull the caulking gun out of his hand, and set it down on the counter, but the look in her eyes told him he was about to find out.

"What's happening?" he asked with a laugh.

Ruby looked like there were countless things she wanted to say, but her eyes did most of the talking. "We can finish this tomorrow. Take your woman to bed, Alec."

The words stiffened him immediately.

Ruby pulled his face down and kissed him, hard and with urgency, like she'd just been filled with something deep and powerful for Alec. He knew where she was coming from. Being here in his mom's house with Ruby was another step in a new direction. Clearly, his mother loved Ruby, and they were about to sleep the whole night together in a bed. Not just any bed, but in the very room that used to be his.

He'd come home. And he'd brought his new love with

him.

She took his hand and led him upstairs. They skipped a few steps, just trying to get there as quickly as possible. His mother's door was closed, thankfully, and from the quiet glow of the TV plus the soft snoring, he knew his mother was out like a light.

Ruby took Alec into his room and closed the door.

Suddenly, things exploded between them. He couldn't kiss her, couldn't touch her, or undress her fast enough. Alec hauled Ruby onto the bed, slid her leggings off, then spread her legs apart so he could push his way up to her panties. Gripping her under her knees, he yanked her until her hot, wet center pressed against his cock. They both moaned at the contact.

When she sat up to kiss him deeply, Alec sifted his fingers through her long hair and pulled it free of its tight bun. Pins pinged as they hit the table. "I need you, Ruby," he muttered as he pulled her blouse apart. Buttons popped, but even Ruby was so far gone that she didn't yell at him for it. She wanted him as much as he wanted her, and she moaned when he sucked her nipples through her lacy bra, but he needed her to be bare. When he freed her breasts, throwing her bra against the football lamp that used to be his as a small child, he palmed one rounded tit and suckled at the other.

She squirmed against him, sifting her fingers through his hair.

"You're so wet, Ruby." Alec pulled aside the silky fabric to reach her pussy, slicking his fingers through her folds, loving the way her head tilted back in sweet agony when he did.

"You make me this wet," she said, pulling her panties to one side, offering her gift to him. She watched him play with her pussy, which only made Alec harder, as he strained against his pants. He felt her get wetter and wetter until she practically soaked his palm with her juices. He wasn't sure how she'd take it, but he had to taste her. Bringing his fingers to his mouth, he licked them clean.

Ruby's mouth fell open, then she wrapped her hand behind his neck and pulled him in for a deep kiss to taste herself.

A flush crawled up her chest, and with a noise in her throat, she reached for his pants' buttons. Within seconds, she'd freed his cock, which was almost painfully hard, and began to stroke him. Now it was his turn to tip his head back and moan. Her fingers pulled and gripped him, and when she cradled his balls in her other hand, he had to push her hands away to keep himself from coming all over her pretty fingers.

But Ruby had other ideas, and he couldn't fault her for where that little wicked mind of hers was going. "I want to taste you, too," she said. She spread her legs apart at the edge of the bed, super fucking sexy, and took him into her mouth.

Alec swooned.

Raking his fingers through the gentle cascade of her hair, he watched, as she wrapped her lips around the head of his cock and slowly pulled it out until it popped from her cheek. She smiled then pushed the whole goddamn thing back in. He felt it reach the back of her throat and thought he was going to explode, but he kept his eyes shut and looked up, thanking the universe for this incredible woman.

Ruby pulled him out then plunged his cock back into her mouth again, building a rhythm all while she held his balls with her other hand.

"Holy shit, babe. You're killing me."

"You want to see how wet I get from this?" she asked, taking his hand and leading it to her soaking wet panties. Damn, she really did love having his cock in her mouth, and she was beyond ready for a good fucking—she was ludicrously horny for it.

Something unleashed from inside of Ruby's soul. In a matter of seconds, he watched this woman who he'd seen from afar be professional and restrained to now being completely unhinged. She sucked and sucked on his cock, guiding it into her mouth and pulling it out with such lustful abandon, Alec knew he wasn't going to last long.

"That's enough." His voice was like gravel, low and almost hoarse with desire. When he pulled away to collect himself, he was astonished to realize his hands trembled ever so slightly. He just managed to pull off her panties and step out of the rest of his clothes without fumbling before leaning down to kiss Ruby. "That…was insanely sexy."

Then, spreading her legs apart and looking down at his woman, his prize, that beautifully trimmed pussy aching for him, he entered her with a delicious slowness. Although it hadn't been that long since their last encounter, it felt like ages ago. A thousand years. He wanted her every day. For the rest of his life, if she'd let him. Slowly, making sure it all fit, he pushed his cock to the hilt inside of her.

She panted, her breath hot and sweet against his ear when he lowered himself onto her. "Hold on to me," he said.

She wrapped her arms and her legs around his body. "Fuck me, Alec," she whispered in his ear.

He didn't need to be told twice. "Yes, ma'am. You tell me what to do. I listen to you. I need you, Ruby. Need you to guide me."

"Good, then fuck me hard. I've resisted you for so long."

"And?"

"Make me regret it."

Pulling out, he thrust back into her sharply, pounding that sweet little cunt, and she squealed with delight. He covered her mouth with his hand, just so his mother wouldn't hear, and Ruby moaned with hot breath into his hand. Their bodies slapped together, and Alec felt a haze cover his vision. If anything, he got even harder being inside her tight pussy, and his balls started to draw up after only a few thrusts. He was going to explode within seconds and had to make sure Ruby was ready for it. He forced himself to slow down.

Ruby moaned in frustration, which only made him

smile. "Don't stop," she said as she dug her nails into his shoulders. "I'm so close."

"Then, look down. Watch as I fuck you." He angled her head so she could see, and then he slowly pushed inside of her and pulled back out again. They both watched their joining, and seeing his cock covered in her wetness only edged his arousal higher. Luckily, Ruby's ragged breaths grew faster, and when she began to undulate in time with his thrusts, he knew she was chasing after her own orgasm without any other thought in her head.

He pressed his thumb to her clit, slowly circling it as he fucked her. He watched as her clit emerged from its hood, tender and swollen. She was close. Her sheath tightened around him, and it took every ounce of his strength not to lose it right then.

"Come for me, baby. Come for me right now." He rubbed her clit with more pressure, giving into her trembling muscles.

Ruby gasped, and as Alec filled her completely one last time, she started to come. Her body shook from head to toe, and as her pussy contracted around his cock, he lost it. He swore as he detonated inside of her, pumping and pumping, filling her, and he didn't know how he didn't manage to collapse on top of her, he was so spent.

My woman, my life. He'd given her all of him.

She'd let him into her life, into her whole being.

They were sweaty and disheveled as they tried to catch their breaths. Zings of pleasure continued to run up and down Alec's spine. He rubbed Ruby's back, and she clung to him, like she needed to hang onto something after the storm of pleasure that had wrecked her body.

Fuck the shower. They could do it tomorrow.

Because nothing—repeat, nothing—could replace the feeling of them collapsing onto the pillows and pulling up the comforter to cover their naked bodies, finding warmth in each other, arms and legs a tangled mess. He wanted to sleep all night this way, with her head against his chest, holding her…protecting her…

Loving her.

15

The trip to visit Alec's mother had been eye-opening. The trip home to Savannah? Not so much. Though Alec had done a good job driving, and for the most part, it was a beeline south down the highway without many turns, Ruby was carsick. At least she hoped it was carsickness and not a stomach bug the day before the big Sports Armour meeting. Because that would royally suck.

"You doing okay? You look green," Alec said, bringing down a window to let in some fresh air for her.

"Better. I'm just nervous about tomorrow." If all went through without a hitch, this would be the first major endorsement contract for one of her very own clients. She had to kill it. She had to impress her father and everyone at the firm, cementing the idea that she was worthy of being there, and each mile toward home reminded her the meeting was getting closer and closer.

"Babe, everything's going to go fine. My ratings are back up. The agent has sent you the paperwork…"

"I know, but anything could happen, Alec," Ruby reminded him. "You know how unpredictable these companies are. The smallest thing goes wrong, and they don't want you representing their line anymore." The more she thought about it, the more the knot in her stomach tightened.

The fact she'd taken time off to visit Alec's mom hadn't exactly helped either. She had to get home, finish her work, and come out tomorrow morning like a mad lion. Preferably a healthy, non-carsick one.

On Monday morning, it was game face time. Alec picked her up at her townhouse looking fine as hell in his snazzy silver suit. She wished they would've had time for a quickie to shave the edge off her nerves, but it was time to go.

"Look at you," Alec said, taking her by the hand and leading her to his car. He couldn't take his eyes off her. Granted, she wore her standard black suit, this time with a pink blouse, which went perfectly with her red, pinned-up hair, but she did look hot in a professional bitch sort of way.

Ruby giggled nervously. "Time to kill it, Alec." She hated to even think it, but she was glad he hadn't gotten into any trouble last night while she slept. How shitty would that have been to wake up this morning before the meeting and seen him splashed in the papers for something gone wrong.

No, Alec was in line, and it had been all because of her. Everything would go perfect today—she just knew it. Time to stop fearing and start accepting that things were going her way. Her career was going up, things with Alec were smooth as silk, and now a dream meeting.

When they arrived, they were treated like rock stars, shown into a large meeting room with stainless accents and red lacquered chairs. A basketball lamp hung from the ceiling surrounded by balls of other sports. Ruby took a seat beside Alec and folded her hands. Even though the company probably knew they were dating, she still wanted to keep things professional.

A tall, older man came in surrounded by other tall, older, handsome men. Apparently, this company was entirely run by former athletes. "Good morning, everyone. Miss O'Brien...Mr. LeBrun, thank you so much for being here." Everyone took a seat, as a young woman closed the meeting room door. "We're just going to cut to the chase. We've been delighted with the turnaround your public image has taken, Mr. LeBrun," the man said, giving Alec a nod. "You've also done some wonderful things with kids' charities lately. Do you like kids, Mr. LeBrun?" the CEO asked.

"I definitely do, sir." Alec beamed, but Ruby could see his knee shaking a mile a minute. She touched it and it stopped moving.

"Do you think you might be having kids in the future?"

Ruby thought it a strange question at first, but then

again, she realized where this was going and suddenly felt a surge of happiness. They were going to offer him a kids' line after seeing his recent appeal with children.

Alec cocked his head and cringed a little. "I do, yes, but not at the moment."

"That's fine," the CEO said. "The only reason we're asking is because we want a long-term commitment, someone who will represent the brand for a while, someone who might be a father in the future. For the image of sports dad, you know. We've seen how you roughhouse with the little ones, how they jump all over your back." The man laughed and looked around at his colleagues. "We love that shit."

"Thank you, sir." Alec looked at Ruby and smiled.

"It's our hope that natural affinity for fatherhood will come through in advertising, in order to appeal to fathers and parents of sporty kids, in general. What do you think you can bring to the table, Alec?"

As the CEOs listened to Alec talk about his love of football, how he was raised by a hardworking mother, and always wished he'd had a father around, he brought a personal touch to his own sales pitch, and Ruby would've loved it if it weren't for the sensation of air being completely sucked out of her lungs.

Relax, Ruby. Everything's going to be fine, she told herself.

Her father would be calling right after the meeting to hear how everything went, and she couldn't feel any more anxious about it. What if Alec fucked up again? What if things didn't work out between them, for some reason, and he went on another rampage, stole another car, or made another scene in the end zone?

Her career would be over. Her father would fire her immediately. Everything came down to this moment, this meeting. As she looked around at all the faces, mainly male, she was reminded that being a woman in this industry was hard enough without your life falling apart around you.

"Well, of course I'm going to want to get married eventually," she heard Alec saying. It sounded like he was talking from behind a glass wall.

"Good, because the playboy bad boy isn't exactly the vibe we're looking for," someone else said.

Playboy bad boy. That's what he'd been all this time, and Ruby had changed him, but could a tiger ever really change his stripes?

The meeting room felt like it was swirling, and Ruby had to stand and excuse herself. "Just need some fresh air, gentlemen. Be right back." She gave her best smile, as worried looks surrounded her, including Alec's, but she knew she had no intention of going back into the room.

She was sick as a dog and had to get out of there before she barfed all over the meeting table. Heading out of the building, she called a *Lyft* car to come and get her then texted Alec: *Feeling terrible. I have to get to a medic center. Sorry, Alec.*

God, this wasn't happening. She wasn't bailing right at the most critical moment. But one thing reassured her—

Alec. He would know what to do, what to say in front of
those guys. He'd been doing a great job so far. Her
presence in the meeting was only supplemental, to make
sure he didn't say anything stupid. No, she definitely had a
stomach bug of some kind and needed treatment right
away or risk fainting in the Sports Armour lobby.

A reply text came in. *No worries, got this. Meet you
there. Text me address once you're there. Love you.*

Love you.

Wow. That was the first time he'd ever said that so
nonchalantly. As Ruby waited for her car, she stared at the
words. He followed them up with a smiley face. She could
wrap her head around that. In love with Alec was how
she'd felt for a long time now, but being the responsible
girl she was, she wanted to make sure everything was right
in place before declaring it.

Just as the car arrived, Ruby leaned over and threw up
all over the sidewalk. The driver, a woman with black hair
and a pretty smile, leaned her head across the front seat
and said, "You okay? I swear, I'm a good driver."

Ruby fought to smile then told her to take her to the
nearest urgent care center. No amount of anxiety had ever
made her feel this sick before. What shitty timing. Her
father would undoubtedly be upset that she left the
meeting. Knowing him, he would've wanted her to stay,
stick it out, even through being deathly ill, but that had
always been one difference between her and her father—
Ruby was the sensible one.

Five minutes later, Ruby checked into the medic

center, provided all documentation, then sat in the waiting room with a plastic bag by her side. Another text from Alec came in telling her they were on a break and everything was going well. Part two of the meeting would be going over of contracts.

She hated the thought that there would be contract perusal without her. *Don't sign anything until I see it. We can always reschedule,* she texted Alec.

The thumbs-up emoji came in, just in time, as a nurse came out to get her. "Ruby O'Brien? Come this way."

Ruby fought to stand, fought not to lose her balance, as she followed the young nurse down a hallway and into a curtained examination room. After the customary questions, she was left alone with a pee cup and a paper bag.

She wasn't sure why, but all of a sudden, it felt like the world was coming down around her. Like she'd failed Alec by leaving the meeting, failed her father, and failed herself. She'd prepared for this meeting and had felt so positive about it, despite the nerves, but now if things went wrong, she couldn't help but feel like it'd be her fault.

Maybe they could give her a shot of something to calm her stomach and still make it back in time before the meeting ended? She would ask the doctor as soon as they came in. But for now, all she had was this nurse popping her head into the room.

"When did you say your last period was?" the nurse asked with a tilt of the head.

Ruby thought back. "October...twentieth?" Was that

right? No, it couldn't have been. Had it really been two months since she'd last gotten her period? She didn't like what the nurse was silently suggesting. After all, she was on the pill, but oh, God…that would explain so much.

A chill ran through Ruby's back, chilling her to the bone.

The nurse shrugged. "Because you're not sick, sweetie," she said. "You're pregnant."

16

Ruby wouldn't answer his texts.

Wouldn't answer his calls.

Wouldn't let him through the gate when he arrived at her townhouse complex.

For days, he had no contact with her and wondered what the fuck had happened to her. All he got, her last communication to him, had been a text while he was still in the meeting with Sports Armour. He'd asked if everything was okay at the doctor, to which she'd replied: *Fine. Leave me alone for a while. Need time.*

Time for what?

Had she sat in that meeting hearing them talk about babies and having a family in the future, and she'd suddenly decided she didn't want to be with him anymore? A wake-up call of sorts? She'd started feeling sick in the car after leaving his mother's house. Had it been too soon to bring her to meet Mom?

Ruby was skittish about them being together, but now

he wondered if maybe he'd pushed all this on her too soon. Insisting they date, insisting she let him make her happy, insisting she come to meet his mother. Yes, something must've clicked in her mind and now he was paying the price.

He hadn't signed the contract, just like she'd said. He'd spoken to Phil, Ruby's dad, who advised him to do exactly what Ruby had said and to give her a few days, because she was more than likely sick and needed time alone. Alec had conceded, but now after practice two days later, he had to see her.

If something was wrong with Ruby, he had to make it right. Correct his fuck-up, whatever it was. Getting into his car after practice, Alec drove by a local bakery to pick up some soup and bread before driving over to Ruby's. He didn't care if she didn't want to see him. Tough—he wasn't going to let her go without a fight.

Whatever it was, they could talk this through.

Besides, if he waited too long, she might accuse him of not caring about her, and only the opposite was true—he *did* care, deeply. But he also didn't want to be pushy, if that was the case. If that had been the root of this problem to begin with. If he examined his feelings too closely, he'd discover things he wasn't ready to accept quite yet—just how deeply that care and concern for Ruby went. But one thing was for certain: he was determined to get her back.

At the townhouse gate, he marked her number but nobody replied. He picked up her phone to call her. The call went to voicemail. He decided to text her instead.

"Ruby, I have your laptop bag that you left in the meeting. You can't avoid me forever," he spoke into the dictation field. "Please let me in. I have soup."

Those must've been the magic words, because the gate buzzed open suddenly.

"Thank you," he dictated into the text. Alec blew out a breath and drove in, curving around the bend to reach her townhouse near the back.

When he saw her car in her driveway, he let out a sigh of relief. He hadn't been sure she really was sick and had imagined her driving off, away from Savannah, far, far from him. He got out of the car, hauling her laptop bag, soup, and the bread all in one hand, his keys and things in the other.

Be ready for anything, he told himself.

Whatever it was, he'd fix it.

When she finally opened the door after his second knock, he immediately felt guilty for thinking she might not be sick. The woman looked practically green, which clashed with her fiery red hair, now a tangled mess around her face. Without any makeup and dressed in oversized flannel pajamas, she didn't look anything like the perfectly assembled woman he knew so well. But this version of Ruby was just as beautiful to him—maybe more so. It was a side of her she didn't show other people.

"What are you doing here?" she croaked. She didn't move to let him inside.

"I brought you soup." He held up the offering. "And your laptop bag." He turned to show her the bag splayed across his back. "Let me inside for a little while. I promise I won't harass you."

She hesitated, but with a sigh, she opened the door to let him in. He instantly made her go sit down while he poured the soup into a bowl and brought it to her, along with a slice of bread and a spoon. Although she insisted that she wasn't hungry, he told her he wouldn't leave until she ate something.

With a scowl, she finally started eating the soup.

"What do you have? The flu?" He scooted his chair close to the table, watching her with utmost concern. "You never told me what the doctor at the urgent care center said."

"Because it doesn't matter."

"What doesn't matter, Ruby?"

She looked like she would engage in discussion with him, but she only shook her head. "Don't worry about it."

"I do worry about it. I'm worried about you, Red. About us." He laid his hand on top of hers. "What's going on?"

She wouldn't look at him, instead seemed focused on the bowl of soup in front of her. "It's not the flu. And don't worry, it's not contagious."

"Not that I'd care. Do you have a fever? Nausea, vomiting?" He leaned over and placed his hand over her forehead, but she pulled away. Something was definitely wrong besides just being sick. "You seem warm. Want me to go find a thermometer?"

She sighed in exasperation. "No. Look, I appreciate

you coming out here, Alec, but you didn't need to. I'll be okay."

Alec wanted to ask, *What about us? Are we okay?*

She looked so pathetic that he didn't have the heart to upset her. Right as he was about to get up to leave, though, she paled and, jumping up, ran from the room. Concerned, he followed her, only to hear the bathroom door slam before the unmistakable sounds of vomiting echoed from the bathroom.

"Ruby? Are you all right?" He knocked lightly on the door.

"Oh, God," she groaned. "Go away. Please."

He wasn't about to go anywhere when she was this sick, but he went back downstairs to give her privacy. After a bit, she returned, glass of water in her hand. She sat down gingerly, and he couldn't help but notice that she seemed thinner, gaunt, and definitely going through something.

"How long have you been vomiting?" Alec asked, sitting on the opposite end of the couch from her.

"It's nothing."

"That doesn't seem like nothing to me."

"It *is* nothing." She shot him a glare. "I usually only vomit in the morning…"

The way she said it…morning…vomiting. Her face paled again, and it was then that Alec knew what was wrong. "Wait. Are you pregnant?" His eyes narrowed. She looked like she was going to faint. He instantly rushed to her side and gripped her by her upper arms. "Ruby, are you? Pregnant?" He could barely get the word out.

Her bottom lip trembled, and she finally nodded, tears welling up in her eyes.

"Holy shit. How long have you known?" He held her close, but she pushed away. Now that he knew her secret, they could talk about it, work this out. So, why was she pushing him away?

Ruby kept her eyes down in her lap. "Since the urgent care," she whispered. "I thought I was going to faint during the meeting. God, I feel so stupid, Alec. I'm so sorry I left you all alone in there."

"Are you kidding me right now?" He tried not to sound too upset, but she wasn't making any sense. "You were sick. You're pregnant. It was totally justified. Oh, my God." Suddenly, he had to stand and pace the room. It hadn't occurred to him that anyone else might be the father, but just to be sure...

"Ruby, the father..."

"It's you, Alec." She full-on started to cry.

"Okay, listen." He ran his hands through his hair. Holy fuck. First, Colleen and now Ruby. Except Colleen's wasn't real, but still, getting the news twice that he was going to be a father was particularly straining. "We'll figure this out."

Although part of him wanted to demand why she hadn't told him the moment she knew, another part of him could barely wrap his head around this news. Ruby was pregnant. With his child. How had this happened, though? She said she was on the pill. An insidious inner voice wondered if she was telling the truth, but he knew that was only trauma speaking. Ruby would never lie to him like Colleen had, and besides, she definitely wasn't faking her nausea and morning sickness.

"There's nothing to figure out, Alec. You don't want kids, and now I've ruined your life again."

"What are you talking about? I love kids. What makes you think I don't?"

A fresh round of tears burst from her eyes. "In the meeting, you said you weren't ready for kids. In the future, maybe, but not now. I should've known at that moment, it was a sign I was pregnant. Everything was going too smoothly for us."

He knew he should be freaking out, but to his surprise, the only emotion he felt was joy. Joy, because he was really going to have the chance to be a father, and this time not with a woman he didn't love either. But with a woman he adored.

This meant Ruby could never run from him again. He would always be a part of her life, and she would be a part of his. They had to make this work. "We're getting married, then." At her shocked look, Alec knew he should've phrased that better. Asked her maybe, not ordered her.

But at the moment, he just needed to convince her.

She shook her head. "Are you crazy? This is exactly what I was worried about, why I didn't want you coming around here. You felt you had to marry Colleen, and now you feel you have to marry me. Alec, I know you're a good guy, but this won't ruin your life, I promise."

"Ruin my life? Ruby, marrying you would be a fucking dream come true. Don't you get it? It's like the universe took that problem away from me—"

"And gave you another. I know." She squeezed tears from her eyes and sobbed into a couch pillow.

"I was going to say, and gave me a brand-new start with a woman I love."

She looked up at him through tears to gauge his response, his eyes. She loved to scan his eyes and make sure he wasn't lying. Yes, there he said it—he loved her. Because it was true, goddammit. "I've ruined everything."

"You've ruined nothing." He sat next to her, one arm around her. She didn't push him away. "It's the perfect time to talk about it. You're pregnant, and I'm the father. I'm assuming you don't want to raise this baby alone. Right?"

"Yes, but that doesn't mean we need to get married. It's not like I'll have to wear a scarlet letter if I have a baby out of wedlock," she pointed out wryly. "You can still have your freedom. Don't worry."

"I don't want freedom, and I don't care what anyone thinks. What I do care about is doing the right thing." He took her hands and pressed her fingers.

"I don't want you to marry me because you feel it's the right thing. You wouldn't have asked me to marry you if it weren't for me being pregnant, so I don't want you asking me to marry me now. Get it? This wasn't supposed to happen." Ruby bawled into her pillow, and Alec knew enough about pregnant women to know he shouldn't push the issue.

For a long while, he said nothing, only rubbed her back until the sobbing ebbed away. "Ruby, I get what you're saying, and I respect your feelings. I'm not going to push this issue right now because you're going through a lot. But I want you to know…that I may not have proposed to you this very week, but I'd already been doing a lot of thinking. We're good together. We should be together. And us having this baby does not scare the shit out of me the way it did when Colleen told me. Okay?"

She coughed out a small laugh.

There it was, that smile. Even as tiny as it was, he loved it. "I'm serious. I'm feeling happy right now. I'm just worried about you. Ruby, this may make things happen sooner than expected, but I love you, girl. You hear me? And we're good together."

"This isn't the way to do things. Getting married because of a baby is one of the worst reasons to get married. A surefire recipe for divorce."

"You don't know that. I know people who got married because of a baby and they're still together."

"Who, Alec? Who do you know?"

"I can't think of them right this second, but I know there have to be some people." Ugh, his argument was sucking. But it was true. Plenty of people in the world got married because of a pregnancy and made it work. Offhand, he couldn't think of any, but they had to exist!

She made a frustrated sound. "Look, if I promised you

that you could be as involved with the baby as possible without having to marry me, would that satisfy you? Because I want you to know, Alec, that it's fine by me. I never meant to ruin your life."

The tears were unstoppable. Like a fountain at the Bellagio in Las Vegas.

"Stop saying that. You're not ruining my life. Ruby…babe…I want to live with you as my wife. I want us to raise our child. Together." He lowered his voice, trying to make her understand. "Colleen promised me a family and then when I found she'd lied, it did something to me."

"What do you mean?"

He looked away. He wasn't sure what he meant. "I guess…I didn't know how much I wanted to be a father until she took it from me." He looked up at her. "This is my chance to do things right. To fix my life. To marry the woman *I* want. Please. Let me do this. It'll be the best for everyone."

She gazed at him a long while, and he thought she would give in. But suddenly, she rose from the couch, like she couldn't bear his touch. His heart sank. "Me, me, I, I," she said. "That's all I hear. I know you think I came into your life just to fix you, Alec. I know I represent change for you. But what about me? What about what I want?"

Of course. How could he be so stupid to phrase his words that way? He just wanted to make sure she understood that he was good, he was happy with all this. Instead, he'd come across sounding like a selfish idiot. "Of course what you want matters," he said, standing to follow her.

But she held out a hand. "Then don't follow me. And don't come back here. I'm going to get some rest. I'll call you soon to figure out the logistics. You know the way out." His eyes followed her up the stairs until she was out of sight.

His heart ached like someone had stabbed it with a butter knife. This couldn't be the end. It couldn't have been so short-lived. Even his mother said it, she was the one. *No, she just needs space*, he told himself. Time to think. He could do that. He could give her space and all the time in the world.

But one way or another, he had to make her understand, make her believe he'd always loved her. From the moment he met her. And not just because of the baby either. But because she was the most wonderful woman in the world.

And now, the mother of his child.

17

She stood before the mirror after her shower, completely naked.

Until this moment, she had avoided looking in the mirror. Avoided touching her belly. Avoided acceptance. *There's no way,* she'd spent all week telling herself. *There's no way I'm pregnant. It has to be a mistake.*

Ruby had always been the good girl, the one with the straight As, the one who did everything right, the one who climbed to the top of her field and demanded respect. The one who took birth control even when she didn't have a boyfriend, for God's sake. Now that she had one, she'd somehow gotten pregnant anyway. This morning, she'd finally gotten around to calling her Ob-Gyn to confirm what the UC nurse had told her.

That a little life was growing inside of her at this very moment.

How many weeks was she? Five...six? If she'd had her last period the week before Alec's fight in the locker room with Connors, then that meant she'd ovulated roughly two weeks after that around the time she and Alec had sex at his house.

Sometimes, birth control doesn't work, the nurse had told her when she felt like the world was crumbling down all around her. Had she started a pack late or missed a pill?

Yes. It happened every month at least once. She'd forget to take the pill then take it as soon as possible. The lapse had to have lowered the probability of it working correctly.

Well, there was no point lamenting it now. The damage was done. Ruby knew in her heart that she was going to go through with it. There was no other way to go. She was old enough, she had a great career, could offer the baby everything in the world, except...what about a father?

Could she marry Alec? Yes, she was crazy about him, found him insanely sexy, and knew in her heart he would make an excellent father, but they only started dating! This was crazy. Ruby shook her head and touched her belly. She wasn't showing yet, but her boobs looked fuller, felt more tender, a lot like being on her period. Her hips looked different, too, slightly thicker and wider. Ruby had always been well-proportioned in stature, but now she felt a bit more swollen.

A life. A little life growing deep within her.

It was so hard to believe.

As alone as she felt, she knew she wasn't. Alec knew about it, and he'd been giving her the space she needed and asked for. He'd been checking on her daily, asking how she felt and if she needed anything, but for the most part, he gave her breathing room. Finally, today, they'd talked about something other than how she felt, and she'd given him the go to sign the Sports Armour docs.

Her father had called to congratulate her, but she didn't feel like celebrating. Her heart tore in two knowing she was keeping a secret from her parents, but she couldn't figure out how she would break it to them.

Oh, hey, guys, you know my client, Alec, right? Yeah, the one who's been getting negative press lately. Well, he impregnated me. Pass the pepper?

There was no subtle way to do it. She was just going to have to come clean. Tell them she was pregnant and that she and the father would work it out amicably. She couldn't marry Alec. At least not now. Deep in her heart, she knew that marrying for a baby was wrong. It was the reason Alec couldn't marry Colleen and told her so. What would make this any different?

No, she couldn't ruin his life. They could co-parent and do great. It'd be fine. Marriage wasn't necessary. Still, it burned her. Always the good girl doing everything right. Well, not this time, apparently.

Ruby dressed and sat at her desk, hoping to focus and get some work done. Contracts needed reading, articles and social media needed perusing, and just because a tiny life was growing inside of her didn't mean the world had to stop. Staring at a contract on her desk, Ruby felt a wave of emotion rising in her chest.

Of course the world had to stop.

Why was she treating this like she had a tooth cavity or a UTI that would go away?

This was a baby, for God's sake! A baby! And she should be happy and celebrating right now. The fact it was a surprise shouldn't steal that happiness away from her. Alec was right—this was a time to feel joy, and she simply wasn't letting herself. So, the next time he called to ask how she was doing and invited her to come over, this time she didn't rebuke him.

This time she said yes.

From the moment Ruby walked into Alec's house, she felt at home. From Alec handing her coffee and giving her a big hug to Henna following her everywhere meowing, Ruby felt like they were her mini family.

"She knows," Alec said.

"How could she know? She's a cat, not a sonogram technician."

He chuckled. "I don't know, but cats know things, dude." Alec looked her over carefully once they reached the kitchen, as if he wanted to touch her but was still trying to respect her space. "You look amazing, by the way."

"Thanks, but I feel like shit."

"Well, that's understandable, but you look fabulous." He gave her a soft smile, a sad smile. Was he sorry he'd helped put her through this? It wasn't his fault, in case that's what he was thinking. "Can I..." he began, then turned away and poured coffee for himself.

"Can you what?" Ruby asked. "Touch my stomach? I guess." She'd already accepted that she was pregnant and desperately wanted to begin enjoying this journey, come hell or high water. Married or not, she was ready to start letting Alec have a part of it, too. It was only fair.

He put down his mug and came around the kitchen island, took her hands, and kissed the top of her head. In keeping with her overflow of emotions as of late, tears welled up in her eyes. "I won't if you don't want me to," he said.

"I do," she said, wiping away the tears. "I do want you to."

"Ruby, I know this has been hard for you this week, ah, ah, ah…" he said when she put up a finger like she didn't want to talk about it right now. "I was just going to say I'm excited. Whether or not we get married, I'm excited for this little guy or girl."

"Are you sure, Alec? You weren't in that meeting. You weren't with Colleen."

"I told you already, I think I was. I have been ready to be a father. It was the idea of having a child with Colleen that freaked me out. But you…" He tipped her face up and kissed away the tears on either side of her face. "You are special. You are amazing, and I hope you'll give me a chance, Ruby, I really do." Then, he kneeled and placed both hands on her flat tummy, pressing his cheek against her. He closed his eyes and breathed her in, breathed in the moment, and Ruby nearly erupted into fresh tears again.

"Oh, my God, I'm like waterworks over here." She wiped at her face with a napkin. "Is this how it's going to be for nine months?" Yes, her intuition told her. Get ready for a ride.

Alec then kissed her tummy and stood to hug her. No sexy kiss, a good thing, because she didn't feel sexy at the moment. He seemed to pick up on what she needed right away, and she felt grateful for it.

"Okay, so you ready to see what I've been up to all week?" His eyes grew wide and childlike.

Ruby cocked her head. "What? What have you been up to? Alec?"

"It'll be awesome, I promise. Come upstairs with me," he said as he took her hand. "I need to show you something."

Ruby's intuition was working overdrive lately, and now she knew what he was probably up to. He better not have gotten a baby's room ready. One, because she still wasn't sure she wanted to live here with Alec, marry him, or was even ready to see a nursery yet. And two, because if she created a nursery for the baby, she wanted to do it her way.

Guys, they didn't know how to do a baby's room. Heading up the stairs, she just knew he'd probably painted it in awful light pink or light blue, perhaps stuck ugly pre-bought stickers on the wall, and gotten one of those terrible plastic-y mobiles for a crib. Ugh, this was going to be bad, she just knew it. Then, she'd be in the awkward position of rejecting whatever idea he'd had.

But when he opened the door to a room a few doors down from his own bedroom, it took her a moment to figure out what she was seeing. Yes, it was a nursery, as she'd expected, but it was insanely gorgeous. The room was filled with light and painted with various shades of green, the walls accented with zoo animals, like giraffes and elephants. There was even a "tree" made of fabric hanging from one corner, and beanbag "rocks" to sit on.

Her hand over her mouth in shock, she stepped inside, her heart pounding like mad. "Alec…"

"I wanted to surprise you. Do you like it?" He sounded unsure. "I know you didn't want to find out the gender, so I went with gender neutral colors. You said your favorite color was green, so that's what the designer went with."

All she could do was stare. It couldn't have been more perfect had she designed it herself. Something about the room made her want to stay, work it out, raise the baby with Alec, with or without marriage, but at least living together. Possibly.

"Ruby, you aren't saying anything. It's freaking me out. Are you okay?"

She wasn't okay, but not for the reasons he feared. Going to the crib—a beautiful piece of furniture made of walnut, the blankets a plaid with green and blue stripes, she could only touch the soft cotton sheets and choke back tears. When she stepped to the bookshelf filled with all kinds of picture books, a sob finally escaped.

He did all this for me.

Because he loves me, and he loves our baby.

"Ruby?" He peered into her eyes.

The thought only made her cry harder, especially when the next thought she had was: *I'm in love with him, aren't I? Yes, I am. Stop being stupid and accept him already.*

"Shit, Ruby, don't cry. Why are you crying? Do you hate it? We can change whatever you want. I told the designer that the mobile was too much, but she insisted—"

Ruby shook her head before shushing him. "It's perfect, Alec," she said through tears. "It's absolutely beautiful. I'm crying because I'm happy. I never could've imagined a better nursery for our baby."

At that, his face transformed into that wide smile she loved so much. He held her close, stroking her back as she cried. When she finally got her emotions somewhat under control, he showed her every nook and cranny of the nursery.

"See the animals on the wall? I did those. Took me forever to get them right, but I think they came out pretty good."

He'd painted them himself?

He'd actually painted their baby's wall art?

Then, Alec pointed to a giraffe stuffed animal that looked like it'd seen better days. "And that's mine from when I was a baby. I asked my mom for it. I told her about the baby. I wasn't sure how you felt about me telling, but it's my mom. You know she's private, Ruby. She won't tell a soul. What she did say was that I would be the biggest idiot ever if I didn't marry you."

She coughed back a laugh, then picked up the giraffe to stroke its soft head. "I love it, Alec," she murmured. Looking into his dark eyes, she said, "I'm serious. I was worried that you'd done this, worried that it would be all wrong, but…"

"But?"

"But you've given me no reason to be afraid of anything," she said, and he sighed with relief. "If anything, you've done everything right."

"And that's bad because?"

"Because I keep feeling like I'm in a dream. Like something is going to go wrong. Like life—or you—can't be this perfect. I don't know what the future will bring. I don't even know how I'm going to feel tomorrow, but I can tell you right now that I love you. Thank you for this." She wrapped her arms around him and melted into his frame.

She loved him. There was no denying it.

"Even though I drive you crazy?"

She nodded, overcome with emotion.

His eyes darkened, and he took an unsteady breath. "God, Ruby, I'm so glad you said that." He cupped her face in his hands, tenderly stroking her cheeks. "I love you, too. I know we're going to be so happy with this baby. I know you don't want to talk about getting married, and this wasn't a ploy to get you to marry me. I just really wanted you to see how excited I am about this. I'm here for you, Ruby. And for the baby."

She threw her arms around his neck, hugging him tightly. He hugged her back, and they stood like that for a while, simply enjoying each other's warmth. Ruby inhaled Alec's scent, loving that he smelled so good. She didn't know what it was—his soap? Some cologne?—but every time she was near him, she couldn't get enough of that smell. She inhaled his shirt, her body heating.

It was the first time she'd felt anything other than fear, sadness, and desolation. It was also the first time she'd left the loneliness of her townhouse in a week. Being at Alec's was good for her, she surmised.

She tipped her head back to look at him. His eyes were dark, searching. His nostrils flared, and she felt him breathing harder. Touching his chest, she pressed a hand against his heart and felt it pound beneath her fingertips.

"Ruby," he said gruffly.

She loved how he said her name. His voice had entranced her the moment she'd first heard it. She stifled a smile, wondering if she loved how he smelled or how his voice sounded more. Standing on her tiptoes, she pressed her mouth to his. He didn't react for a millisecond, but then he took control of the kiss.

I lied, she thought to herself, *I love the way he tastes the most out of everything.*

When he pulled away, he tipped her chin up the way he loved to do. "You know what made you pregnant, right?" he asked.

"Sex?" She laughed.

He shook his head. "My super sperm. It blasted right

through that birth control and made it all the way up there." He flexed his arms and chest. "You gotta admit, that's pretty damn impressive. Am I right?"

Ruby slapped his chest and rolled her eyes. "Oh, you would say that."

That night, he made her dinner, and when he took her to bed, when he thrust inside her, completely bare, completely hers, she reveled in it. The openness. The freedom. The lack of worry, if only for one night. She whispered how much she loved him, and when they came together, Ruby knew they were meant to be. It didn't mean they needed to get married, though. She'd stick firm with that. But no matter her own reservations, or her fears about her father or her job, or about the future in general—they were destined to love each other. And their little one on the way.

18

With each day that went by, Alec's restlessness grew. Not only because he had a baby on the way but because he couldn't do much about it. Ruby had let him back into her life, and that was good, but he still hadn't been able to convince her that getting married was the best thing for them. According to Ruby, she still believed Alec wouldn't consider marriage, much less having kids, if it hadn't been for this surprise being forced on him.

She wanted to be with him. She accepted and even rejoiced that they loved one another. But because of the way things went down with Colleen, with Alec telling her he couldn't marry her and pulling out of their engagement, Ruby seemed to think that she and the baby were a similar situation. It didn't matter how many times he told her that it wasn't—that he was actually excited about the possibilities with Ruby, that she should move in with him immediately—she would shake her head and say he was just being a good guy.

Since when had being a good guy been a bad thing?

Those excuses drove him insane, so much that he had to get away for the evening. He called up Kyle and Heath, agreeing to meet them down at the bar for a while. Ruby was home working, and there was no practice tonight.

"Jesus, you look like shit," Kyle said, as Alec and Heath sat across from him at Duffy's, their local hangout. "What happened?"

Alec had asked that his two buddies meet him for drinks, citing he had some things he needed to tell them. They'd agreed without asking for details, but they had no idea how deep the rabbit hole went. They were, however, about to find out.

"All right, you guys know that Ruby and I have been seeing each other," Alec began with a heavy sigh.

"Is that what you kids are calling it these days?" Heath laughed, grabbing a napkin.

Alec gave him a dour look.

"Shit, buddy," Kyle said, ordering a round of beers for the three of them. "Alec's serious. So, what's up? What's going on? You guys having problems already?"

"No, that's just it."

"Is Colleen giving you shit about Ruby?" Kyle asked.

"Actually, she is, but I mostly ignore her. The problem is, things have been great. Really great. It took Ruby a while to accept my feelings for her, which are strong. I mean, you guys know how great she is."

Heath nodded. "She's pretty fucking awesome. And Camille loves her for you. She talks about it all the time."

"Yeah, so I even took her to meet my mom, which

you know I never did with Colleen. I just felt...I don't know...like she was the one."

"I fail to see the problem, buddy." Kyle sipped from his beer, passing the other two down the bartop.

Alec knew what he was about to say wasn't going to sit well with his buddies. He'd already told them a mere three months ago that Colleen was pregnant, even though that ended up being a lie. Would they make fun of him for saying it again, only with another woman this time? "The problem is...Ruby's pregnant."

Two pairs of eyes stared back at him. Quiet. Assessing. Then, they looked at each other. Then, Heath burst into laughter. "Are you fucking kidding me?"

"Great," Alec said, "thanks a lot."

"No, I'm just..." Heath gripped his shoulder. "I'm shocked, but I'm happy for you. Right, Kyle? We're happy?"

"Super happy, bro. Like, thrilled to death. I'm not kidding." Kyle raised his glass, and the three of them toasted. "To Alec, the most fertile one of us three. I suppose you're getting engaged soon?"

"Guys," Alec said, shaking his head. "That's just it. We're not. Ruby doesn't want to get married. She's convinced I proposed because I'm just doing the right thing like I did with Colleen," he finished before taking a long drink of his beer. "She thinks I don't want kids for a while, because of something I said in the Sports Armour meeting. I don't know how to convince her that I've always been crazy about her and I'm proposing because I want her. Even since before Colleen."

Heath whistled. "Damn. I thought Camille and I had a complicated relationship."

"Uh, who has a complicated relationship here? Me." Kyle raised his eyebrows. "I'm the one dating a princess, you know."

"Yes, and you'll be her Prince Charming shortly, buddy," Heath teased.

"Of that I have no doubt," Kyle said. "So, what are you going to do?" he asked Alec.

"I don't know." Alec pressed his forehead to the bartop. "Honestly, I see things her way. I love her. I believe I would have asked her to marry me sooner than later, and that discovering she was pregnant speeded things along. But I love her. I really love her. I don't see marrying her as a duty or burden, but a natural progression in our relationship. It would have happened eventually, I know that. Why can't she see it, too?"

"There may not be anything you can do," Kyle said. "She has to see it for herself, and the only way to do that is to give it time."

Maybe Kyle was right—maybe it would just take time. All he could do was keep showing Ruby how much he loved her and hopefully, everything would fall into place.

"Another thing..." Kyle drawled. "Have you tried groveling?"

Heath nodded. "Sounds like you need to grovel, big time."

"But I didn't do anything wrong." Well, maybe it was his super sperm's fault, but hell, it wasn't like he'd orchestrated getting her pregnant.

"Doesn't matter," Heath said. "You're a charming guy, Alec," Heath said.

"And that's bad?"

"In this case, kind of. You go on press conferences to convince people of shit all the time. Ruby knows this. Ruby's the one who encouraged you to do it whenever you were in trouble. Plus, the big one—Colleen told you she was pregnant and you didn't hesitate to propose to her. Hell, even when you found out she was lying, you refused to tell anyone. You're all about doing the right thing, even when it means acting your ass off. Yes, this time it's for real, but you can see why she'd have her doubts."

"She's worth fighting for, right?" Kyle asked.

"Fuck yeah, man." Alec looked up at them. "Never would've gone through this for anyone else."

"Then, you don't think twice about it. Just prove yourself over and over. Grovel. Eventually, she'll see the truth, just like Arabella did with me."

Alec winced at the reminder. Due to Kyle's asshat father, Arabella had once thought Kyle had sold her out to the media. Thankfully, things had worked out for his friends in the end. Was it possible he and Ruby would have the same shot at happiness in the end?

"To Ruby seeing the truth." Heath raised his glass, then Kyle and Alec followed.

"No, to the women who make us grovel," Kyle said.

They clinked glasses.

"To the women who make us grovel," Alec and Heath said at the same time.

19

Ruby walked into the O'Brien PR offices for the first time in two weeks. As far as anybody knew, she'd had a terrible stomach virus that had knocked her out, kept her bedridden, but now she was back and ready to return with a vengeance.

Along the way to her office, everyone congratulated her on the Sports Armour contract. *Way to go, Ruby. Congrats for corralling Alec, Ruby. How did you do it, Ruby?* Everyone wanted to know. What special magic powers did she possess to make Alec LeBrun, NFL Bad Boy Extraordinaire, fall in line and behave like an exemplary model citizen?

She'd done it. By just being herself, giving him the evil eye when he needed it, and cracking her whip whenever he fell off the wagon. He'd done it, too. Love was an amazing motivator, and he'd wanted to prove to Ruby that he could be the man she needed.

He'd succeeded far more than he could have planned.

Just by being Alec. The talented football player. Good friend. Generous hearted man who did house chores for his mother and played "tackle" football with kids with cancer and designed a nursery for his unborn child. With each hour that passed, he was starting to break down Ruby's fears that he only wanted to marry her because of the baby. Because truthfully, hadn't he shown her how much he cared for her before he even knew she was pregnant? Maybe it was she who needed to have more faith in Alec. She'd always had that faith in him as a football player. Could she have it in him as the man she loved?

Could she believe that her situation with Alec and the baby was nothing like what he'd had with Colleen and everything about what fate had in store for them so they could have the happily ever after they deserved?

She was thinking yes, and that made her heart feel lighter than she had in weeks.

So, then, why did she get a bad feeling, suddenly, when her father stuck his head out of his office upon hearing her return and demanded she enter his room immediately?

"My office. Now."

A chill ran through her.

Was it the contract? Did it fall through? Did Alec do something stupid last night that just came out in the news? Her body fluttered with anxiety, which, mixed with pregnancy symptoms, was proving to be a recipe for disaster. "Yes, sir," she replied automatically.

She couldn't help but compare his tone to all of the

times he'd yelled at her as a child for doing something wrong or not living up to her potential. *A B+! Ruby Marie, you can do better than that. I don't care how hard that test was. You're going to make up this grade until it's an A+.*

She shook off the memories. She wasn't a little girl or even a teenager: she was a "grown-ass woman," as Alec liked to put it. To keep her mind steady, she thought of him, of his love for her and their baby. Both gave her the strength to walk into her father's office and face his rage for whatever had happened.

She shut the door, but before she'd even sat down, Phil barked, "Is it true?" He whipped around and slammed a hand onto the desk, which made Ruby jump. "Are you pregnant with Alec LeBrun's child?"

The blood rushed from her head, and she staggered to sit down. How had he found out? Swallowing, her throat dry, she croaked, "Yes, it's true. But let me explain, please."

Phil's face looked like a volcano about to erupt, mottled with various shades of red and pink. "Ruby Marie, dating him was one thing. It was supposed to make him appear favorable in the public's eyes. No one told you to go get pregnant!" he yelled.

This was definitely not how she wanted to tell her father that he would soon be a granddad. Tears rose into her eyes, but she pressed them back. "It wasn't part of the plan, Dad. Things haven't happened the way you thought."

"And here I was, thinking you were sick at home. I've given you the benefit of the doubt and made excuses for you to everyone. Meanwhile, you were lying to me. I don't know what makes me angrier—that you're pregnant or that you've lied to me and your mother."

"Dad...I've been waiting for the right moment to tell you." Ruby wrung her hands and tried to figure out how he could possibly know. The only person who knew was Alec, and there was no way Alec would have thrown her under the bus.

Unless...

"I'm not a fool," her father continued. "I saw your face in that interview outside the restaurant. Your relationship didn't just start with that 'celebratory kiss,' did it?"

She shook her head. "No."

"Of course not. You have to be at least five or six weeks along." He shook his head in disbelief. "I can't believe you would do something so stupid and completely outside the bounds of decency."

"Decency? Dad, Alec and I are in love. He's asked me to marry him, and I'm beginning to have faith it's not because he feels it's duty, but because he truly wants me and the baby in his life forever. I know it's not the way we wanted everything to go down, but it's all going to be okay. I know it is."

"You slept with a *client*, Ruby. That's the first rule of professional boundaries. Never sleep with the client. And two, you lied about it. Three, you kept it from your own father."

A hot flush of humiliation crawled up Ruby's cheeks,

but she refused to show her father how upset his words made her. "I'm sorry I lied to you as a boss. I am. But I'm not sorry I hadn't told you yet as a father. You can be very hard on me, Dad. So much that I've hated myself for two weeks now, all because I got pregnant. I'm not the A+ child you've wanted me to be all my life. Sometimes I'm B+. So I got pregnant first, then got thinking about getting married after. So what. Life's not perfect, and neither am I. But if you love me, you'll be happy for me."

Phil stared at her with hurt in his eyes.

"I wanted to tell you when I was ready, not when you found out," she said. "You'll have a grandchild at the end of this."

"Ruby, right now, I'm talking to you as your boss." Sitting down heavily, Phil put his head in his hands for a moment, his shoulders slumped. Finally, he looked her in the eye. "Although I'm happy for you, I'm going to have to let you go."

No.

"You knew from the beginning that this kind of behavior would result in instant termination. I hate to do this. I really do, but if I don't let you go, it will set a bad precedent for the team."

Tears filled Ruby's eyes, but she held her chin high, refusing to let them fall. Everything seemed to come crashing down around her. How had she thought her father would react any differently? A thousand times, she'd warned herself that this would happen—falling in love with Alec would terminate her position as his publicist.

She cleared her throat. She needed to know who'd ruined her life. "How did you find out about this?"

Phil made an annoyed sound. "Your boyfriend did. Said he wanted to fess up because you wouldn't. Even asked for my blessing to ask you to marry him. Noble of him, wasn't it? Wish you would've told me yourself, Ruby."

Her mind stopped completely. There was no way. This couldn't be true. Alec had told him? When he'd promised he wouldn't?

All of the hope she'd been feeling about their future fractured into a dozen pieces.

She should have known better. He'd been too perfect. There had to be something wrong with him, and here it was—confused loyalty. Why would he have gone behind her back and done this?

"He called you?" Her voice trembled. She didn't know why she even asked. It would only twist the knife in deeper.

"He emailed me, of all things. Rather a surprising thing to get in my inbox last night." He looked at her now with some concern. "Are you going to be all right? I know this isn't what you wanted to hear, but you have to understand that you've put me between a rock and a hard place. You know image and reputation are everything."

She nodded. At this point, she didn't care about getting fired anymore. She could only think about Alec and why he would tell her father about them like this. A sudden thought occurred to her...had he done it to push her toward marriage?

Unfettered rage began boiling up inside of her. First, for trusting and believing in Alec, and second, for what he'd done. After she packed up her things and left the building, feeling like a scarlet letter was affixed to her forehead, she walked to her car with heavy steps.

The idea that he'd done it to force her hand at marriage blossomed in her mind.

If she lost her job, she would have no choice but to marry him, wouldn't she? It was what Alec wanted badly, the figurative nail in the coffin. She'd have nowhere to go. And with a baby on the way, it would be difficult, if not impossible, to find a new job before she gave birth and had to go on maternity leave anyway.

She couldn't deal with him right now.

She had to think of how to solve this on her own, the way she'd always been before she fell for manipulating Alec.

Through a foggy mind, Ruby struggled to open her car door. She barely noticed that her box of things tumbled all over her backseat, or that she was sitting in a parking garage, gasping for breath. She felt like the walls were closing in on her, and it took everything in her not to give in to panic completely.

Alec had trapped her to get what he wanted. To do his *duty*.

With no concern for Ruby's concerns whatsoever.

Ruby drove straight to Alec's. She needed to know the truth, hear it from his own mouth. Forcing away the fear and devastation long enough to drive herself safely to his house, she arrived within record time. When she didn't see his car in his driveway, though, she worried he wasn't home.

I wouldn't be home either if I'd pissed a pregnant woman off, she thought miserably.

She was about to drive away and figure out what she was going to do next when she saw Alec walk out his front door to meet her.

"Ruby! What are you doing here, babe? I mean, I'm happy to see you. Don't get me wrong." He leaned through the car window for a kiss, but she pulled away.

Lying, manipulative Alec.

"How...?"

"How, what? Are you okay? What's wrong?" He took in her wet cheeks, her mussed hair, and her red eyes. "Is it the baby?"

She could only shake her head, and the trembling started all over again. Alec opened the door and helped her inside the house. She didn't want him to touch her, yet at the same time, she longed for his embrace. She wanted to burrow into his strong arms and let him take away all of the uncertainty and pain.

Pain he'd caused.

He held her hand all the way to his bedroom, but she didn't have the energy to protest. He set her down on the bed with a gentleness that almost made her cry again, but she had to be strong.

"I can't believe you, Alec."

"Ruby, tell me what happened." Alec tried to embrace her, but she pulled away. He gave her a hurt look.

"I just got fired," she whispered.

He blanched, then his face creased with anger. "Your father? What for? You're the best employee he has. What bug crawled up his ass and died?"

She looked at his face, nearly ready to strike. Why would he even need to ask? It was his fault to begin with. "You don't have to act like you don't know," she replied, her voice tired. "My dad told me you sent him an email telling him I was pregnant with your baby."

Alec stared at her. Words were lost on his tongue. He couldn't speak. Then, he exploded. "What the fuck?" When she flinched, he kneeled in front of her and took her hands. "Not you, baby. I'm sorry. But what the fuck is your dad on? I would never do that. Why would I do that when I promised you I wouldn't say a word?"

"That's what I want to know!" she cried. She wanted to believe him so badly that it hurt. Her heart clenched in her chest. "But why would he lie to me? He has proof that you sent him that email. Why would he make this up?"

Alec rose, shaking his head in disgust. "How the hell would I know? I didn't send him any email. I haven't told anyone. Well, I told Heath and Kyle—I admit—but, Ruby, you have to believe me, babe…they wouldn't tell anyone."

"They're not the ones who emailed my dad. You did."

"I swear, I didn't." He scoffed and ran a hand through

his hair. "You're an adult, Ruby, not a child. You can sleep with and have a baby with whoever you want. You can't lose your job all because you fell for somebody."

"Not just anybody, Alec—a client. I got pregnant by a client," she added just to drive her point home.

He huffed. "A client who's also a grown-ass man and doesn't need anyone telling him who he can and can't fall for. I knew what I was doing, you knew what you were doing, and unless you're going to tell me I forced you to be with me—"

"No! Alec, never think that. I wanted you, and I want this baby." Her eyes filled with tears, and she tried to brush them away. But it was no use. They kept coming no matter how hard she tried to suppress them. "But I also know you wanted to marry me, and when I didn't say yes right away…"

"What are you saying?" His voice was low, uncertain.

God, should she accuse him? What would this mean for their future?

But if it walked like a duck and talked like a duck…

She rose from the bed. Having Alec stand over her only made her feel worse. "I'm saying you told my dad our secret to trap me into marrying you. Once I lost my job, I would have nowhere else to go, especially with a baby on the way."

His jaw dropped and he cocked his head. "I can't believe you're saying this. Why would I do something like that to you? I love you." He moved to touch her once again, but Ruby wouldn't let him.

"I don't think you did it to be malicious," she allowed, her heart heavy, "but you're the type of guy who gets his way. You did what you had to do. But even though I can't marry you now, you'll still be in our child's life. I promise you that." She braced to leave. She'd said her peace, and that was it.

"You're going to marry me, Ruby, because you love me and I love you, and we're going to be a family." He wrapped his arms around her and tried to kiss her, but she pulled away and pointed at him.

"Don't do that. You think I'm weak and only need a kiss from you to make everything okay? It doesn't work like that in the real world, Alec. I'm not a fairytale princess and you're not my prince who can fix it all with some charm."

For a moment, she almost didn't care he'd lied to her. She loved him so much that part of her would forget this ever happened. But she also knew how to stand her ground. Because she was Ruby O'Brien—no-nonsense, practical, strong woman who made things work her way, and no amount of manipulation could change her, no matter how sexy and good-smelling Alec may be.

In a word—he fucked things up.

With a willpower she didn't know she possessed, Ruby pushed him away. A sharp sob escaped her throat, and when Alec murmured her name, she turned and ran from his house, her heart breaking into a million pieces.

20

The first thing Alec did once Ruby left was check his email account.

There was no sign of a sent email in his name.

What in the fuck was going on? Could Phil O'Brien be making shit up just to fire his own daughter, get back at her, and prove his point that she wasn't ready to work at his firm? What asshole father would do that? Alec couldn't imagine himself ever doing such a dick move to his own little girl.

A parent loved, a parent supported, a parent scolded when necessary but never, ever did they sabotage his or her child's own success. Alec thought of the one woman who'd always had his back despite it all and got in the car to see her.

"What's going on, baby?" Carolyn asked as soon as she saw him.

"Ruby got fired, Mom. I'm not sure what happened, but she believes her father's bullshit that I emailed him and told him she was pregnant. I never sent an email. But now, she's livid, and I can't do anything about it."

"Who sent the email?" she asked.

Alec loved his mom. Loved her so much. She immediately believed her son, the way it should be.

"There's no email, Mom."

"Not when you check your account. But couldn't someone have deleted the message? What about on your server? Would it still be there?"

Alec stared at his mom. He hadn't even though of that option, and his mom had? "I didn't realize you were so tech savvy."

She shrugged. "I email you, don't I? Now who else knows Ruby is pregnant?"

Alec explained how he'd told Heath and Kyle, but they were solid for life. Buddies who would never betray him in a thousand years. Of course, betrayal always came from the people you least expected, but Alec was pretty damn sure there was smeared shit written all over this.

"What about Colleen?" his mother asked.

Alec paused. Colleen would have reason to do it, but Colleen didn't know about the pregnancy. He hadn't told her, and neither of his buddies would dare talk to that woman. "Mom, it's a mystery."

"Well, you'll figure it out, I'm sure. But listen, honey. You do what you need to do for yourself, that child, and Ruby. When your father left, I did what I could to make him stay, but he had his mind made up. Your father was a scared man, not ready to tackle fatherhood, whereas you're my mature, intelligent son who does the right thing."

"I try, Mom. I don't always succeed."

"But you will," Mom said with a smile that conveyed her utter confidence in him. "Convince her that you love her. Do whatever it takes. Make sure you want to be together for her, as much as it is for you. A woman wants to feel cherished, Alec, and that's something I never got from your father, but I sure as hell got it from you."

Alec tried to say something in return, but all he could do was choke back his tears as he hugged his mother tightly.

"Okay, boys, listen up," Coach Reddick boomed from the front of the room. "We've got Pittsburgh coming up this week and they're going to be a tough challenge, even in our own house. So let's keep it focused right now, hear me?"

For Alec, focusing on football for the next three hours was a godsend.

His mind needed a break or at least a change of subject from Ruby, Ruby, Ruby... Ruby. After returning from his mom's house, he had tried a shower to clear his head. He'd tried cooking. He'd gone for a long run, then a long bike ride, then a long swim. No luck. Alec had even given yoga a chance to calm his stormy mind. Nothing.

Masturbation was a mistake. A huge mistake. He needed Ruby to turn him on. The second he touched himself, images of his gorgeous, redheaded beauty flooded his mind and no matter how much porn he watched, the girl was always Ruby.

It'd been days since he'd spoken to her. He missed her terribly.

Coach's angry rants about running the wrong route or not keeping two hands on the ball or whatever else he's screwed up on were a great distraction. But with the lights dimmed for the film and his head tucked into his chin, Alec soon found his eyes slipping closed. Sleep had eluded him the last few days. Normally, his coach's voice sounded like nails on a chalkboard, but this morning, he felt his shoulders staring to sag, as Coach's drawl sounded more like a soothing lullaby.

Heath had to elbow him a few times, but he either eventually stopped or the overwhelming sensation of tiredness finally took over. He didn't quite remember fully falling asleep but when loud cheers and cat calls filled the room, Alec jerked awake.

It took him a moment to remember where he was and then a moment after that to figure out why the guys around him were making all that noise that disturbed his nap.

"Wassup, lover boy," Hewitt called from the front, twisting around to grin at Alec.

"Who you dreaming about, LeBrun?" Plough added.

Martinez poked his head over the other guys. "Hey, Heath, he pitch a tent?"

Alec had no idea what the fuck was going. Beside him, Heath was cracking up and his only response was to point to the screen up at the front of the room.

Ruby.

It was the first game of the season, the game against Sacramento judging by some of the jerseys of the fans around her. His woman—not his woman at the time, and may never be again—sat in the stands with some friends, laughing and watching the game. Her hair was in that tight knot, but a wisp had escaped and fluttered around her face. She looked so beautiful, so happy.

For a moment Alec forgot all his confusion about what was going on and blocked out the jeering and teasing from his teammates. All he wanted to do was watch her, lose himself in Ruby O'Brien's smile. It was everything joyous and right and worth fighting for in this world. All right there on the screen. But how was Ruby's photo up there during the team's film review…

"LeBrun!"

The snarl of Coach's voice pulled him right back to the present, and he wiggled in the chair to sit up straight. "Yes, Coach?"

"While you've been having yourself some little beauty sleep back there, the boys and I have been trying to solve a mystery that's been bugging me."

Alec scratched the back of his neck and looked sheepishly at everyone's eyes on him. "Sorry, Coach. Been getting little sleep, but I'm on now. Fully awake."

"You better be. Know what mystery that is, LeBrun?"

"Um, no, Coach, I don't think I do."

He'd been embarrassed by his coach before. They all had. The best thing to do was say as little as possible and let it run its course. Coach was like a boulder rolling down a hill when anyone messed up. Best not to stand in the way.

Coach sucked in a deep breath for his tirade and began, "Well, Cinderella—"

"Sleeping Beauty," Martinez corrected.

"What's that?" Coach asked.

"You mean Sleeping Beauty. Cinderella was the one with the pumpkin and the talking rats," Martinez explained. "Our boy back there's got drool all over his chest."

"I think they were mice." Plough laughed.

Coach exhaled loudly and ran his hands over his face. "I'm too old for this shit." He sighed. "You boys done comparing pretty princess notes?" Coach shook his head at Plough, who shrunk down in his own chair. "Like I was saying, Sleeping Beauty"—the coach turned his glare back on Alec—"I was wondering why you were always late getting off the line. And you know what I discovered?"

Alec tried to stay humble and listen. "No, Coach?"

"I looked at the tape and discovered something. The whole pre-season, you were never looking at the ball on the line of scrimmage before it was hiked."

"Coach?"

"LeBrun, you've been looking in the complete opposite direction the entire time. Right up into the stands. And so I had a mystery on my hands, a mystery to solve. So, do you know what the boys and I did just now?"

"I'm scared to find out, Coach."

The room tittered with quiet laughter.

"We tried to figure out what kept drawing your attention away from the fucking ball that you were supposed to be fucking catching." The other players in the room made 'ooohh' sounds like in middle school when a kid got sent to the principal's office. Coach put his hands on his hips and walked toward Alec. "And do you know what we found?"

Alec felt his cheeks grow red. He smiled sheepishly. He knew where this was going. "Sorry, Coach."

"Sorry?" Coach threw his hands up in frustration and clocked Alec behind the head. "LeBrun, you're out there to win football games. What the fuck are you doing searching the stands for your publicist? Every goddamn time a snap was taken of you, you're looking off to the left, off to the right, your neck always swiveled in the fucking direction of Red O'Brien."

It was true that he'd been crazy about her since even before Colleen. Every practice, he'd been showing off, trying to capture her attention, disappointed when she wouldn't look at him. He just didn't know there'd been photographic evidence captured of his enrapture.

"Ruby," Alec said.

"What?"

"Her name, Coach," Alec muttered, still staring at Ruby up on the large screen. "Her name is Ruby."

Coach gripped both sides of his hair and growled. "That's not the point, loverboy! The point is you're risking your fucking career staring at some lady. Don't you guys have porn or something? Martinez, I know you do. Can't you just show him some good porn to get it out of his system?"

There was laughter and joking, but Alec's eyes moved back to the frozen image of Ruby laughing at the game. It took another whack on the back of his head for Alec to realize Coach was still yelling at him.

"You need to get your head in the game, all right? I want you to stop doing this...this...bullshit. And play ball!"

But Alec's wheels had begun turning, and when Alec's wheels turned, there wasn't much anybody could do about it. Ideas sprouted and became action, and action made them into reality.

"LeBrun, you hear me?"

He'd always known exactly who he wanted—Ruby O'Brien in the stands, watching him. Now he just needed to go after it.

"Coach?" Alec asked.

"What?"

"How many more tapes do you have? Photos of me looking at Ruby?"

His coach frowned and crossed his arms in a huff. "A whole fucking lot, unfortunately."

Alec grinned.

"What in shit's name are you grinning about, LeBrun?"

"Coach? Can I borrow them?"

21

Sometimes, things go right in life. Sometimes they don't, and you have to roll with the punches. As much as Ruby had been hoping Alec would be her man, she was glad she found out now that he wasn't.

Less heartache later on.

So, he'd betrayed her. He'd given into his own ego and talked to her father without consulting her first. It was a typical Alec LeBrun move, and Ruby was only upset that she hadn't figured it out earlier. Of course he would go behind her back and talk straight to her father. He'd taken the phone out of her hand that one time in order to tell her father what he thought of him.

He was all about him—alpha and egotistical.

She wouldn't lament her pregnancy from him, though. What happened happened, and at the time, she was head over heels with Alec. No matter what happened, she felt secure that she could tell her baby that he or she'd been conceived in love. It was true—Ruby had loved Alec. A stupid move, but it was the truth.

Now, it was time to tell Alec it was over. She drove to the game after having eaten some saltine crackers to calm her stomach. She was moving into her second trimester and had barely begun showing, but she was feeling it a hundred percent of the way. *Breathe in, breathe out. Courage, Ruby.* Courage to do the right thing. After the game would be the best time to do it. She couldn't risk going to his house and getting caught up in his web of manipulation. Before she knew it, she'd be back in his bed, getting all dazzled by his smile.

No, it couldn't happen again.

As she found her seat and watched the game, she remembered her love of football, what had brought her to the stadium to begin with—the crowd, the lights, the smell of pretzels baking in the concession stands. She couldn't let Alec ruin that for her. No matter what, she'd always love the sport and vowed to support the Bootleggers, no matter what.

Even if the man who'd lied to her was currently out there on that field, working his ass off for a win. Hopefully, he wouldn't get into another fistfight now that things weren't going too well in his world. And if he did— oh, well—it wasn't her problem anymore now that she didn't have a job as his publicist.

"Hey, you."

Ruby looked to her left and spotted Camille, Heath's wife, scooting down the seats to come crouch next to her. She sat on the step, making sure she was out of the vendors' path. "Hey, Camille. How are you?"

"I'm good. I'd ask the same about you, but I actually already know how you're doing." Camille put a hand on her shoulder, looking at her with so much compassion that Ruby's eyes widened. But then she remembered that Camille's boyfriend, Heath Dawson, was one of Alec's best friends.

"He told Heath I'm pregnant?" Ruby whispered.

Camille nodded. "More like bragged about it. He's happy to be having a baby with you, Ruby. But I also know about the email your father received. Not because Alec was trying to betray you, but he's so upset. He needed advice. And well…" She chewed her lip.

"And what?"

"And he didn't send that email, Ruby."

Ruby swallowed hard and instinctively pulled away from Camille's touch. She was surprised when Camille didn't let her go. "Camille, I know Heath and you are Alec's friends, and you want to believe he wouldn't do something like that but—"

"Colleen sent it, Ruby."

Shock reverberated through her. "What?"

"Colleen's a bitch, and we'd never be friends, but she and I have a friend in common. Someone I've done private photographs for before. She knows Heath and Alec are friends, and well, she's always liked you, Ruby, so when she heard Colleen talking about what she did…"

"What did she do, Camille? And how could she do it? How did she know I was pregnant?"

Camille smiled sadly. "Look at what you're doing right now, Ruby."

Camille's gaze lowered and Ruby's did too. She immediately saw that she was holding a hand protectively over her belly. Guarding the precious creature she and Alec had created.

"Something as simple as this? She guessed?"

Camille shrugged. "She wanted to be pregnant with Alec's baby so badly. It wouldn't be a difficult leap to make."

Ruby shook her head. "Alec was so proud of his super sperm. It would *kill* her. But the email was sent from Alec's account."

"They lived together for a month when they were engaged, even if they were sleeping in separate bedrooms. She had access to his email. She saw him type his password one time and even got pissed at him for it."

"Why get pissed?"

"Because his password was REDRUBY. Ruby, Alec's had his eye on you for a long time, apparently, even when he was engaged to Colleen."

Ruby couldn't blame Colleen for being pissed. But, *oh my God.* All that time he was with Colleen, he never belonged to her. He belonged to Ruby. He'd told her that time and again, and while she hadn't necessarily doubted it, this was the first time she truly believed it. "She sent the email from his account, then probably deleted it from his SENT folder so he wouldn't see it."

"The email server should still have a record of it, not

that that matters. If you still think Alec sent it—"

Ruby shook her head even as tears welled in her eyes. "I don't. I can't believe I ever did."

It might've been November, but the chill coming over Ruby then wasn't from the weather. It was from what she was hearing.

How could she have thought he would do something so horrible? Had the stress and confusion of the last couple of weeks so blinded her that she couldn't believe the very man she'd loved? The very man with whom she'd created life?

"Oh, come here, hon." Camille pulled Ruby into a hug right there in the stands.

Shame and relief filled Ruby's heart. "Thank you so much for telling me this. It clears up a lot."

Ruby wished she could hate Colleen for the trouble she'd caused, but she couldn't muster up the pain it would take to feel that way. Colleen was a troubled girl who'd lost a great guy. For whatever reason, she couldn't handle the rejection and hated that her man had always been in love with someone else.

Someone unattainable.

And that someone had been Ruby.

She cheered on her favorite team like she had all her life.

Only her heart felt utterly relieved. She'd come here with the idea of breaking up with Alec, but as it turned out, she was going to tell him she'd been wrong about him. She had pegged him for a manipulative liar, and she couldn't have been more ashamed. The manipulative liar had been Colleen, not him. He had told Ruby about Colleen's tendencies to be that way, and yet, she'd never thought of her one moment.

Instead, she'd blamed Alec.

There was so much fixing to do. So much starting over. But at least she knew one thing—he loved her. He'd always loved REDRUBY. She smiled into the cool November wind.

After halftime, Ruby held her breath, as she watched the Bootleggers return to the field. They were up 14-0, and yet Alec didn't seem to be in one of his happy dance moods. Instead, he looked focused down on that field, less like a kid and more like a mature man. A man whose life had recently changed.

At one moment, she lost sight of him, but then again, the defense was set to start this quarter. More than likely, he was lost in the sideline crowd, planning his next move. As she thought about all the things she needed to tell him after the game was over, the jumbo-tron zoomed in on his face. She almost cried.

But then…

"Ruby…"

She froze, half-wondering if she were hallucinating, but then, she turned and saw his face right next to her. In the stands! A cameraman was with him, and she instantly realized it wasn't some vision or dream. It was Alec with a microphone.

Up to something.

"What are you doing?" Her purse almost fell from her fingers. She looked around at all the smiles and cheers coming from the fans cheering his name.

"I need you to listen to me, please."

She covered the microphone with her hand. "Alec, I know I was wrong about my dad—I know what happened."

"I know what happened, too. I figured it out after I talked to my mom."

"Your mom?" Ruby asked.

"Yes, she's a pretty smart woman, you know. It's about Colleen."

"And the email she sent?"

"Yes. Listen, we'll talk about it later. Right now, they only gave me a few minutes to do this. I missed you, baby. Come with me." He kissed her cheek and took hold of her hand.

And just like that, she wanted to throw herself into his arms. He smelled like sweat and grass, but his expression was all Alec. His eyes gleamed, full of love, and she knew that grin of his wasn't for the crowd's benefit—it was for hers.

He tugged her along, down the steps, through the level walkways, down the spirals, all the way through the tunnels and onto the field. She could barely keep up. "Alec! I can't run that fast."

"Come on, Ruby!" He was running and laughing, which made her laugh, too.

This, she thought.

This is a moment I'll never forget. This craziness borne of Alec's crazy mind. His crazy ideas. His crazy love for her. A love that now she knew was real. Had always been, even long before he could admit it to her.

The tears started falling now, even as she ran. "I'm so sorry, Alec," she called out, as they approached the field. "I should've believed you. I should've known you wouldn't do something like that to me." She held her belly, as her breath ran out, and she couldn't speak anymore.

"Babe, you were scared, and you lashed out. It's okay." He pulled her into his arms, hugging her tightly, all the while the cameraman was still capturing everything on the jumbo-tron. "Ladies and gentlemen, boys and girls...see this woman right here?"

The stadium erupted into applause. Half the team wolf-whistled, and Alec grinned at her. Ruby couldn't think, couldn't be angry, couldn't do anything but love this moment. Loved the attention he was lavishing on her.

How could she have ever doubted him?

"I fell in love with a woman. A woman I definitely didn't deserve, but we men never deserve our women, do we?"

The crowd cheered through the smells of sweat and beer and popcorn, as Alec led her to the very spot where they first made love.

"Tell me you're not going to..." She couldn't finish her sentence. She was afraid it'd be captured in the microphone for all the world to hear.

He squeezed her hand. "I wanted Ruby for my own the first moment I saw her," Alec said, his voice now more somber. "I saw her across the room, and I thought, 'Damn…she's the one.'" The stadium cheered louder. "I thought I was crazy, but I realized I wasn't. I'd just met the woman I was meant to love for the rest of my life."

Ruby began crying, really crying, and her vision blurred.

"I had no idea then how much that love would grow. It grew and grew into something even bigger than us." Everyone on the sidelines looked at the big screen, and Ruby thought she looked like a swollen, pregnant, crying thing there in the jumbo-tron, but she didn't care.

She'd been to more Bootleggers games than she could probably count. She'd been to one where it was below freezing and it was all the fans could do to pound their gloves together in muffled claps. At another one, the team had been down by twenty-one in the first quarter and it didn't get much better after that. Hell, she'd even been to the stadium when it was empty and filled with nothing but her moans.

Yet, she couldn't remember a time where it felt quite this quiet. Solemn. Almost holy. The fans were all in on this. Her heartbeat filled her ears.

"Watch," Alec said.

And suddenly, there, on the screen, were videos of her. Of Ruby on the sidelines laughing with another publicist. The camera panned from her to Alec as he was lining up for a play. But he wasn't paying attention to the ball being set on the line of scrimmage. Instead, he glanced at her like a distracted boy. After the plays, he still glanced at her. In fact, in every shot, he was looking at her.

One clip ended, and another began. Over and over, Ruby saw Alec's distraction. Over and over, the camera revealed her smiling face. One video after the other captured Alec's fascination with his own publicist, the ginger in the crowd.

Ruby felt like her knees might give out, and it wasn't because of the sprint through the stadium. How had she not noticed him looking at her all that time? How had she not realized she was the object of his affections, not the football, not the opponents, not the cheerleaders or the fans. How had she thought, the whole time, that he was a mischievous playboy interested in everything but her?

The proof was right in front of her.

Ruby knew Alec was an expert at getting people to like him. He was a charmer who knew when to turn up a smile, when to put on irresistible puppy eyes, knew how to make reporters love him. But she never knew that his hijinks had been mostly for her, to get her attention and respect, to get her to look at him. Now it was clear as day.

Ruby never considered that his showmanship had all been for her benefit.

Because there on the screen, bigger than any movie she'd ever seen, was the same man she'd always loved. But instead of a devilish smile, instead of an end zone dance or an acknowledging wink, when gazing at Ruby, he was just Alec. Nothing more.

Just a man in love.

Another clip started and this one was from an after-game interview still on the field. It must have been a win, because he gave that classic smile that made everyone fall for him. The reporter asked him a question, but he was too distracted and his face shifted behind him.

Still standing there catching her breath from the stairs and losing it from the scenes unfolding before her eyes, Ruby and all seventy thousand people in the stadium finally saw what caused the shift in Alec's attention. In the video, Ruby passed behind him. His eyes followed after her until the reporter repeated her question for the fifth time, and Alec looked at her like he forgot entirely she was there.

The whole crowd laughed. In the next clip, Alec tried to wave to her in the stands and she didn't see and he awkwardly tried to pretend that he was smoothing back his hair. Ruby felt tears spring to her eyes. Her eyebrows creased in confusion when what would be a different clip came up on the screen. A recording of the draft. She remembered the day clearly. Cameras had been everywhere. Even in the clip that was playing she could count at least fifteen others. No audio, but this one zoomed in on Alec who'd just been selected by the Bootleggers. He was listening to Ruby talk, nodding along in his new jersey. Ruby remembered how much her legs had shaken walking up to him to give him her pitch to hire her as his publicist.

She knew a thousand others had already done the same and thought the chances of him picking an unheard newbie were slim to none. But she'd been damned determined to try. She'd told him, "Hey. All those other guys are blowing smoke up your ass. Pick me if you want someone to push you, challenge you, and make you your best." It'd been a bold thing to say, but she'd been real with him a hundred percent.

In the clip, she offered out her hand and Alec smiled and shook it before she turned around and left. Ruby remembered running straight to the bathroom after that. But the clip didn't end there. Alec turned to his mother, who'd been sitting just a few feet away, and said something. Ruby was surprised when it changed to Alec's face on the screen, in the locker room clearly recording himself.

"Hey, there, Miss O'Brien," he said. "I found this video of the first day we met and I wanted to show it to you."

Ruby stood frozen.

"There at the end, I know you can't hear it, and I'm guessing you can't read lips, though who knows. You're full of surprises. But I'll tell you just in case." On the screen, Alec smiled. "I said, 'Her. It's her.'"

A peanut shell dropping would have sounded like an explosion in that moment.

"You asked me to prove it to you, Ruby," he said. "That was me. This is me. I've always wanted you. Always will. And now, I'm asking you…" Alec dropped to one knee, and Ruby's hands flew to her mouth. She let out a sob when she watched Alec get down on one knee in front of her.

Oh, my God...

He pulled out a small box from inside his sweaty football pants. She would've laughed if this wasn't the most wonderful thing that had ever happened to her. "Ruby, Red, babe...I've loved you from the first moment I met you. I love you so much I'm dying with it. I can't breathe or live without you. Marry me, Ruby. Marry me and make me the happiest man on this earth?" Looking into her eyes, he said, "Ruby O'Brien, I love you."

She cried harder when he opened the small velvet box and found her ring inside it. A beautiful, sparkling huge ring that she couldn't examine too closely at the moment, because of how hard she was crying. All she knew was the ring's sparkles looked like starbursts through her tears.

"Yes, I'll marry you, Alec." Ruby sniffed, wiping her tears then laughing.

"SHE SAID YES!" Alec shouted into the microphone, slid the ring onto her finger, then lifted her into the air. He twirled her around and around. The crowd cheered, music played, and Ruby couldn't stop laughing. He tossed the microphone over to the cameraman and whispered in her ear, "I love you, Red. The baby is only the cherry on top of everything, but make no mistake, you're my fucking delicious sundae." He kissed her.

And life was absolutely perfect.

22

Alec sighed, admiring his woman.

Ruby took a deep breath, her full, swollen breasts pressing against her top. It was getting cold outside with the windows open to his room, but he'd always wanted to snuggle under the blankets with a woman he loved, and now was his chance. Desire stirred in his gut. He wanted to give in to it, let the tidal wave wash him away.

All his dreams were coming true. Ruby was the mother of his unborn child, she was here, in his arms after an amazing day, and all had mended between them. He'd made things right, just like he'd said he would. As Ruby gazed at the view, then gazed at him, the air seemed charged with electricity.

"I love you, Red. Marrying you has nothing to do with duty but needing a lifetime with you. Even so, I'd never lie to you. Never manipulate you. Don't ever doubt that again," he said.

"I won't."

"I put a ring on it, you know."

She smiled. "I know."

He took her into his arms and kissed her long and deep. She moaned low in her throat, and he knew she felt the connection between them as much as he did. He kissed her harder, wrapping her arms around his neck, pressing those gorgeous tits against him. He deepened the kiss as he stroked her jaw and cheeks before tracing a line down her throat.

Such a perfect woman. And now she was all his.

But it was his turn to moan when her tongue touched his bottom lip. She tasted like spun sugar and lilacs. Something about being pregnant had made her even sweeter. A ripe, full moon filled with maternal potential. She was sexier than she'd ever been, though he wasn't sure how that was even possible. Was he dreaming? But then he felt the softness of her breasts against his chest, and the hardening of his cock confirmed that this was no dream. It was real, and he was never letting her go.

"Stay with me tonight," he murmured.

She hesitated. He took that as an opportunity to kiss her again. If there was anything he was good at, it was seduction. Convincing. He licked the seam of her lips, coaxing her to open, and she capitulated without a small mewl. He couldn't get enough of her taste, and his hand trailed down her spine until it rested right above her ass.

"Stay with me," he repeated.

With glassy eyes and a flush on her cheeks, she whispered, "Yes, sir."

"Ohhhh…you're doing that again. Fuuuck," he groaned.

His heart soared. Lifting her into his arms, he carried her from the balcony over to his bed. Ruby kept kissing and licking his neck, his jaw, her hands pressing against him like a cat kneading. Alec flipped on a single light before laying her down on the bed. Her hair had fallen from its pins, strewn across his bed like tendrils of fire. How he loved her hair. Would their baby have her hair, her eyes? He hoped so. He wished the baby would get everything of Ruby's.

Though it could have his smile. But that was it.

Ruby sat up and began to unbutton her blouse. He watched her, drinking her in, and with every inch of creamy skin revealed, his restraint continued to break. She smiled at him, obviously enjoying tormenting him.

"You're killing me. Go faster," he growled.

She clucked her tongue. "So impatient."

"Hey. It's been weeks since we do this."

"And now you get to make love to a pregnant woman." She chuckled.

"Even sexier." There was nothing flippant about his comment. He meant it with every word. Something about seeing her expanding belly, slightly rounded with his seed, his flesh and blood growing inside of her, made him want her even more.

She reached for the clasp of her bra behind her back, but then she seemed to think better of it. "Nah. I think it's your turn." Shit, he'd strip naked in five seconds flat if that was what it took to see Ruby naked. He tossed off his shirt, shucked out of his jeans, and was about to tear off his boxers when she let out a laugh. "You're supposed to take off one thing, then me, then you—"

"Fuck it." He crawled over her. "I don't give a damn." He kissed her, and she arched underneath him. They kissed and touched, and finally Alec got that bra off of her, and he groaned aloud at the sight of her naked breasts. Full and creamy with nipples the color of raspberries, they were better than in his fantasies.

He leaned down to lick the tip of one breast, swirling his tongue around her nipple until she was panting. He loved how responsive she was, how she threw herself into lovemaking head-on like she did everything else in her life. Playing with her breasts for what felt like hours, he enjoyed every second until she begged him in a breathy voice to continue. But he wouldn't relent. He wanted her wet and ready.

He sucked and licked and nipped, loving her taste and the smell of her skin, wondering how he could ever let her go in the morning. She was his everything now. And she carried within her his entire hopes and dreams. His future.

Under him, Ruby writhed and grasped at him and drove him into a frenzy of lust. Never the passive partner, she pushed at him, and although he was twice her weight in muscle, he let her push him onto his back. Now straddling him, her dark red hair spilled down her shoulders, she looked like some kind of goddess. He didn't know if she'd come to reward or punish him, but at this point, he hardly cared which. She ruled him like she ruled the moon.

"I have you where I want you." She smiled before leaning down to kiss his chest. He groaned in agony. "All of these muscles. I wanted to get my hands on you since the moment I saw you," she admitted.

"Oh, really?"

"Yes, really. Don't act like you don't know how you drive women crazy. Going shirtless all the time, wearing those pants that leave nothing to the imagination…"

He laughed. "Only because I wanted to drive *you* crazy."

She kissed his chest. "Well, it worked. Now, you're going to pay for it."

Alec had to admit he was intrigued by this side of Ruby. She'd always seemed so contained, but he loved when she let loose. When that hair came down and she became a being of passion in bed, a woman who sometimes liked to take control and at other times relinquished. He could live with that.

His smile widened, and he grunted when her nails raked down his belly.

Her hot little tongue followed the path where her nails had been. Frissons of sensation moved through Alec's body, and his cock pushed against his boxers, begging to be freed. He needed her to take out his cock, stroke him, see those fingers grasping him, but Ruby was like a playful mermaid, refusing to be tamed, frolicking freely. When he bucked his hips, she smiled and kissed his navel. "Didn't I say patience was a virtue?" she said breathlessly.

"You're driving me insane. Fuck me already, woman."

She laughed, still wearing her pants, but he could feel her heat through the fabric. She rubbed her pussy against his cock, and they both groaned. God, if she didn't stop this, he'd come in his boxers like some teenaged boy. Gritting his teeth, Alec willed himself not to lose control. *How am I this worked up already?* he thought desperately.

"Ruby..." he warned when she danced her fingers along the waistband of his boxers. "You're playing with fire."

"I like playing with fire."

At that, he tipped her over onto the bed and took over once again. "Then, you chose the right man," he said. "And you'll thank me when I'm kissing your pussy and you're screaming my name."

She turned bright red to match her hair, and her breath increased, deepened. Her nipples hardened under his touch. He wasn't about to withdraw his promise. Kissing down her body, he unbuttoned her pants and yanked both legs and panties down her body until she was completely naked. *Finally.* Her soft white skin was dotted with freckles, although her belly and thighs hadn't seen much sun and were a shade paler. Alec licked at her hip, tracing the crease between thigh and hip, and Ruby inhaled a quick breath.

He could smell her arousal, which only turned him on more. Gently touching the curls on her mound, he kissed her right above her pussy. To his delight, he loved the constellation of freckles there.

She shifted on the bed, restless. Dipping a finger between her swollen lips, he parted her, like he would a flower. She was already wet, and her juice coated his fingers. Alec couldn't stop himself from burying his nose in between those silken petals.

"Alec," she moaned.

He tongued her, tasting her essence, and she moaned, loud and low. He loved that sound. Tasting her and playing with her until she bucked and cried out, he thrust his tongue inside her quivering sheath. She shivered, and he knew she was close to climax already.

But he wanted to be inside of her when that happened. Giving her one last, leisurely lick, he kissed her curls before getting off the bed then grinned at her dazed expression. He palmed his cock, brushing his thumb over the sensitive head. Ruby licked her red lips, then crawled over to the side of the bed where he stood. She covered his hand with her own, and together they stroked his length.

When she kissed his cock, Alec almost didn't have the willpower to push her away. But he'd come on her pretty little fingers if he didn't stop her. "Lie back and open your legs for me."

She did as he asked, shyly spreading her legs open. "Like this?"

He grinned. "Just like that. Show me everything."

Where had this sex goddess come from? How had he gotten so lucky? For months, he'd dreamed of her, then he thought he'd lost her, and now here she was again. With him. Giving herself to him completely. He could finally take her as hard and fast as he'd dreamed about for weeks, only this time, he'd have to soften things up.

Now, she carried his child and he wanted her like he'd never wanted anyone.

"You know, every time we've had sex, your hair is down. I remember wanting to see your hair down for so long. But you know something?"

"You want to fuck me with my hair in a bun," she guessed.

"How did you know?"

"Because you're you, Alec. Like I don't know you."

"Like you don't," he said, smiling. He loved that they'd reached this new level in their relationship where she knew every thought he was thinking. Slowly, he pressed inside of her and watched her face as he did. She took that bottom lip of hers between her teeth, and it took everything in him not to pound her hard. To force himself to go slowly, to savor this. To make love to her slowly, sweetly…

"Oh, Alec," she purred and undulated under him. "I'm so full, oh my God…"

She was full of his cock, full of his being and soul. He wished he could possess her in every way, make her completely his, but there would be a whole lifetime to do that. For now, he was just thrilled she'd said yes.

"So full of your cock, Alec…"

Jesus, she couldn't keep talking like that and expect

him to maintain any type of self-control. He kissed her, but the taste of her on his tongue only made things worse. His cock pulsed. Pulling out, he slowly thrust back inside her tight sheath, starting a steady rhythm. Ruby wrapped her arms and legs around him, as Alec gritted his teeth. She was so tight and wet, it was almost unbearable.

The way she looked at him, the way she touched him, the way she clenched around his cock every time he thrust inside her willing and soft body, every movement sent him higher toward his climax, sent his balls cuddling up against him in preparation for release.

Ruby started panting, a red flush climbing from her chest to her cheeks. He knew she was close, and he picked up his pace. "You can fuck me harder, Alec," she said, giving him permission, though he held back, not wanting to hurt her.

"Are you sure? But the baby…"

"I'm fine. Just do it."

He slammed into her, and she squealed. Drawing up her legs to open her up further, he pounded into her, stroking her body with his cock. He watched as she tipped her head back, exposing her pale throat, and he licked her skin as she started to climax, loving the taste of her skin. She moaned loudly, and when he brushed his thumb over her clit, she screamed and exploded in waves of pleasure.

Finally, he let himself come, too. He thrust one last time before his climax hit him like a freight train. He poured himself into her, spurt after spurt, and just barely had the strength to collapse next to her so as not to crush her. They both struggled to breathe for a few moments. The room smelled of sex and sweat and Ruby, and Alec inhaled the scent, breathing it into his lungs. The most beautiful scents on the planet.

He kissed her neck. "I love you so much," he said, playing with her hair, pulling it away from the sheen of sweat on her face. "I love you, I love our baby, I love our life. Thank you, Ruby."

"For what, baby?"

"For rescuing me. I'd been waiting for you for a long, long time."

She smiled against his skin, contentedly falling into a luscious deep sleep, and as she fell away, he kissed her eyebrows, sighed, and dreamed of his future.

EPILOGUE

When Ruby's water broke, Alec had been the one to keep his cool. At first, Ruby thought she'd have to console him, but when those contractions hit her like one tsunami wave after another, suffice to say she was the one who'd relied on him. To remember to bring the bags for the hospital, to bring the paperwork, the birth plan, to call her parents…

On the drive to Savannah General Hospital, Ruby had squeezed his hand so hard, she thought she'd break a finger, not that he complained. And when they arrived, her doctor had informed her she was only dilated three centimeters.

"It'll be a while," Dr. Fincher advised. "I'd recommend getting yourselves comfortable for now."

Ruby couldn't figure out how to get comfortable when her body was in agony. The contractions had been long and heavy, and she'd cursed Alec and his entire family tree more than once. To his credit, Alec had kept his cool, placing cold washcloths on her forehead, massaging her shoulders, back, and feet and simply being there to support her.

He'd been great.

And she loved him all the more for it.

There was no way she could've given birth without him. And when she'd finally hit ten centimeters dilation, she'd pushed and screamed and screamed again, as Alec urged her on with each contraction. When she felt there was no way to keep going, spent in a heap of sweat and tears, Alec had encouraged her.

"You can do it, baby. I know you can," he'd said, squeezing her hand. "Just one more push."

Finally, at 1:32 a.m. on July 5, Daniel Alexander LeBrun had been born, twelve hours after they'd arrived at the hospital. He came into the world screaming his full dark head of hair off. With deep brown eyes, like looking into Alec's, Ruby swore the baby made the same face she did when she was irritated with his father.

Early that morning, Ruby awoke from exhausted sleep to the sound of a baby crying. It was still an odd sensation, the knowledge that she'd had a son with Alec. As she blinked, the room dark, she heard movement.

"I'll get him," Alec rumbled.

Although Ruby had told Alec he could go home to get sleep—the last he'd have for a while—he'd insisted on sleeping on a cot in their hospital room. Never to move from their side. Always to bring her everything she needed. The birth had gone smoothly, and although it had hurt like hell, Ruby had to admit it hadn't been as awful as all the horror stories would tell you.

Then again, she might've just been lucky in comparison.

She couldn't help but beam full of pride, the smile of a contented mother, when Alec placed their son in her arms. Daniel fussed, clearly hungry, and Ruby placed him on her breast as the nurse had shown her. Immediately, the baby began eating with gusto, and she and Alec both laughed at his funny little faces and sounds.

"That's my boy," Alec said with pride. He touched the silky hair on the baby's crown and smiled at Ruby. "Have I told you yet that I love you?"

Her heart swelled. "No." She laughed. It was their little game.

"Damn. I have to get better at that." He smiled, his heart full of joy.

She pulled him in for a kiss. "You tell me every single day."

"Whew." He leaned his head against her shoulder and watched as their son nursed. "I love you, too. I love our son. I'm so happy that my heart could explode." Alec kissed her lightly, as he sat on the hospital bed with her. Right now, they were the only three people in the entire world.

Nothing else mattered.

Nothing else was happening.

Only the birth of their perfect little family.

As Daniel finished eating, Ruby lifted him and patted

his back. He let out a loud belch, which both of his parents thought was the most glorious sound they'd ever heard. They praised the newborn, their laughter lulling Daniel to sleep in his mother's arms.

Alec and Ruby had married a week after the infamous proposal at the Bootleggers' game. It'd been a small ceremony, just close friends and family. Although Alec hadn't been fond of the idea, Ruby had insisted on at least inviting her father. She'd hated the thought he wouldn't be at her wedding. When she saw him, she'd fallen into his open arms.

Tears had sparkled in both of their eyes. "Congratulations, sweetheart," Phil had said. It wasn't perfect between them, but it wouldn't have been right without her father there. After all, he did love her. And maybe firing her was just the push she needed to start her life anew.

Now, she was free. Free to explore options, free to work for herself, and now that she'd be home to take care of a newborn soon, maybe it was time to start her own business. There was time to think about it, but for now, she was just happy to see her father smiling again.

By the end of the short ceremony, there hadn't been a dry eye in the audience. Everyone was thrilled for them— Heath, Kyle, Camille, Arabella, Ruby's family, and of course, Carolyn, Alec's mother had driven down from Charleston to see the special moment come to life.

The memories all crashed inside her mind, as Ruby held her son. Her son—she had a son. She could barely believe it, even with the baby asleep in her arms. She'd never known she could love someone as much as she loved Daniel and Alec, and to think that last year at this time, she thought she'd be alone for the rest of her life.

How quickly things changed.

"You need to get some sleep," Alec murmured. "Let me put him back to bed."

Ruby almost told him no, but then she yawned. "Okay."

Alec took the baby, turning to Ruby, saying, "Check it out, Red. Football hold."

Ruby laughed. Too hard and it would hurt her body. She had to admit she loved seeing the big football player holding a tiny newborn. The contrast was startling, and yet, Alec held his son like he was the most precious being in the entire world. Ruby couldn't stop the tears from brimming. She'd been a total watering pot for months now. Stupid hormones.

After he put the baby down, Alec got onto the hospital bed with her. He didn't really fit, but she'd missed his warmth next to her. "Thank you," he said as he kissed her forehead. "For our son."

She smiled sleepily. "You're welcome."

As he murmured words of love in her ear, she fell asleep in his arms.

Ruby looked up from her laptop and smiled, while Alec stumbled into their bedroom and flopped face down onto their bed.

"Finally get him down?" she asked, moving a hand off of her keyboard to run her fingers through his tousled hair. Poor thing hadn't slept much for the last four months since Daniel had come into this world. The little sucker wanted to take everything in, always staring around the room, as Ruby or Alec carried him, sang to him, even begged him to please go to sleep.

"I think he's going to be a coach," Alec said. "Because God knows, he owns me. Tells me what to do like a little bitch."

Ruby giggled and slapped his arm. "Don't say that about the baby. Just last week, you swore he was going to be a wide tight end, like his daddy. And the week before that it was a kicker," Ruby said with a laugh.

Alec lifted his head from the bed. "Well, that's before I heard the lungs on him. Good Lord. As if I don't hear enough screaming from Coach."

Ruby caressed her husband's cheek, and he leaned into her touch.

"Knowing us," she said, "he won't end up in football at all. He'll insist on doing his own thing entirely."

"And I'll support him one hundred and fifty-nine percent."

Alec gave Ruby's hand a sweet kiss.

"Oh." She grinned. "Well, then I'll have to give him one hundred and sixty percent."

"Such a competitive woman." He grabbed her legs and slid her along the bed, then lifted her into his arms as she shrieked. "All right, lady, time to get ready. We have guests coming in twenty minutes."

Ah, yes, the barbecue. Alec had been wanting to have one ever since the baby was born, but she'd wanted to wait a while until she was up to it. Now that it was chilly outside, and the Savannah humidity had burned away, now was the perfect time.

"What should I wear?" Ruby asked, getting up and opening her closet.

"Nothing. Go naked, please. Except for some shoulder pads and knee socks." He winked at her, and she stuck her butt out at him. She loved the way they played, loved that Alec had brought out that sassy, playful side in her, loved that she could feel like herself around him.

"I don't think the guests would appreciate it," she said.

"Oh, yes, they will. Well, the guys will, anyway."

Once they'd gotten dressed, brought all the food outside, including the cooler, and set up to watch a football game since it wasn't their week to play, they began opening the door, one time after another, letting in their friends and family. After only an hour, Daniel woke up and screamed through the speaker until Ruby went and fetched him, bringing him to the backyard, bundled in a blanket for everyone to say hello.

"Here he is!" Ruby brandished the baby like he was the main dish. Barbecue ribs, be damned. Nothing more yummy than her little munchkin.

"Oh, he's so beautiful!" Arabella, Kyle's girlfriend

screeched. "Doesn't it make you want to have a baby, Kyle?"

"Yeah, Kyle, don't you want to have a baby?" Heath chided him, clapping a hand on his shoulder as he walked past to grab a beer from the cooler.

"Duchess, we just got married," Kyle said.

"So? You know that as a princess of Salasia, heirs are very important."

"We'll get there. Right now, I'm enjoying having you to myself. Hell, I already have to share you with a whole country."

"And you're doing it marvelously, sweetheart," Arabella said, blowing Kyle an air kiss before cooing at Daniel.

Ruby patted Kyle's shoulder and went on to find Camille sitting in one of their rocking chairs.

Camille was about six months pregnant, her baby bump round and adorable. She and Heath had found out they were having a boy and had already picked out a name—Peyton Andrew. Emma could barely contain her excitement at having a baby brother and had wholeheartedly approved of the name, saying it definitely belonged to a future football player.

Ruby looked forward to meeting Peyton and was sure he and Daniel would play in the backyard together while Ruby and Camille watched their husbands play on TV.

Camille, Arabella, and Ruby all fawned over Daniel's cute smile while Heath, Kyle, and Alec all watched, beers in their hands, cracking manly jokes but really, amazed at the families they'd started.

Ruby overheard Heath say, "I can't complain, man. Life is fucking amazing, you know? Every time I see Camille and Emma, Camille pregnant with my baby…" He couldn't finish his thought. "It's just awesome."

Alec nodded and stared at Ruby with a smile. "Yep. I know what you mean."

"Me, too," Kyle said, his gaze on his princess. Then he blinked and shook his head. "Stop making me look bad, though. I'll be the happiest man alive when Bella gets pregnant but that can wait a year or two."

Heath and Alec just grinned.

"Sometimes you have to take your blessings as they come," Alec said. "Can't plan for everything, and I wouldn't have it any other way."

Alec winked at her.

He had embraced fatherhood without hesitation. The moment Daniel had come into his world, he'd fallen head over heels in love with his son, and even more for Ruby.

His career was flourishing too. The Sports Armour ads had been filmed and would air at the start of the new season, plus a new ad campaign was being laid out by Sports Armour, along with new offers from Nike and Reebok. Alec's image had undergone a complete transformation. Their marriage hadn't stayed a secret for long—despite his and Ruby's best efforts—but when the cat had gotten out of the bag, Ruby had told him they'd be better off using it to their advantage.

She became his full-time, freelance publicist.

Her father hadn't liked it at first, but there was nothing he could do about it.

The public ate up his love story, and when they'd discovered he and Ruby were having a baby? Suddenly, he'd been on every magazine cover, and photos of them together appeared on Instagram every day. It had worried Alec at first, the intrusion on their privacy, and she understood his worry that some might view the publicity as some kind of sign that he valued his career more than family. But day by day, she'd been allaying his fears, assuring him that so long as it didn't cross certain lines, it was okay to share their lives, their happiness, with the public. He didn't have to worry that Ruby would ever interpret his actions as duty or showboating or manipulative ever again—she knew her husband for what he was. A good man.

The best man. The hottest, sexiest, most-fatherly man on Earth.

"Does it ever not feel so...overwhelming?" Kyle asked no one in particular. Ruby glanced over at him and saw his gaze was on Arabella again. Lord, the man was smitten. "Like everything's just too perfect? Don't you feel like it's unfair to have it so good?"

Heath shrugged. "Maybe a little, but it will just get better and we get to enjoy that. Cheers, dude." He clinked beer bottles with Kyle and with Alec. "To life."

"To our unbelievably amazing lives," Alec corrected, staring at Ruby.

The friends enjoyed their evening together before

Camille and Heath needed to leave to pick up Emma from her father's. Kyle and Arabella left soon after, leaving Alec and Ruby to themselves and the baby.

Cradled in his father's arms by the fireplace, Daniel was an adorable, sweet, sleepy bundle. Ruby was pretty sure he'd be huge in no time with the way he drank milk and was filling out fast. Sitting in their living room, listening to music, while Ruby worked on her laptop, nobody had to say anything. Every so often, Alec would lean over and kiss Ruby's hair, neck, and cheek.

She'd close her eyes and wonder how she got so lucky.

"You know, I'm glad you decided to break the rules for once," he said after some moments of silence. "Otherwise we wouldn't be sitting here tonight."

She smiled at him. "And I'm glad you decided to listen to me and play by the rules, otherwise we definitely wouldn't be here tonight."

Daniel's eyelashes fluttered, and when he opened them, his face screwed up like he was going to start crying. Ruby took him into her arms and rocked him, her voice soft and soothing. Daniel finally fell back asleep. "Let's get to bed. Our talking is keeping him up."

"Let's get to bed so I can rock your world."

"You are so smooth. Not." Ruby laughed and led her husband into Daniel's amazing, zoo animal nursery. But yes, slipping under the covers with her husband would be so good right now. Maybe they could even have sex for hours like they used to do before Daniel came.

Together, they put their son to bed and watched as Daniel squirmed around then finally settled into a comfortable position. They each kissed his little forehead and cheeks before Ruby pulled up the side of the crib, covering him with a light blanket. "Good night, my little football player," she said.

"Good night, my little freelance publicist."

Ruby scoffed and elbowed Alec. "Good night, our huge game-changer."

"Truer words were never before spoken." Alec picked up his wife and carried her into their bedroom, while Ruby laughed into his neck. Climbing into bed together, her husband wrapped his arms around her, as they stretched and yawned for the third time in five minutes.

"Wow. We may need to postpone that world-rocking session until the morning." She laughed, cuddling against his chest. Making love in the morning before the baby awoke was her favorite thing to do anyway.

"Fine by me…" Alec kissed her forehead. And before he'd finished his thought, he was fast asleep, his large chest rising and falling in tune to his breaths.

Ruby slipped out of his arms, turned off the light, and snuggled back against her husband. "Good night, Alec. I love you." Only the sound of his snoring replied. But she knew he loved her, too. He'd told her. And then he'd never, not once, stopped showing her.

Thank you for reading Deep Inside.

If you enjoyed these characters, be sure to check out Book 1,
Down Deep, Book 2, *Royally Deep*, and Virna's
other sexy contemporary romances!

Here's a sneak peek of Book 1 in the Kiss Talent Agents
eries, *Lip Service*, about sports Agent Hunter Kiss and Dani
Chase, a woman determined to protect her little brother.

LIP SERVICE Excerpt:

1

Hunter

"Hunter, baby, you up? Breakfast is almost ready."
Shit, I think as my eyes flash open.

I stare up at the ceiling and listen to the sounds
coming from my kitchen. Female humming. Cabinets

opening and closing. Dishes rattling. To my left, sunlight peeks through the shades. I fumble for my phone, check the time, then mentally curse again. Viciously. Not only because I overslept, but because I'm pissed as hell at myself.

"Hunter?"

"Yeah," I finally call out. "Coming."

I throw back the covers, get out of bed, pull on a pair of sweats, then splash cold water on my face. Arms braced on the counter, I stare at my reflection in the mirror and curl my lip in disgust.

"You stupid bastard," I mutter.

Exhausted from a string of eighty-hour work weeks and too much to drink, I'd apparently done something I haven't done in ten years—fallen asleep immediately after having sex with a woman.

The same woman who was now frying bacon by the smell of things.

The same woman whose name I can't seem to remember.

I'd met her at Gatsby's last night and taken her home with me, another rarity. Usually I prefer going to a woman's place so I can make an easy escape, but she'd been visiting from out of town and had been curious about where I lived. Getting a hotel room had seemed like too much trouble and before I knew it, here we were. She'd been good with her hands at the club, even better in bed. Wild and crazy in the sheets.

But I still can't remember her name.

When I walk into the kitchen, the pretty blonde looks up and offers me a warm, beautiful smile. If I was anyone else, if I wasn't Hunter fucking Kiss, the smile would probably melt my heart.

But I *am* Hunter Kiss and I don't have time for this shit.

I notice she's wearing my grey cashmere robe, the one that normally hangs on the back of my bathroom door. That annoys me. When I see my laptop where I left it on the kitchen counter, however—with the screensaver activated, telling me she'd tried to access my files—any notion I had of politely eating breakfast with her before nudging her out the door vanishes.

"Good morning," she purrs. "You hungry? I thought we could eat and then spend the day together."

"Yeah, that's not happening."

She frowns. "Sorry?"

"My screensaver is still on." I raise my brows, but I don't lay into her as much as I should. Yeah, she was nosey, but it wasn't her fault I'd fallen asleep even after I'd made it clear last night I wasn't looking for anything more than mutual gratification. Talk about giving a lady mixed signals. Still, I want her gone. "Listen, last night was great, but I've got to get to work. The café next door has amazing pancakes."

Her mouth open and closes. Her face turns red. Finally, her eyes narrow. "You're a dick."

I contemplate her words and shrug. I'm not trying to be even more of an ass; she just happens to be right.

"Which is why you really wouldn't want to spend more time with me than you have to," I say softly.

"Fuck you," she scoffs as she rounds the counter and passes by me to stalk into the bedroom.

It's on the tip of my tongue to apologize, but I force myself to remain silent. Ten minutes later, she blows out of my apartment. For a few seconds, I feel guilty. She was a nice woman, for the most part, and great at giving head. But mostly I feel relief. And determined not to make the mistake of actually falling asleep with another woman again.

I make coffee and pick up my phone to call Trisha, my personal assistant. She informs me she already rescheduled my morning meetings.

"Have I ever told you how much I love you?"

"Yes, you've told me a million times, Hunter. I love you too, and before the sound of those words makes you shriek in horror and run away, you know I mean that in a brotherly way."

"Right," I chuckle. "How's Gwendolyn?"

"Let's say it's complicated and leave it at that."

"Women are so damn difficult." I take a sip of coffee, immediately regretting the decision as it's still too hot to drink and singes my lips. "Honestly, I don't know why you don't just switch teams. I happen to know a handsome guy who would be just your type."

"Is he a little over six feet tall with an athletic build? Brown hair and hazel eyes?"

"Yeah, I think we're talking about the same guy."

"Yeah, I know that guy, and he's only my type because he's even more afraid of commitment than I am. Plus, he's like my brother, too, and assuming I was ever strictly dickly, I'm not into anything taboo."

"Everyone's into something crazy behind closed doors." I grin widely then ask, "Have you confirmed tomorrow's meeting with Cross?"

"Actually no. When I called him, he hemmed and hawed a bit. Literally."

"Yeah, well, he's a good old Southern boy. But he's also the best upcoming quarterback in the country, and what do you mean he hemmed and hawed? He was damn excited about the prospect of signing with me and going pro last we talked."

"Apparently that was before his sister got to him. He let slip she has concerns."

"Is this the same sister who left twenty-five messages the past week?"

"That's the one. She's not your biggest fan."

I snort. "I'm not afraid of his sister."

"Seeing as I'm the only one who's actually spoken to her, I can say in all seriousness: You should be."

I roll my eyes. "You're being ridiculous. Signing Cross is basically a done deal."

"Yeah, well done deal or not, he mentioned he might want to include the sister in the meeting."

I blow out a breath. "Fuck. But fine. By the time I'm done with him and his sister, they're going to be drooling with dollar signs in their eyes."

"I hope you're right. Anyway, will you be gracing us with your presence soon?"

"I'll be there within the hour."

I end the call then jump in the shower. When I'm done, I hear someone pounding on my door. Is it the blonde? If she "forgot" something, better to give it to her now rather than risk her coming back. She knocks again, this time more aggressively. My robe is on the floor where she left it and I figure, what the hell, she's already seen all there is to see of me. So I grab a towel, sling it loosely around my hips, and throw open the door.

Only to find myself staring not at the blonde, but a short curvy woman with hair dark as midnight stalking away from me toward the elevator. When I open the door, she twirls around, and my brows pop up. She's busty, with large tits that jiggle when she turns, tattoos, hot pink highlights in her hair, and the darkest eyes I've ever seen. Her mouth is pouty. Her skin is a light tan with hints of freckles. And she'd be gorgeous but for the scowl on her face.

"Hunter Kiss?" she calls, still some distance away, her voice so deep and throaty my dick twitches.

I brace my hands above my head on the door jamb and lean forward with a grin.

Her eyes widen as she seems to suddenly notice I'm only wearing a towel that can slip at any moment. I can practically feel the trail of heat her gaze leaves as it wanders over me. I subtly flex my pecs, grinning when she zones in on the movement. "That's right. And you are?"

She blinks then shakes her head as if to clear it. "I'm Chad Cross's sister. And you can take this phone and shove it up your ass," she says just before tossing something at me that hits me in the face—hard.

1

Hunter

"What the fuck!" I roar, automatically raising a hand to my left eye, which stings like a motherfucker, while automatically lowering a hand to hold on to my towel. Or maybe it's a subconscious move to protect my nuts from a different type of sneak attack.

"Oh my God, I'm so sorry!"

The apology comes immediately, but I barely hear it. Whatever hit me in the face—I'm assuming it's the phone she so rudely suggested I have intimate acquaintance with—stunned me more than hurt me, but for a few seconds I'm practically frozen in shock. Sure enough, I catch sight of a smart phone at my feet. When I lift my gaze again, Cross's sister is right in front of me and she looks every bit as shocked as I feel, maybe even more so. Her face is pale, one hand covers her mouth, and she looks like she's about to cry. Insanely, I feel the urge to comfort her, which I viciously shove away even as I let go of my towel, grab her wrist, kick the phone out of the way, and drag her into my apartment, ignoring the little squeak she lets out when I shove the door closed, spin her around, then pin her against it. Vaguely I'm aware that my towel has dropped, but I don't care. I'm pissed and want answers.

Yet I still manage to register how soft and luscious she feels pressed against me.

With wide eyes, she swallows hard then says, "Let me go!"

"How about you explain what the *fuck* that was about and *maybe* I'll let you go," I say between gritted teeth, distracted by the way the pulse in her throat is fluttering. In contrast to the colorful art on her arms, her throat and chest are unmarked, and I have another insane urge—this time to lean down and lick her. To my surprise, when I glance up, I see a flash of desire in her eyes. Dark eyes swimming with fire complimented by her dark hair, pink highlights, and arm tattoos.

I like it. Too much.

"You're naked," she chokes out.

"Yeah, well forgive me for dropping my towel when a strange woman assaults me."

"I—I didn't mean to assault you. I just came to return your phone."

"Not my phone."

"Fine. The phone you gave my brother."

"Didn't give your brother a phone."

She struggles against me. I lean in, giving her more of my body weight, and she gasps.

"You're lying!"

"No, I'm not. And fair warning—you keep rubbing against me like that, and you're going to get a whole hell-of-a lot more than you bargained for. Or is that what you were hoping for?"

She turns bright red but manages to stare unflinching into my eyes. "You wish."

I shift my knee slightly, pressing the weight of my leg against her thigh. "Gotta say, you picked an unusual way to proposition me but big points for getting my attention."

"Yeah, that's it," she sneers. "Word on the street is that you are an absolute monster in the sheets, and silly me, I couldn't resist."

"The word on the street is seldom right, but I think just this once, the street might be onto something." I cock my head and pass a quick look over her. I strengthen my grip around her wrist and dig my knee deeper against her. "So what are you into? Domination? Submission? Humiliation?"

She blinks and swallows a nervous lump in her throat. There's something different in her eyes now, something that tugs on my heartstrings.

Fear.

"Seriously?" I shake my head in disbelief and let out a groan before staring up at the ceiling then abruptly releasing her. I plant my hands on my hips, noticing the way her gaze drops to my naked dick.

"You've got a lot of nerve being scared of *me* considering what just went down. Then again, you're obviously a crazy person. The question is whether I should call the police or get you medical attention."

But she doesn't appear to be listening to me.

Her cheeks blush fire-engine red. Her mouth opens and closes like she's a fish sucking in air. Her eyes are wide as saucers, her gaze no longer edged with fear but filled with a mixture of awe and hunger. I swear she looks ready to bow down and worship me. Or rather, worship my dick. Seeing it gets me horny as hell, making me swell right in front of her eyes.

She blushes even harder, which for some reason I find completely adorable.

And hot.

Finally, she takes a shaky breath then lets it out slowly, as if she's really struggling to collect herself. "This hasn't exactly gone according to plan," she finally says even as she rubs at her wrist, which is slightly red. I'm hit with a frisson of guilt that turns into a mix of amusement and grim satisfaction when she stares at a point just above my right shoulder, obviously unable to make herself look at my monster cock again. Too bad because it's desperately craving her attention.

She licks her lips nervously, and asks, "Can you put on your towel? Please?"

I want to tell her to go to hell. My eye hurts like a motherfucker and chances are I'm going to have a shiner. But remembering that look of fear, the fact this is Cross's sister and she might be able to help alleviate the concerns Trish talked about, I finally grab the towel, and wrap it around me. "I'm covered."

She looks at me hesitantly, as if she's not sure I was lying about having covered up, but when she sees I was telling the truth she looks equally relieved and disappointed, which makes me stifle a laugh.

"Look, I really am sorry...about your eye. I meant to toss you the phone with a little attitude, not ream you with it. Honest. I'm not usually the violent type. You have to believe me."

"Lady, I don't know you."

"I'm Dani Cross. I'm Chad's—"

"Yeah, I know. You're Chad Cross's sister. The one who's called and spoken to my personal assistant on several occasions."

She scowls. "So you admit you've ignored my messages asking you to call me back?"

I lower my hand to my towel, for a brief second seriously tempted to drop it again just to check her attitude, but instead I ask, "Is that why you threw the phone at me?"

"No. Well, sort of. But not the only reason," she says, her mouth sulky.

Jesus. Now I want to bite her plump lips. "Look, Ms. Cross—"

"Dani," she interrupted.

"*Ms. Cross*, number one, I don't know you. Number two, you don't know me. And number three, just because you're pissed at someone doesn't give you the right to assault them."

She raises her chin. "I didn't *mean* to assault you. Not like that, anyway. I just meant to aggressively toss a phone at you."

"Besides me not calling you back, what else can you possibly be mad about that would justify you *aggressively tossing* a phone at me?"

"Hey, I'm not proud of what I did. But I know the rules prohibiting agents from bribing potential clients, which is what you were clearly trying to do when you gave Chad that fancy phone."

I spot the phone where I kicked it. "Pfft. It's not that expensive. But again, not my phone. I don't know who gave Chad that phone but it wasn't me."

She frowns. "He said it was an anonymous gift and I assumed... Oh!" She bites her lip as her eyes light with realization. "Maybe it's *another* agent and you've got some competition."

"Some *unethical* competition. Because as you just noted, agents are prohibited from giving gifts to potential clients. Another reason why Chad should sign with me and not someone else, don't you think?"

Her mouth flattens into a thin line. "No I *don't* think. I don't think Chad should sign with *any* agent. He should stay in college, not risk his health and his future by going pro, at least not before he earns a degree."

Ah. So that's what all her phone calls and Chad's sudden concerns were all about. I study her for a moment, then I run a hand through my hair. She might be a whacko but she is also the sister of one of my potential clients, so I need to get this crazy situation under control. "Look, I have breakfast. It's cold, but why don't we sit down, have something to eat, and talk about what's going on."

Her expression suddenly turns to one of outrage. "I'm not eating the breakfast that Amy prepared."

"Amy—?" Realization dawns. *Amy.* The name rings a bell now. The name of the blonde who'd so recently warmed my bed.

"I know I'm going to regret even asking this question, but how the hell do you know Amy? And what does she have to do with your brother and the fact I'm going to make him a star?"

"She's just further proof why I don't trust you. And I told you, Chad can be a star after he finishes college."

"With his talent, he doesn't need a degree."

"That's not for you to decide."

"The hell it isn't. Your brother was born with a gift, and I was born with the gift of giving credence to his gift."

"I know how this works," she scoffs and tosses a flustered hand through the streak of pink highlights in her hair. "You promise him the world, but nothing is ever guaranteed. He could get hurt during training and never actually play."

"It's an obvious risk, yes, but it's a risk he has to take. Your brother is going to be the greatest quarterback in the League. There is a small window of time open for him. The longer he waits to play, the less successful he's going to be. Talk about no guarantees in life. He could get hurt walking down the street, lose his scholarship and never have a shot at anything. Right now he has a chance to fulfill his dreams and make a ton of money in the process. Not many people get that chance. He can always finish college later. Don't you want what's best for your brother?"

"Of course I do, you bastard. It's why I'm here."

"You're not a pleasant person."

"Pot meet kettle."

"Pot came to kettle's door and hit him with a phone. But I have to admit, the memory is actually starting to turn me on more than piss me off. Have any more pent up aggression you want to get out? Because I can think of a few things that would be far more pleasurable for both of us."

"I'm sorry," she coos, mocking me. "But since I'm obviously not your type, let's not waste our time."

"You have no idea what my type is."

"Amy. Amy is your type. Not a fat chick with pink highlights, piercings, and tattoos."

I scowl. "Fat?" I look her up and down, taking in every curve. *Sexy yes, but not fat.* "You're not fat." I shake my head.

She snorts.

I narrow my eyes, for some reason, determined to convince her of my sincerity. She's much shorter than me, so I have to crouch to meet her at eye-level. She's right about one thing, she's definitely not my usual type.

But maybe I could use a new type. I tilt my head slightly.

"You're gorgeous. Crazy, yes, but gorgeous and your body rocks." I can't help but give her the once over again. "Plus, Amy's gone. You're still here, despite trying to do me bodily harm. What does that tell you about my type?"

She averts her eyes before finally murmuring, "That you're a sadist."

"Maybe if you're the one holding the crop. What do you say? I've got one you can try out."

She makes a sound like she's holding in a scream.

I'm not going to lie, this banter is incredibly entertaining. There's something about this girl that just sets me off, in more ways than one.

"You think you're funny." She steps up and points a finger at my chest, which I quickly grab before she can poke me.

"I didn't make it this far in life by being a—"

Violently, she pulls her finger out of my grip. "You have no regard for others, so how the hell am I supposed to trust you with my brother?" She pauses as if she's waiting for me to say something, to say anything, but for once I'm content to let her spiel her bullshit.

"I came here on a mission. To get you to talk to me. But running into that poor girl downstairs, who was in hysterics as she stumbled out of the elevator, that enraged me. And that's why I threw the phone instead of handing it to you. Because I wanted to kick your ass, for that crying girl downstairs and for every other girl you've ever been a complete dick to."

"Because men have been dicks to you?"

"Yes! You know the only man who hasn't been a dick to me? My brother." She paces away from me. I'm watching her carefully in case she decides to pick up something and fling it at my head, when suddenly her shoulders slump. Looking as if she can barely stand anymore, she sits on my couch and drops her face in her hands. "I just don't like this," she groans. "I don't like the idea of my brother foregoing college for this pro football bullshit. He can get hurt, be paralyzed!"

I sit beside her and place a hand on her shoulder. "Look, I understand your concerns. But your brother has talent, and this is his shot at making it big. It's not tomorrow, or in a few years. It is now."

"But what if it's a mistake? What if it ruins his future? Sure football helped him with college, but he's so much more than just a football player."

Every drop of concern for her brother is genuine. This isn't about her, it's about someone she loves. I haven't run across someone so selfless in a long time. I can't just push away and ignore her concerns. According to Trish, this woman has substantial influence on her brother. The promise of fame and money obviously isn't swaying her, so I need to do my job and find out what it's going to take to seal this deal. "Look, you don't want to eat breakfast, fine. Let's go get lunch or something, and I'll explain why I think this is best for your brother."

She hesitates, but the fear and animosity that had been

radiating from her in spades seems to be dwindling.

"This could change Chad's life in the best way," I press. "This opportunity is huge, and I think you at least owe it to your brother to hear me out."

She bites her lip, then finally nods. "Okay, we'll talk. But lunch has to be within walking distance because I rode my motorcycle."

"I don't know why that surprises me." *Nothing should surprise me when it comes to her.* "It's okay though, I can drive."

"Let me guess," she says with a smirk. "You drive a Porsche?"

I can't help but crack a wicked grin. "A Cayman."

She smiles tightly. "We're walking."

BOOKS BY VIRNA

Kiss Talent Agency

Book 1: Lip Action (Simon)
Book 2: Locking Lips (Caleb)

The Bedding the Bachelors Series

Book 1: Bedding The Wrong Brother (Rhys)
Book 2: Bedding The Bad Boy (Max)
Book 3: Bedding The Billionaire (Jamie)
Book 4: Bedding The Best Friend (Ryan)
Book 5: Bedding The Biker Next Door (Cole)
Book 6: Bedding The Bodyguard (Luke)
Book 7: Bedding The Best Man (Gabe)
Book 8: Bedding The Boss (Eric)
Book 9: Bedding The Baby Daddy (Dante)

Home to Green Valley Series

Book 1: What Love Can Do (Quinn)
Book 2: The Way Love Goes (Conor)
Book 3: I'm Gonna Love You (Brady)
Book 4: Best Of My Love (Riley)
Book 5: Because You Love Me (Sean)

Hard as Nails

Book 1: Hard Time (Street)
Book 2: Hard Case (Slate)
Book 3: Hard Core (Axel)
Book 4: Hard Place (Jericho)
Book 5: Hard Act (Davis)**

Going Deep Series

Book 1: Down Deep (Heath)
Book 2: Royally Deep (Kyle)
Book 3: Deep Inside (Alec)

Say You Love Me Series

Book 1: Say It Sexy
Book 2: Say It Sweet

Rock Candy Series

Book 1: Rock Strong
Book 2: Rock Dirty
Book 3: Rock Wild

Para-Ops Paranormal Romantic Suspense Series

Book 1: Knox: Chosen by Blood
Book 2: Wraith: Chosen by Fate
Book 3: Dex: Chosen by Sin

**Coming Soon

ABOUT THE AUTHOR

Virna DePaul is a *New York Times* and *USA Today* bestselling author of steamy, suspenseful fiction. Whether it's vampires, a Para-Ops team, hot cops or swoon-worthy identical twin brothers, her stories center around complex individuals willing to overcome incredible odds for love. Bedding The Wrong Brother, which begins the Bedding The Bachelors Series, is a #1 Bestselling Contemporary Romance and a USA Today Bestseller.

Virna loves to hear from readers at www.virnadepaul.com.

CONTACT VIRNA HERE

Website: www.virnadepaul.com
Twitter: @virnadepaul
Email: virna@virnadepaul.com
Facebook Fan Page: www.facebook.com/booksthatrock